D0977153

Advance Praise for

The Murder Mystery Race

"What impressed me about *The Murder Mystery Race*, which is appropriately targeted to grades 7 to 9, is young author Andrew S. Cohen's command of the art of storytelling. He exhibits this talent with striking confidence and bravado. This is indeed an extraordinary publishing debut that points to a bright and productive future."

—**Raymond Benson**, author of
The Mad, Mad Murders of Marigold Way

the MURDER MYSTERY RACE

ANDREW S. COHEN

A PERMUTED PRESS BOOK

The Murder Mystery Race

ISBN: 978-1-63758-826-0
ISBN (eBook): 978-1-63758-827-7

Cover art by Cody Corcoran
Interior design and composition by Greg Johnson, Textbook Perfect

Permuted Press, LLC
New York • Nashville
permutedpress.com

Published in the United States of America
1 2 3 4 5 6 7 8 9 10

For my sister, Jordan Cohen
and my parents, Natalie and Aaron Cohen.

Contents

1

The Knife Thrower

Where am I? How did I end up here?

I stand on the sidewalk next to a familiar road. I notice a bakery and a parking lot to my left. It is pitch-black outside, and I inexplicably get an eerie feeling. I am tired, befuddled, and I feel paralyzed. I watch as cars whiz by; their headlights flash into my eyes.

I feel drowsy, as if I could just drop down to the ground and fall asleep. I turn my head. I see the Knife Thrower, armed to the teeth with knives. He is wearing jeans and a black leather jacket. He is staring at his next target…me. I widen my eyes in alarm.

Behind me is a parking lot where I see several people. The Knife Thrower takes his eyes off me and throws his first knife at a woman in the parking lot. Fear consumes her face as the blade is buried in her chest. The woman sinks to the ground, and her agonizing cries turn to silence. The Knife Thrower throws the next knife at a man, slicing his forehead, and decides to finish him off with another to the temple.

The Knife Thrower throws numerous knives into peoples' shoulders and stomachs. I start to run away, but that's when the Knife Thrower brings his attention back to me. I quicken my pace in terror. The first knife comes flying in on my right side; fortunately, it misses, but by less than an inch. The Knife Thrower keeps going after me. When I turn my head, I see a knife coming toward my face. Adrenaline shoots through me, and as I sling my body back, the knife soars over my head. The Knife Thrower seems to give up and return back to the massacre at the parking lot to find his next victim.

I keep running. I can feel the sweat running down my body. Tears trickle down my cheeks in apprehension. I turn my head back to make sure I am far away from that parking lot, but as I do, something trips me. I try to lift up my body, but the Knife Thrower has somehow appeared in front of me. He kicks me in the chest, and I fall to the ground helplessly. "Please don't!" I beg desperately.

The Knife Thrower draws his knife and goes for a stab, but I miraculously grab his wrist. I twist it and grab the knife, then kick him in the stomach while spinning him around, and then I stab him through the back. I don't stay to watch the gory scene. Instead, I run home, but when I get to my driveway a figure appears in front of me.

"It's not safe to be out late at night by yourself," the Knife Thrower says with a smirk.

I gasp in horror.

The Knife Thrower shoves me against my mailbox and has his hand pressed on my chest. "Surprise. You stabbed me in my back, Andrew! It hurt!" Then he draws a knife and swings it down to my head....

I wake up with sweat covering my body, my heart pounding, and my eyes widen in horror. *It was just a dream*, I think, *but it can easily happen today*.

I glance at my calendar. Today is Friday, March 6, 2054. I need to get ready for school—I have an eight-thirty Zoom call. Due to recent events in town, kids have been doing online classes. I sigh and walk to my bathroom. When I look in the mirror, I see my exhausted self, my brown hair and brown eyes, which remind me that I was most likely adopted. Both of my parents have blonde hair and blue eyes, so I always wondered how they ended up with me. By the way, my name is Andrew Mikaelson. I live in Wayverlyn, New Jersey.

Things have been annoying with school lately. Everyone in my town is in danger. I have had nightmares recently. I have been very cautious of my surroundings. Everything is brutal.

I brush my teeth and head toward the stairs. I don't see my dad because my parents are divorced. My mom recently got married to someone else, who is my stepdad. He's very nice, but a little bit of a kiss-up to me, acting as if I like him and we are good buddies. My real dad lives all the way in Trenton, which is a few hours away.

When I walk downstairs to the kitchen, my mom cheerfully greets me. "Hey, good morning."

"Morning," I mumble. Then I ask, "Mom, when will this all be over? I want to be in person when I'm doing school! And live a life where I can feel safe to go outside."

"Once the police catch the man who's behind all this stuff, you'll be back in school in no time," my mom replies.

If you're wondering why the town I live in is Zooming for school, it's because of the murders. It isn't safe to go outside. Not at all—otherwise you could be stabbed by the Knife Thrower. That's the name of the man who is responsible for all the murders. I didn't know any of the victims.

Then my mom says, "Listen, I know it's hard for you using the Zoom app for school, but to make you feel better—"

"Yes," I abruptly interrupt her. "I know back in your time, in 2020 and the year after, that you had online school for a long time because of that virus." I am annoyed, because she has told me that about one thousand times.

"Hey!" she shouts. "It's true and it stunk, but the police will soon catch this guy before—"

"Before we get killed," I interrupt again.

"Andrew," my mom says, "we'll be fine."

All of a sudden, my stepdad, Jonah, walks in holding a baseball mitt. "Hey, bud," he says excitedly, "wanna play some ball before school starts?"

"It's literally 7:30 a.m.," I respond rudely. "I just woke up about thirty seconds ago."

"Hey!" my mother snaps at me. "Be nicer to your father."

"Step," I correct. I've been a very moody person lately because of Jonah. When we would talk or hang out like normal people it was fun, but when he suddenly started acting like we were best friends or something, I developed different thoughts about him.

Jonah dejectedly says, "All right," and leaves the kitchen.

My mom whispers, "Don't speak to your stepfather like that! He's trying his best to be nice to you, and you keep pushing him away." I sigh. "Look!" my mom says. "I know that you and every single child in this town are going through a rough time, but don't take it out on Jonah. Think about all the families whose relatives have been murdered! *Think about what they're going through.*"

"Okay," I reply. "Sorry."

I march to the fridge and grab an apple for breakfast. First, I wash the bright red apple and take a big bite into it. It is very sweet. I keep eating.

Once I finish, I go upstairs to my room to get ready for the day. I get dressed in black pants and a long-sleeve blue shirt. I wait until 8:29, then open my medium-sized computer. I click on the email app and see a message from my teacher, Karry Rolenstein. In the message it has a Zoom link that I click on. My computer says: *Waiting in 5th Grade Karry Rolenstein's meeting. Host will let you in soon.* At 8:30 I am let in.

I see my teacher and twenty other students. Every day we have a one-hour Zoom meeting focusing on two different subjects. After the meeting I do a bunch of work that was assigned. But because it's Friday, that means it is creative day, where we do something else instead of two subjects for Zoom. But we still get homework to do over the weekend.

To begin the class, Ms. Rolenstein says, "We are going to go around and say what we want to do when we grow up. Then you will go into breakout rooms with a partner. One person will be with me because we have twenty-one students."

I later learn this is because one kid didn't want to turn on their computer at all because they were nervous that the Knife Thrower would hack into their computer and track them down.

"I will call on you one by one." She calls on the first kid.

"I want to be a police officer!" she says.

"I wanna be a pilot!"

"I want to be in the MLB."

"A doctor!"

"A teacher!"

Finally, Ms. Rolenstein calls on me. She asks, "Andrew, what would you like to do when you grow up?"

I think about that for a moment. I had considered careers such as a doctor, a physicist, a biologist, maybe even an astronomer, but I don't have much interest in science. I'm pretty skeptical about me ending up as some kind of scientist. What about somebody who wants to work in government? Eh, politics is boring and seems stressful, based on my limited knowledge of how the government works. A firefighter? Meh. How about a prosecutor maybe? That sounds fascinating. A judge? "Actually, I want to be a lawyer," I answer.

"Interesting," she replies. "Okay, let's move on."

My teacher keeps calling on other students. If you're wondering why I would like to be a lawyer when I grow up, it's because I am very interested in law and solving crimes, which means that being a detective would be another good job for me. Except for the fact that it can be a dangerous job, and I wouldn't want to possibly get hurt.

I once went through a phase where I wanted to be in the FBI, but my mother burst my bubble and told me that it was too dangerous. I was very upset that day, but now that I'm older it makes sense why a mother wouldn't want her child to be in the FBI. Right now I want to be a lawyer, but I also want to solve this mystery in town and find out who the Knife Thrower is, which doesn't relate too much to being a lawyer.

After everyone has answered, my teacher says, "Okay, now that everyone has shared what they want to do when they grow up, we will go into breakout rooms in pairs. You will practice your job with your partner, and your partner will give you feedback. For example, if my partner is Luke and he wants to be a major league baseball player when he grows up, he would show me how he swings a bat or how he throws a ball, and then I would tell him how he could do better. Off you go!"

In the seconds that I am loading into my breakout room, I am hoping that I will end up with my teacher. The reason is, I don't really know how much kids my age understand about law and courts. I'm not saying that my classmates are simpleminded; I am just saying that ten-year-old kids don't usually learn much about law.

The main reason I know about law is because of TV. I know it seems like an odd resource for knowledge, but it's true. Maybe I'm not learning how lawyers should really be acting in court because, come on—the lawyers have to break out in a fight in a good law movie or TV show. I am cognizant of how lawyers should behave in court, but from TV I learn a bunch of laws and what roles certain people play in the profession.

To my luck I am paired with Ms. Rolenstein! She begins with, "Well, hello, Andrew. How are you doing?"

"I'm good. How are you?"

"I am blessed beyond measure," she says happily.

And yes, I know that when someone says, "I am blessed beyond measure," it can really bug the crap out of you. Yes, you are happy for them or whatever, but really? Who says that? It's especially annoying when you're having a bad day and someone just acts so jubilant. I'm not having a bad day, but nothing so far in my day is making it good.

"So, earlier in class I remember you saying that you want to be a lawyer when you grow up. Isn't that correct?"

"Yes," I say.

"I have a question for you. If you are representing someone in a trial, and while you're doing some research, you come across a video that is proof of your client being guilty, what would you do?"

I am speechless. I have no clue what to say. Then she says contemptuously, "Think about it. That's something extra for your homework." Well, it is strange for somebody to say that so roughly, because they also happen to be the person who just a minute ago described themselves as "blessed beyond measure." Again, who really says that?

"Okay," I say. "I'll think about it."

"I have another question for you," she says. My gosh, now I wish I'd been paired with a classmate instead of my garrulous teacher. Conversation is not fun with her. "Let's say that your client is very rude, and you do not want to protect him or her in the trial. What would you do?"

"I'll make sure none of my clients are like that," I say.

"And how is that?" Ms. Rolenstein asks.

"Before I defend someone accused of committing a crime, I'll get to know them first so I can see who I'm defending," I remark. And I feel like a genius for saying that. My teacher expected me to be in a dilemma on what to say, but I answered her question perfectly. I stated my answer strongly—and also with a bit of attitude to show how much I supported my answer.

"That's a good idea," Ms. Rolenstein admits. You could tell, based on her voice, that she was taken aback by my answer. I was pretty shocked that I was able to come up with something so good so expeditiously. "Well, time's up. I'll invite you to the main session. See you," Ms. Rolenstein says apprehensively, seeming to want to end our conversation—which, trust me, I did as well.

"Bye," I reply.

She leaves the breakout room, then I do. Once everyone is in the main session, Ms. Rolenstein asks, "So, how did it go?" Many kids put their thumbs up and smile, while I just nod yes. Other kids smile too, but reluctantly, because it's still early in the day. They were even doing this class in their pajamas. I've done that before. We all did in those days.

Ms. Rolenstein says cordially, "Well, that is phenomenal." I bet she is the only teacher who acts kind to her students so early in the day, which I am grateful for because last year my teacher was an old grump. "Now, if you look on Google Xortic you will see a doc. I want you to write on that doc five paragraphs about what you want to do when you grow up and why. Use font size 14. As a requirement, you need your paper to be over one page. You all know how to structure this. The first paragraph is an introduction, paragraphs two through four are reasonings to support your statement, and the final paragraph is your conclusion. So, everyone can now turn their camera off and get to work."

After I turn off my camera, I take a deep breath and start to write about why I want to be a lawyer when I grow up. It is because I find law very appealing, considering all the mysteries and the "arguments" lawyers have in court. Well, that isn't such great reasoning. I need more valid reasons. I think for a while. Sometimes I'd type three sentences and decide that it was a piece of garbage and delete those sentences but end up writing the same thing again.

Finally, I finish writing my paper, and I personally felt rushed doing it. Afterward, I realize that I have to edit it. Therefore, I slowly read it to make sure my grammar is correct. There were numerous spots where I had misplaced commas. To my surprise I didn't spell one word wrong. Or at least I don't think I did.

At 9:29, my teacher announces, "Cameras on." Right then, we all turn our cameras on. Ms. Rolenstein goes over the homework. She says, "I would like you to complete pages sixty-two through sixty-seven in your math workbooks, read for twenty-five minutes, and write a summary about what you read, then share it with me. There should be a doc on Xortic, which has the links to watch a science video and another video for social studies. You may now leave, but stay on if you have questions."

I leave the Zoom meeting and walk downstairs into the kitchen to start some of my homework. When I walk in the kitchen, I see Uncle Jeremy. He is Jonah's brother who has been living with us for the past month. He sleeps in the basement and is a very deep sleeper. He sits on his phone a lot and always seems busy texting people, like some teenager addicted to their phone.

I suspect that he came up into the kitchen about five minutes before I came here. I like Uncle Jeremy. I usually call him Uncle J. I like him a lot more than Jonah. One reason is that Jonah sees me as a weak and very clueless person. He's always trying to help me with things that I know how to do. I appreciate that, but it's been getting super annoying. Whereas Uncle J sees me as an independent, strong person. If I ever ask him to get me something, he just replies, "Get it yourself. The fridge is like five feet away from you." I like that because it shows that he thinks of me as a person who is capable of doing things. Uncle J is like a friend to me, not a third parent. We always goof around together.

As I walk into the kitchen, Uncle J says, "Hey, good morning! What's up?"

"Nothing much," I reply. "How about you?"

"I'm great. One sec, I've got a surprise for you," Uncle J says excitingly. He leaves the kitchen. I am very curious about what this surprise could even be because I don't ask for much. Uncle J returns to the kitchen holding a big box. "Guess who got you the new 4TX game console!" he exclaims.

Ah, the 4TX console. It's the newest console that video games are played on. I'm not a big video game guy, but I would feel horrible telling Uncle J that I don't like his gift. I'm very happy that he wanted to surprise me, even if it's just the thought he put into getting me something. He'll probably be playing the game late at night and I'll be a parent to him shouting, "It's getting late! You better stop playing that game!" That is actually very funny to think about, so I giggle for a moment, which Uncle J probably sees as a show of gratitude.

"There's a new mystery game that we can play, and you have to find out who did the crime. You search houses in the game and a bunch of other stuff!" Uncle J is very happy, as you could probably tell.

"Cool!" I shout. "I've got some schoolwork to do, but after that, I will one hundred percent play with you."

"And it's Friday! We could stay up late!" Uncle J adds.

I then start to do my math pages—that is, until I notice Jonah murmur something. I can't tell what, but I lean into the table, like I'm asking, *What did you say?* Jonah just rolls his eyes and hides behind his newspaper. I read what is in a big font on the back of the newspaper. It says ANOTHER MAN KILLED BY THE KNIFE THROWER. I see a small caption that says 63-YEAR-OLD JIM MARCUS WAS STABBED FOUR TIMES BY KNIVES THROWN AT HIS CHEST. There is some other stuff that I can't read because of the small font, but it is definitely not anything good.

I was about halfway through multiplying fractions when my mother says ominously, "Guys I have some news for you, and it's not good."

"What is it?" Jonah asks, lifting his chin up, interested.

"Mr. Smith was killed," my mother says gloomily.

Jonah sighs and shakes his head disappointingly.

"Who is Mr. Smith?" I ask. Perplexed, my eyes twitch around as I shift my gaping look from one adult to another, hoping that somebody will give me an answer.

My mother and stepfather stare at each other. Jonah then asks my mother Jamie, "Jamie, can you tell him?"

"Tell me what?" I ask anxiously. Something feels a little fishy right now. Uncle J stares down while saying, "I'm going to get back to doing what I was doing," which is really an indication that he doesn't want to be in this conversation.

My mother sighs. "It's a long story. If you must know, about fifteen years ago, Jonah was falsely accused of murder."

"WHAT?!" I shout. "How have you never told me that?! And what does that have to do with this Smith guy?"

"Let me finish," my mother says calmly, probably thinking it would chill me out. "While Jonah was in court, the prosecutor was this Mr. Smith."

"Why would you become friends with someone who was trying to put you in prison?" I ask Jonah.

My mother sighs again, seeming a little agitated. "Let me finish," she repeats. "Luckily, Jonah and his lawyer won the case. A few years later, Jonah ran into Mr. Smith and they made peace. Mr. Smith went on for a while about how terrible he felt for accusing him of such a callous crime. Jonah accepted the apology, because that is the good person he is."

"I'm so sorry," I say to Jonah.

"It's fine." Jonah looks dejected but then seems to have felt a rise of happiness, thinking about something positive to change his mood. He seems somewhat nostalgic.

Then my mother begins to speak. "What we're worried about is that maybe the Knife Thrower might go after your stepfather."

"Why would the Knife Thrower target *him*?" I ask.

"I have a name!" Jonah corrects, but I ignore him.

My mother resumes, "The point is, people still think that your stepfather is guilty, and if one of those people is the Knife Thrower, he or she might have a lot of hatred toward Jonah."

I nod. There is silence for a moment until I say, "Well, I'm going to finish my math homework."

I keep on doing my homework, but I can't stop thinking about how bad I feel for Jonah. Even though I still don't like him much, it isn't because he's some random stranger who all of a sudden came into my life. It's because I don't like him as a person. I'm starting to have a little less hatred toward him, although I feel like Jonah is the kind of person who would most likely be guilty of murder but the least suspected. Like how it is in all the movies. I decide I'm probably overthinking, though, like how I always do. I take a big breath and clear my mind of mysteries.

After a little while I finish my math homework. Next, I watch my social studies and science videos, which are surprisingly amusing. I then start to read for twenty-five minutes and then write a summary about it. The reason why I'm not saying so much about my homework is because it's quite boring. I finish my work around 10:45. I plan on having lunch around 11:15 so I will have some time to do absolutely nothing, which I love.

All of a sudden, my mother walks over to me. "I've got some more news for you," she says somberly.

"What is it?" I ask, assuming that somebody else just got stabbed by the Knife Thrower.

My mother says, "About five minutes ago a class Zoom call was going on and the Knife Thrower somehow logged on to it. From now on you won't be doing any school at all."

"Well, how can you be sure that it was the Knife Thrower?" I wonder. I was glad that I wouldn't have schoolwork, but I felt nervous about what the Knife Thrower had done.

"He was wearing the same dark mask he wears, and he was holding knives. Also, he logged in with the Knife Thrower as his ID."

"How'd he get into the Zoom? Wouldn't the teacher have let him in the meeting if the teacher is the host?" I ask.

"The police have already thought of that. They are going to question the teacher tomorrow," my mother replies. "My friend Ali's husband works at the station and Ali informed me."

"Oooh, can I look through the door when the teacher is being questioned?" I inquire excitedly.

"Um, with the Knife Thrower out there, *no*! Even if I'm with you, it's too risky," my mother tells me.

"What if I bring a weapon?" I suggest.

"Are you crazy!?" my mother shouts.

"I guess," I concede reluctantly.

My mother exhales. "Just promise me you won't go."

"Okay," I lie.

"Thank you." She seems very relieved.

No way I wasn't going. It would be so interesting to watch that teacher be found guilty. Even though the Knife Thrower is out there, I'll just bring a few steak knives to kill him if I come across him. I mean, how hard could it be?

I figure I might as well practice right now. I go to the kitchen and grab knives that are as large as butter knives but have sharp blades. I then go in my backyard and pick up a few pieces of leftover wood that had been used for floors. The pieces of wood are very large and dirty. I dust the dirt off, then go to the garage and grab red spray paint and a shovel.

I carry the heavy materials to my backyard. I feel relief once I drop it all. I sigh while staring at everything, intending to build a knife range. I'll start by digging holes about six inches deep. Next, I will line up all the wood in the holes, making sure that 80 percent of it is sticking above ground. After that, I will move all the dirt that I dug up so it's all around the wood. Then, I'll spray-paint a human body on it. Next, I will throw knives at the wood.

Will I be a master at this in the next twenty-four hours? No. But, I will be just a little bit better at throwing knives, which I have never tried before, and I assume I am bad at it.

I sigh and start my work. I plunge my shovel into the dirt. I keep on digging deeper and deeper until I think that my spine is going to split in half. I then let go of the shovel and stand up.

I grip my hands back on the shovel and keep pulling and pulling up until it flings backward! I turn around and I see Jonah covered in dirt. "I…I am so sorry!" I apologize.

Jonah moves his body around like a hip-hop dancer to get the dirt off him. "It's fine," he says. "I just looked through the window and saw you. I was wondering if you needed any help. You seem to be struggling."

"Yeaaaaah, I'm fine," I lie, because I didn't need help from him.

"Are…are you sure?"

"I'm fine, thanks for asking. Just please leave," I say in exasperation.

I put both my hands on Jonah's arm, turn him around, and give him a light push.

"W-what are you even doing?" he asks.

"Um, uh, a science project," I lie.

"Are…are you sure that you don't need help? Because—"

"Yes, I'm sure! Now go!" I order, while pointing to our house. He seems a little offended. "Go!" I shout again. Jonah then starts to walk backward into the house until his foot hits a rock.

He mutters something about me being some ungrateful or annoying kid. Jonah stomps into the house while wiping some dirt off his crimson shirt. Then he shakes his head. I am very curious about what could be going through his mind right now, but I for sure know that he doesn't like me so much anymore, which is fair. I go back to my digging, wondering whether I will be able to build this knife range before tomorrow.

Suddenly, Jonah is back. "Are you sure that this is a science project?"

"Here we go again," I mutter so he can't hear me. "Yes, Jonah!"

"Well, what's with the knives?" he asks, while pointing to them.

"Can you just go?" I ask, feeling very bothered.

"As your father, it's my job to make sure that you're safe," he says, like I'm a piece of gold.

"Stepfather. And you're the only person who is in an unsafe position," I say, so this phony will walk away. I then pick out one of the knives and attempt to throw it. (Not at him, of course.) I throw it like a baseball, and it spins forward and forward until it hits the back of a wooden chair on the patio. The knife is pinned into the wood. I begin panting, not believing what I had just done and why.

"What did you just do?" Jonah asks.

"Um, I guess for some reason I threw a knife." I shrug, acting as if what I did was totally normal. I did want to get some anger and bad energy out.

To be honest, I was a pretty good knife thrower. I was impressed with myself. "That was actually pretty cool," Jonah tells me.

"You think?" I ask.

My mother storms outside. She seems to be going mad. "What's all the racket?" she hisses. She then notices the knife jabbed into her house. "W-what did you two do?"

"Well, it's a really funny story." I chuckle, hoping I wouldn't get in trouble. "It was him!" I quickly say while pointing to Jonah. "All him, not me," I say in affirmation.

"What? Jonah?!" my mother shouts. "Why did you throw a knife at our house?!"

Jonah stumbles over his words. "Wha–? Th-that was him! I was going to help him and then he threw dirt on me, then threw a knife at the house!"

"Is that true?" my mother asks.

"No," I say.

"I'm leaving this backyard, but when you two decide who gets punished, come to me!" she orders. She then stomps into the house while shaking her head.

I feel relieved. "Whoo, that was a close one. You wanna try?" I take a knife out of my pocket and offer it to Jonah. Instead, he rips the knife out of my hand and throws it into the dirt.

"This is RIDICULOUS! You can't blame me for a knife you threw! Why do you treat me like I'm garbage or something?!"

I shrug. "I dunno."

"I'm telling your mother right now!" Jonah shouts.

"Okay," I simply reply.

"Why aren't you scared?" he wonders.

"I'll just go to Uncle J and he'll do something," I say.

"Uncle J?" Jonah says with confusion. He scoffs. "The man who claims that he can't afford rent for one month at an apartment but can buy the newest gaming console? You go to him to help you with something? He is not a reliable person. What if he's keeping secrets from you?"

"Yeaaaaaaah," I say calmly. Jonah is a man who gets jealous very easily and could get very sensitive and angry at the same time.

"I'm telling your mother about what's going on out here!" Jonah yells.

"Okay." I shrug to further exasperate Jonah.

Jonah makes a fist and stomps away. I get back to building my knife range. Maybe I was a little rude to Jonah, but if he was in my shoes, he would've done the same. It's already been about twenty-five minutes since I started building the knife range, but I think it will be worth it in the end. For some reason, while I'm digging, I'm very determined, like I'm looking for gold or something precious. I start getting tired and sweaty.

Finally, after a long time, I am done digging. Now it's time to put the wood in the hole. I pick up a long and heavy piece. I feel like a construction contractor.

* * *

I remember a few months ago when Jonah woke me up at 4:30 a.m. on a Saturday morning to go fishing for five hours. It was the dullest day of my entire life. We didn't have much conversation, and on the mini boat we had runny eggs, burnt sausage, and undercooked bacon. I was literally breathing on my bacon just so it would be hot, and for the sausage I bit off the burnt parts and spit them into the lake. The eggs—I just didn't eat them. I had one bite of the runny egg whites and about two-thousand pounds of pepper, but after that I was absolutely disgusted.

After an hour or so we went back to land to get more bait. At that time, I found a box of matches on the muddy ground. I wiped the dirt off and brought them back to the boat. About fifteen minutes later we caught a fish. I was very happy in those twenty-five seconds. I looked at the trout for a moment, thinking that anything other than the bacon and eggs would be good. I then lit two matches and put them under the fish for a long time, then took a bite into it. And it was the most disgusting thing I ever had. Since that day, I have refused to eat any seafood. Even crab, which was my favorite before that fish incident.

I'm going to guess that Jonah had the time of his life out there, but as you can see, I did not.

About four weeks ago something very fun happened: Uncle J and I went on a two-week trip to Israel! I asked him how he got the money for this. He told me that he won the lottery, which was a big surprise as well. It was very fun, although Uncle J was hardly there during the days. He left early in the morning and came home late at night. I was on my own. I had a map, of course. When I asked Uncle J why he was hardly there, he said he was going to places to create fun surprises for the night. The surprises were revealed every three days and were very lame. Uncle J was probably spending all the time in Tel Aviv looking for some futuristic, expensive technology.

All of a sudden I hear, "Hello, Andrew. Are you busy?"

I turn around. It's Uncle J. "I'm free," I say.

Uncle J is holding a stack of parchment and an unopened can of beer. I stare at it with confusion. "By any chance do you know Persian?" he asks.

"Huh?" I reply.

"The language," Uncle J says. I shake my head in bewilderment. "Russian?" Uncle J asks hopefully. "Preferably Persian."

I feel slightly discombobulated. I am quite shocked that Uncle J can list a language besides what he calls "American."

"What do you need?" I ask.

"I-I..." Uncle J stutters. "You can't tell anyone, okay?"

I nod.

He takes a deep breath. "I'm in the CIA."

2

The CIA Agent

"WHAT?!" I shout.

"SHHHHHH!" Uncle J says louder while putting his index finger on his lips.

"What?" I say again. I'm laughing in my mind, thinking that this is just a sick joke.

"Look—"

I cut him off. "Why would you be in the CIA anyway, and how could you do it?" Uncle J is about to say something until I say, "What I just asked was a rhetorical question. It actually makes total sense. You seem to have a lot of money, and the whole time when we were in Israel you were probably doing some secretive tasks. Or you could've been in some other Middle Eastern country."

Uncle J sighs. I then give him a death stare, hoping for him to say something. I just don't know what I want him to say. I mean, he's in the CIA. How often does your uncle come up to you and out of nowhere say *I'm in the CIA*. Yeah, I was right. Hasn't happened to you.

Did my mother know? Did my stepfather know? I quickly turn around for a second, hoping nobody is behind me. Something interesting enters my mind. I remember when, not long ago, Jonah said to me that I shouldn't go to Uncle J when I needed help. Jonah also mentioned to me that maybe Uncle J was keeping "secrets" from me. Was that hinting something about him being in the CIA?

Uncle J says, "I have to fake an act about my identity. My real name is not Jeremy. It is Parzin."

I am shocked. This meant that Jonah and my mother had to know about this! "So, your brother and my mother know that you're in the CIA?" I say, feeling perplexed.

"Not exactly," Uncle J, who I should now be calling Uncle P, replies in a muffled voice. He seems very sly now.

"What's that supposed to mean?" I say, while crossing my arms. I am very annoyed right now. I can completely understand why Uncle P won't tell me, but I feel indignation rise through my body. From my toes, to my foot, to my ankle, to my leg, to my thigh, to my hip, to my stomach, to my chest, through my neck and my head.

Uncle P replies, "I told them that I am in the FBI."

My eyes widen. Why tell the truth to me but not his sister-in-law or his blood relative?

"But," Uncle P says in a proud way, like giving me an order, "you *cannot* tell them. Anyway—"

"Why lie about being in the FBI?" I interrupt. "I mean, it's a very secretive job." I pause. "Just like the CIA."

"Oh." My uncle chuckles. "Oh, my friend, if the FBI was ranked one to ten on how secretive they are, they're about eleven."

"That's off the chart," I correct him.

"Exactly, but the CIA, you ask. That's about six thousand, I'd say. See the difference? Back to what I was saying earlier—"

I stop him. "Is this going to take a while?" I ask.

"Yeah, sort of," he admits.

"I'm going to go back to what I was doing," I say. "I'll be listening."

"Okay," Uncle P replies. "I lied to your stepfather and mother about my identity. I told them that I am in the FBI. But I'm really in the CIA. I actually have a net worth of seven-point-one million dollars, and—"

"Okay, now you're just bragging," I say, annoyed and starting to envy his great bank account.

Uncle P sighs. "My boss assigned my life!"

I am very confused. What does it mean for someone's life to be "assigned"? That made no sense. Uncle P then says, "My boss forces me to live a fake life. He says that it makes me seem less suspicious about being in the CIA. When I'm talking to other people besides you, my cover is that I'm an entrepreneur. It stinks being forced to live a fake life, but I love being in the CIA. It is pretty cool. I actually own a million-dollar condo in New York City."

I gasp. Wow! All of a sudden, my uncle, who claims he can't afford one month's rent for an apartment, owns a fancy condo in NYC. "It's a nice place," Uncle P says happily. "Very modern. I love it. Although I haven't been there since I crashed here."

"So, your boss forced you to live with us, and luckily my mother agreed to let you stay here?" I ask. Secretly, I am assuming that my uncle can figure out who the Knife Thrower is. I mean, considering he is in the CIA, he is probably very intelligent. I feel very honored to know this when his own brother does not.

"Correct," he responds.

My voice changes to a serious tone. "Why are you telling me all this?"

He shrugs. "I'm not sure. Back to what I was saying earlier, I was wondering if you knew the Persian language?"

"I don't," I reply wearily. "Why do you ask such a strange question that you already know the answer to?"

"Because I was wondering if you wanted to go into a kid training session for the CIA," Uncle P replies lightly.

I can't even process what my uncle just asked me. Me? Me in a CIA training session?

I knew what he said, but just to double-check (because what he just told me was crazy), I say, "Huh?" I am completely bewildered.

"I was wondering if you wanted to go into a kids' CIA training session. Whoever's in it needs to be able to speak Persian and some other languages. Well, one of seven," my uncle says solidly. "Which include French, Chinese, Spanish, Arabic, Russian, and one more that I am forgetting, but you get the point."

I think about it for a moment, then sigh. "I'm interested, but my mom won't let me be in the FBI when I'm older. I think she would be absolutely horrified to find out that I'm even training for the CIA, and to be honest, it seems too risky. The FBI may be dangerous, but the CIA? Err...like you said earlier, in a ranking of how secretive it is, you said six thousand."

I would have loved to do training for the CIA, but if my mom didn't know, then I would feel bad. In my opinion, the CIA is an ominous job. Unless you're sly, clever, and a good liar.

"Well..." he replies.

My eyes get bigger. "Well, what?" I feel very muddled, and my uncle all of a sudden seems very peculiar.

"Once you're eighteen..."

"Hmm?" I ask.

"When you're eighteen, you'll be out of the house and you can do what you want with your life," Uncle P says, as if it isn't a big deal.

"That is true, but it wouldn't feel right," I say. Right now, I'm not so interested in being in a CIA kids' training session. And that's due to my mom. Her being overprotective is a bit annoying sometimes, but in the end I'm always grateful for it.

Uncle P nods. "Tonight I need to travel to Saudi Arabia. I'll be gone for a week."

"So, what's your excuse for why you're leaving?" I wonder.

"That a friend invited me to a lake house for a week," he says.

"You're a very clever person," I admit.

"Right you are," my uncle says, then chuckles.

"So, Jonah nor my mom know your occupation? Why don't you just come clean?" I ask. "Then when you lie to go out of town, it's like you know that we know you're lying while my mother and your brother don't know that I know what your real job is."

"Your mother told me to not say a single word to you about me being in the FBI. It's going to be a whole thing...and plus, your mother would be furious that I lied about my job and that you know the truth, especially when she told me not to tell you what really wasn't true!" he says.

I am so confused. I then hit myself to make sure I'm not dreaming.

"What are you doing?" Uncle P asks.

"Um, uh, n-nothing," I stammer.

"Not about how you just hit yourself," he says curiously. He pauses. "What are you building?"

"Can you keep a secret?" I ask.

"That's a stupid question." Uncle P then cracks open the beer.

"Why?" I ask.

"Keeping secrets is how I get paid and help our country," he says.

"Right," I say. "Anyway—"

"I'm an honest man," Uncle P says while taking a sip of his beer. "What your building looks like is a group of trees after a hurricane hit." Even though the attention I got was negative, I like the honesty.

"I'm building a knife range," I whisper.

"A what?" Uncle P asks, seeming startled.

"A knife range," I repeat. Based on my uncle's face, it seems like he just saw flying pigs. I go on to explain, "I want to sneak into the police station and listen to Knife Thrower suspects be questioned. You know my mother, and of course she told me that I couldn't go, but I'm thinking that if I become a good knife thrower, things could be okay. Because if the Knife Thrower comes after me I'll throw that knife right back at him." I use my hand to express everything I'm saying, as if I'm playing a game of charades. My uncle seems befuddled, trying to process what I just said. "Isn't that a good idea?" I ask.

"*Yeaaahnoow.*"

I am probably the most confused I have ever been in my entire life. "What are you saying?!" I yell. I thought that my uncle was a straight-up honest man. "Speak clearly in English."

"Kid," he starts with. "You've got a big imagination, and that is all I have to say." He sips his beer.

I am getting very irked. "Add details," I say desperately, angrily.

"Well..." He takes another sip of beer. "Erm..." I roll my eyes. "Okay, back to your thing," he remembers. He snaps his fingers. "To start, you sound a lot like the Knife Thrower." My eyebrows raise up, questioning Uncle P. "And two, don't you think that your mother will see you practicing knife throwing?"

I think about that for a moment. A little while ago I got away with throwing a knife because I blamed it on Jonah. My uncle goes on. "And three, you might turn into a serial killer. You might end up having fun throwing knives. You might consider it a hobby," he says gently, because he knows that what he just said is very aggravating.

"Wha-what?!" I feel like some kind of lunatic after this pep talk my uncle just gave me. His first two statements were true, but no way would I end up as a serial killer. In fact, I was trying to stop one. "What do you think I am? A psycho?"

He shrugs with annoyance. "You really think that a person would end up as a serial killer defending themselves?" I ask. He chuckles. "What?" I wonder. It's weird how people could change so much in twenty minutes. He keeps chuckling and I keep getting more and more vexed. "WHAT?!" I finally shout. "What is so funny?!"

He immediately stops laughing after my voice rose so much that I seemed like a roaring lion. Uncle P then says, "Some dude who used to work with me did a lot of self-defense so he could avoid serious injuries and even death, which is the right thing to do, of course. Anyway, he was a crazy guy. He couldn't control himself, and he ended up becoming a serial killer." I am very confused. "My point is I don't want you going down that path," my uncle explains.

"Well, you've done a lot of self-defense before. Shouldn't you be worried about yourself?" I ask.

He sighs. "Yes, but all I'm saying is that it's a waste of your time as well and—"

"Go back to me ending up like the guy who worked with you," I order. Was my uncle even thinking? I knew better to not end up like a serial killer.

"I don't know," he says. "Anyway, I don't think that is a good thing for you to be sneaking out to defend yourself. And what you were telling me is that you will practice throwing knives. Then you'll sneak out, but what if your mother catches you out of the house or something after you've done a lot of knife throwing? People get used to things they do. Your intentions are that you can defend yourself. But if you do it a lot you might like it. For example, when you started to play some sport, maybe you didn't like it, but after you played it a lot you loved it."

I then realize that my uncle is right. Plus, I'd just be putting myself into a lot of danger.

"My point is," he says, "if you're going to try something, it shouldn't be throwing knives. And remember how I'm honest, right? You can't go into town without the risk of getting injured by that creepy knife-throwing guy."

I know that he is lying there. Most of the Knife Thrower's victims were killed at night. I didn't go out in town at night, anyway.

I sigh, then say, "Okay, I understand what you're saying."

"Good," he replies. "Now, there are some more things I need to share with you about me being in the CIA." I wonder what else he could possibly say that would be interesting, but I pay attention. Uncle P then says, "What I'm doing in Saudi Arabia is going to make me risk my life." He grits his teeth.

"What are you doing?" I ask.

"Me and only two other guys have to sneak into a building, the Burj Rafal. We have to steal 4,298 pieces of paper in less than two hours. This is our first task. We have everything planned out, and we know everyone's working hours. We know how we're going to sneak around. Here, lemme show you a picture of the building."

I lean over to see my uncle's iPhone 30. It has thirty cameras on it! Back in the old days, my mother told me that the iPhone had only one camera at first. I can't imagine how annoying that was. I look at his phone and I see a picture of the Burj Rafal. It's a very tall, clear-looking building. I see a caption that says, *Burj Rafal is 308 meters, which is 1,010 feet tall.*

"Whoa!" I say with excitement. The building is exquisite! "It looks so pretty!"

"Seems pretty nice, huh?" Uncle P asks.

"Yeah," I agree.

"Well, at nine o'clock tomorrow morning there's going to be some action," he says excitedly. I grin, finding this talk entertaining. "Want to see what I'm going to wear as my disguise?" I nod. He then pulls up a picture of a piece of clothing that looks like a white gown. "That's what I'm wearing," my uncle says proudly to keep me entertained.

I study the picture. "Is that a *thobe*?" I ask.

"Yes," he replies.

We sit in silence while I study the picture. I notice four white buttons on the top middle of the garment. The clothing is like a robe made from bedsheets. I like the photo because I always find different cultures very interesting. In 2051 I went to a museum with my mom and dad before they got a divorce. There were 203 display cases—one for every country. Each case had the country's flag, most popular food, most common clothing, animals that have habitats there, and pictures of traditions. My father told me that in the year 2020 there were only around 190 countries.

Going back to the *thawb*, my uncle says, "There are many different colors that they come in, and they are for men and women."

"Wow," I say with surprise. We stare at each other. "What happens if you don't make it?" I ask.

"What do you mean?" he replies.

"L-l-l-like…" I keep stammering. I sigh while my uncle looks at me with confusion. "If you don't survive," I finally say.

"I'm not going to die," he says, most likely to make me feel better. "Sure, there is a risk of dying, but that risk is so small." He puts up his left hand and forms a circle, then turns it so it gets smaller, and smaller, until the circle is gone.

"And what is your plan if you get caught?" I ask.

"I won't," he says proudly. "But if somehow we did, our plan is to jump."

"Huh?" I ask. "What does jumping do?"

Uncle P takes another big gulp of beer. "I'm sorry that I wasn't so clear," he says. I knit my eyebrows in bewilderment. He continues: "Me and the other guys will be tied onto very long ropes. We will be in a chopper. Next, we'll jump from it. We'll crash into a window and get in and get all the papers we need. Then we'll grab all our stuff and if we're caught, we jump out of the window. Then we'll get pulled back into the helicopter."

I am so shocked. I know that the CIA does *crazy* things, but this? All I can think is—*wow*!

"Then where will the helicopter fly?"

"Well," my uncle says, "we are afraid if the people in the building have a cartwixziz." He doesn't answer my question.

"What's that?" I say. *Cartwixziz*? What an odd word, I think. Saudi Arabia is a strong country, and I've learned from the news that it has been making big, new, and strong weapons. They are in third place with the best military out of all countries on the continent of Asia. The top two are Japan and Iran. My parents told me that some country, I think called Hina, was around? I'm always pronouncing it wrong. They told me that Japan bought all the land in Hina. They said it happened in 2038. I was not even born then.

"I'm not asking about things they have, but where will the helicopter fly to?" I ask.

"Zigzags and up at the same time," he replies.

Next, I ask, "And what is a cartwixziz?" I assume it's a bomb or a gun, but I still ask.

"It is a big gun. It shoots out grenades and bullets at the same time," he replies.

I thought that seemed like something that would cost $100,000. Or maybe things were either more expensive or cheaper in Saudi Arabia. It seemed very interesting. "Sounds cool!" I exclaim.

"Not unless it kills your uncle," Uncle P says, while laughing.

"What?!" I shout, hoping he's joking.

His laugh stops right away. He nudges me and says jokingly, "*IIIIII'mm kiiidiing*."

"Okay," I say, trying to hide my worry of his possible death.

His phone starts to ring. "One sec, I've got to take this. It's my boss," he says.

He then walks inside the house. Whenever Uncle P got something expensive, I would be very mystified wondering how he had the money. My mother would usually speak badly about him when he slept till noon, which I now realize was probably because he was up late on calls. Anytime my mother would say something bad about Uncle P, I couldn't care less, while Jonah would list positive things about him, saying he needed us. I'm not exactly sure what he'd told my mom and stepfather about being in the FBI, but maybe it was just an act to keep me from knowing the secrets they had with Uncle P. Maybe he told them that in the "FBI" he wasn't getting paid enough and that's why he came here. If my uncle did come clean to my family about me knowing he is in the CIA and how he lied to them and he disobeyed my mother, she would be outraged. She would probably get over it as time went by, but maybe keeping it secret was for the best. In my opinion, if you're in the CIA, you shouldn't tell anyone.

I start to think about school. There would be no school till the Knife Thrower was found. The circumstances leading up to now was making me think that the Knife Thrower would never be found. Well, maybe not *never*, but not for a long time…

I've also been wondering how many people the Knife Thrower will kill until he or she stops. Would I be killed? Anytime I asked my mother if I could get killed, she acted as if I'd said, "I just washed the dishes." Meaning she would be very shocked.

This had only been going on for about a week, because that was how long the Knife Thrower had been around. My goal for the day is to stay as far away from Jonah as I possibly can. I don't really have any other plans for the rest of the day, so I figure that when Uncle P is done with his call we can hang out. I remember earlier when my mother told me how Mr. Smith was murdered and how he had a background story with Jonah. It was for sure interesting.

All of a sudden Jonah is right behind me. With my mother. They seem to be in a very serious mood. "Am I getting punished?" I ask quickly. Usually when your parents suddenly come up to you and start with the "you are an amazing child and I love you so much, but…" the horror goes on from there.

"What?" my mother exclaims.

"You're not being punished," Jonah says, seeming baffled by that unexpected thing I'd just said.

I stare at them with perplexity. "Then what is going on?" I ask.

"I was wondering if you wanted to go ax throwing with me," Jonah says.

Hmmm, I think. "What do you mean when you say, 'with me'? Why not 'with us,' as in your wife, too?" I ask.

"She doesn't want to go," Jonah says nervously. I stare at them, feeling puzzled. There's dead silence. "So, do you want to?"

"No, I'm fine. I'm about to hang out with Uncle J. He's just on a call with one of his CIA agents." And in that moment, I knew I messed up.

Jonah and my mother look at me with shock. "Oh," I say while chuckling. "We like to joke about it because we, um, w-w-we think that it is so cool."

"Okay, I don't know what you two talk about," my mother says, as if I am a lunatic. "And go ax throwing with your father!" she orders.

"Step." I correct that every time. I may have seemed like a smart aleck when I did that, but I didn't consider Jonah like a father to me.

"Okay, wise guy," my mother says annoyedly.

I grit my teeth, then sigh. "Fine. Let's go."

"We will have some amazing stepfather and stepson time!" Jonah says with excitement.

"Uh-huh," I reply sarcastically.

"I'll get the keys. Meet you in the car," he says cheerfully.

I haul myself to move. "Listen," my mother says in a nice way. "I know you don't want to hang out with him, bu—"

"You came out here because you didn't think I would listen to him," I say.

"Uh-huh," she admits. "Now go! And be nice!"

I drag myself to the car. I put my seat belt on, and Jonah says happily, "We're going to be out for three hours and—"

"Three?!" I cut him off. *Are we really going ax throwing for three hours?* I ask myself.

"Yeah!" Jonah says with confusion.

I remember my mom telling me to be nice. "I am just so surprised that we're going to have so much fun together!" I say with enthusiasm. Sometimes it is the right thing to say a white lie.

"Yay," he says.

3

The Knife Attack

We're driving in the car on the busy roads for thirty minutes, and I listen to Jonah going on and on about how fun ax throwing is. I think it will be fun. I feel like it will get stress off me. Well...I actually know it will. I did it once when I went to Montana. I live in New Jersey, so it was a long flight. Once we finally arrive Jonah lets out a holler with delight. The building has a western style, which wasn't surprising.

Jonah goes up to a man working at the counter and says, "Two people for three hours—one adult, one kid." He then hands some money to the guy.

The guy takes the money and puts it in a drawer. He then walks over, and we make eye contact. "You ready to have some fun wit' your daaad?" he asks. He has an accent like someone from *Chicaaaaaaaaaaaago*. Jonah thinks that those Illinois people are funny.

"Yup," I reply. I knew that right now was not a time to correct "dad" to "stepdad." Because—you know—common sense.

"Well, I hope you two have some fun," he says with excitement, probably hoping to get me energized.

We open a door and there is a big ax range. There are eleven sections, but we go to the first one because it's closest to us. There are five axes. Little bits of wood are sticking out, and I wonder if I'm going to get some blisters.

"All right!" Jonah says gleefully. "You ready to throw some axes?" I nod. "I'll go first," he says with excitement. About ten yards ahead of him is a target. Very big. I wonder how good he'll be at this…or how good I'll even be.

He then throws the ax. It flies through the air spinning and spinning, and it hits the bull's-eye! I am shocked. I jump as my eyes get wide! "And that's how you do it," he says victoriously.

"I wanna try," I say anxiously. I grab the ax out of the target as I struggle for a moment to free the weapon. I stomp back to where Jonah is. I bring the ax back over my head, then chuck it. It spins in the air. Fast. Then it hits about five inches under the bull's-eye.

"Good job, kid!" Jonah exclaims. The ax is buried hard into the target.

"Thank you," I say, but I'm annoyed.

My ax may have been close to the bull's-eye, but the fact that Jonah's hit the bull's-eye bugged me. "You know, if you turn around there's an archery set you could do," he suggests.

"What do you think?! That I don't have the strength to get a bull's-eye?" I say competitively, not even bothering to look behind me.

He puts his hands up as if I were going to harm him. "Whoa, whoa, whoa, there's no competition." Jonah giggles a bit, and I guess it was to play with me mentally.

I roll my eyes and turn around. There are six archery ranges. They each have one bow and five arrows. To the left there are six knife ranges. They have targets and five knives each. "Whoa!" I shout. "What's with that knife range?"

"Well, I didn't tell you because you could easily get hurt," Jonah says softly.

"Did you just think I wouldn't notice?" I ask.

"I dunno," he replies.

"That is pretty pathetic that you think I'm so ignorant," I say rudely. "Well, I'll be at the archery range. See you." I give him a dismissive wave even though we're about ten feet apart.

I walk to the range. I put my hand on a black steel bow. It's a bit big for my size, but I pick it up because I want to give it a go. I haven't done archery in a while, so I don't know if this bow really does fit me and it is just supposed to feel awkward at first. I pick up an arrow and fix it into the bowstring. I draw back.

I hold still for a while, which requires a lot of energy from my right arm. The string is touching the side of my chapped lips. I breathe heavily. I stare at the target like it is a piece of fragile glass. I don't even bother to blink. I keep breathing very heavily. I then lick my lips. One second later I let go. The arrow flies to the target. It finds the left side of the tiny bull's-eye! I'm shocked! I blink several times to triple-check I'm not imagining. I take a deep breath, then smile. It feels nice to let my sore arm swing down. I then shout, "Hey Jonah, come look!" He dashes over.

I look over at his target, and it has three axes right in the bull's-eye. I sigh, feeling a little less proud of myself. Jonah then says, "Nice job, buddy!"

"Thanks," I reply.

"So, was that your first try?" he asks.

"Yup," I say.

"I'm going to try that." Jonah seems a bit jealous of me, making me a bit prouder. He grabs the bow from my hand and then snatches an arrow. He quickly loads in the arrow, slowly draws back the bowstring, and lets it go, sending an arrow right above the target.

I quietly chuckle. I guess Jonah was so angry and anxious that he didn't even bother to find somewhere to point the arrow.

"Hey!" he shouts. "Not funny!"

"Okay then," I say sarcastically, while still chuckling.

"Hey! I didn't laugh at you when you missed the bull's-eye in ax throwing," he protests. "Your moment of skill with archery was just luck."

"Well," I start off with, "I was only five inches away from the bull's-eye when I threw the ax. Plus, I never said you couldn't laugh, and I actually hit a target at least when I chucked that ax."

Jonah seems stumped. I take the bow back from him and get the third arrow. The arrow is leaning on the steel bow ready to be launched. I breathe heavily, and the bow is leaning on the right side of my lips. I stare at the bull's-eye knowing I have to hit it to prove to Jonah that my first shot wasn't lucky. That puts me under some pressure, and I can tell that Jonah is behind me and will decide if I am a good archer or not based on my next shot. Ugh. I just want to twist and shoot this arrow right through him.

I take a deep breath and calm down so I don't mess up my shot, because that is what happened to Jonah when he got too frustrated and anxious. I start to squint. My eyes are focused on one thing and one thing only: the bull's-eye. I take one deep breath, then BOOM! Right next to my other arrow is the arrow I'd just fired.

Jonah jumps back in surprise. "Whoa," he says at first, seeming impressed. "Nice job," he says, shifting his voice enviously.

I smirk, proud. He then goes back to his ax throwing while I finish off my two arrows. They are both quite close to the bull's-eye. Next, I grab the five arrows from the target. I turn around and see that Jonah seems to be struggling. I hear many sighs from him. I want to surprise him, but not in a rude way. I drop four of my arrows, and the one I am holding I get ready to shoot. Right when Jonah throws his ax I shoot my arrow. Not at him, of course, but at his target. My arrow hits the ring surrounding the bull's-eye. Jonah's ax is right next to my arrow. He turns around. I see his crimson face turn into an even brighter shade of red. "What did you just do?!" he shouts. I don't respond.

Until I say, "What's the big deal?"

"You could have killed me!" he shouts.

"Okay, mister, I can't even hit the target when I shoot an arrow," I say while laughing a little bit. "I actually hit a couple of bull's-eyes."

His face gets even brighter. He now seems a lot more mad than nice. He takes a deep breath. We make eye contact, and I lower my eyebrows as if I were questioning him about something. He then says, "I am sorry for yelling at you earlier. Just don't tell your mom," he begs. "Please."

"Yeah, no," I say ominously.

"Wha-what'd you mean, *no*?" he asks.

"I mean no," I reply.

He sits there staring at me with anger. I turn around and continue my archery. I then feel bad. I turn around and say, "Okay, I won't tell Mom."

"Thank you," Jonah says, seeming relieved.

All of a sudden someone enters the ranges. It's Uncle P!

"Uncle J!" I shout because Jonah doesn't know that I know his real name is Parzin.

"Hi!" he shouts back.

"How'd you know we were here?" Jonah asks.

"I asked your wife," Uncle P answers, then walks to the knife range.

"Whoa, whoa, whoa," Jonah says. "Don't use knives in front of a child."

Uncle P replies, "What does he care?" I smile. "Okay, I'm going to try this," he says excitedly.

I was thinking Jonah only said that because he thought my use of the knives in the backyard earlier was going to be for violence. Well, actually it was. My plan is to kill the Knife Thrower. I wonder how I would be doing if I had continued practicing on that knife range. Would I be horrible? Would I be good? Would I still be building the knife range? I would've probably been exhausted right now if I had kept digging and carrying that wood.

Sure, ax throwing and archery were fun, but sometimes Jonah couldn't admit he was wrong against a child. Like when my mom left for fun short trips with her friends on some weekends, Jonah and I would play a lot of monopoly. Yes, I know it's a very old-fashioned game, but I find it fun. He calls it cheating when he doesn't realize I land on his green properties. The rule is, if the person who owns a property doesn't say something after ten seconds...welp, better luck next time, because in our house you don't get to collect rent. Once, I let Jonah win. Next time, he bet on his watch and I bet a hundred dollars. I won because I didn't let him win.

Back to what we are doing now, Uncle P takes a knife and throws it! It spins through the air looking like it is going a hundred miles per hour. Uncle P had thrown the knife like a Frisbee. The knife then sticks right in the target! "And that's how you do it," he says.

I see the happiness in his face. I walk over, dropping my bow and arrow. "How did you do that?" I ask. He gives me a stare like I'm a moron. Which, to be fair, sometimes I am. "What?!" I exclaim. Jonah looks over, seeming very bemused.

Uncle P then whispers, "I'm in the CIA. You don't think I've needed to learn how to use a weapon besides a gun?"

"Ohhhh," I say loudly and nod.

"Shhh," he whispers.

I think for a moment whether I should be doing this. After some thought I say, "Can I try?"

"Sure," he replies.

I grab a knife. The blade is silver and shiny. I look more closely at the knife. It is black at the bottom with a steel texture. There are about fifteen serrations at the bottom. Sharp. The lights in this area glare on the blade. I look up at the target, getting ready to throw the knife. I lick my dry lips, breathe heavily, and stare at the bull's-eye. I wonder if I'll seem like the Knife Thrower. And then I throw the knife. Spinning only a few times in the air, it hits the upper left part of the target, then falls down! It was because the bottom of the knife hit the target! "What?" I say with confusion.

"The bottom of the knife hit the target," Uncle P says.

"I know it did!" I say quickly. "But how did yours—"

"How about we take a step back with the way we throw this thing," Uncle P suggests. "All right?" I nod. "Okay, so when you throw this, try to make it not spin. Try to have the knife go fast, but without spinning. And make sure it's horizontal." He then stops speaking. "What are you waiting for?"

"Oh," I say, confused, because I thought he had more to say.

I grab another knife and wrap my hand around the handle. It feels very wet. I take my hand off the handle—it turns out that it was wet from my hot and sweaty palm. I wipe my hands on my shirt. Uncle P looks at me with confusion. I shrug and then throw the knife. It goes straight, straight, and straight…until it falls down due to how slow it was moving.

I sigh. I realize what I'm doing and how unsafe it is. I even wonder why Uncle P was letting me do it, although he had stopped me from building a knife range earlier. Maybe this is a once-in-a-while thing. Actually, I think this will be my last time throwing a knife. Not my kind of thing. My mother wouldn't be proud. She wouldn't mind archery, though. So, I say to Uncle P, "I think I'm going to go back to archery." He nods, and I walk over to the archery range.

I notice some silhouette deer dummies used for bow and arrow practice. Who knew that there would be a practice range for hunting in a town like Wayverlyn?

I start to wonder why a knife range even exists, especially in our small town right now. I guess that the Knife Thrower comes here a lot. There is this one man who I suspect to be the Knife Thrower. His name is John Bryans. John is a very shady man. He lives in the house that is known as the Mines of Murder. There is a tale that, about thirteen years ago, seventeen teens walked into the house. It was abandoned then. Only five came out. One year later twelve skulls were found. Two years later John bought the house when someone put it up for sale.

John is currently thirty-nine years old. He wears a black hat and sunglasses with a black coat. Everyone finds him scary. The house is called the Mines of Murder because the skulls were found in a mine underneath the house. It's weird that such a big area can be under a house. No one knows what happened the night those teens entered the house. People claim John killed them! Personally, I don't like to think about it. It scares the living daylights out of me. Anytime I do, I usually turn around to be cautious after thinking about something so scary. So again, I turn around….

There's the Knife Thrower! He is wearing a black mask and a black leather jacket.

He's holding knives, and I worry I'm going to be his next victim! I scream at the top of my lungs, then Uncle P and Jonah notice him. Uncle P comes running toward me. He grabs me and we go to Jonah. We're trapped! The Knife Thrower hurls a knife that goes into the wall right next to us! I don't know what to do. He keeps throwing knives, but we don't have to duck or move. Not one knife has gotten even close to us!

Suddenly, there is rope hanging from the ceiling and he climbs up, holding a basket. I'm so curious about what he's doing, but he just climbs and climbs. Uncle P, Jonah, and I look at him with bewilderment. Once he is almost to the ceiling, he throws another knife! I dive to my right because this time it almost split my head. He throws another one aiming for my heart, but I move just in time! I pick up one of the knives and throw it up at him! It hits the Knife Thrower's arm, causing a big cut. I see blood gushing. It is the goriest thing I have seen in real life. He groans in pain. He then drops the basket because it's too heavy for his hurt body to hold. All of a sudden hundreds of envelopes drop! They all fall down like a hard rain. Somehow, he is still holding on to the rope, hanging.

I quickly run to the archery set, grabbing a bow and a few arrows. Without aiming I send an arrow up. It's heading right to the rope, but the rope is so thick that the arrow does nothing, I was hoping it would disappear into the Knife Thrower's temple. The Knife Thrower loses his balance and falls off the rope, but he has a soft landing due to all the envelopes on the ground. He then quickly pulls out a red envelope from his pocket and throws it like a Frisbee to me. I'm so curious about what's in it. He then throws another knife that is blood red, but strangely, it doesn't seem like he was trying to hit me with it. It was actually less of a throw and more of a toss. He then dashes out and gets away.

I'm shocked. I think I'm going to pass out.

What will my mother think? I wonder. I probably won't be able to leave my house till I'm forty. I look at the red knife. It is about nine inches long and has a big black *A* on it. I put it in my pocket, but it sticks out, so I put my shirt over it to hide it.

The man who Jonah and I saw at the front desk earlier dashes in. "Are you guys okay?!" he shouts.

"We're okay," Jonah says, while panting.

We all go together and hug. Not with the man who was at the front desk, though. Uncle P sighs with relief. Without hesitation I crumple up the red envelope so it fits in my pocket. I don't even bother to tell anyone about it. The man from the front desk says, "I'm Adam, by the way."

"Nice to meet you," Uncle P says. "Would you like us to help you pick up all these envelopes?"

"Oh no, it's fine," Adam replies reluctantly.

"No, we insist," Uncle P says.

Adam smiles. We all start to pick up the envelopes and put them into big garbage bags Adam gives us. What's weird, though, is that all the envelopes have no letters in them. I'm very confused. As I toss the envelopes into the bag, I look over to the area where the Knife Thrower had fallen. There is some blood from his arm that's almost dried. I look in my pocket and stare at the red envelope. I think I'm going to keep it…at least until I open it. I look around and then think about the red knife I got. I want to look at it, so I shout, "Hey! I'm going to go to the bathroom."

"Would you like me to be near the bathroom as well?" Uncle P asks. "We just encountered the Knife Thrower."

"I think I'm okay. He is long gone," I say.

The three adults nod in affirmation that it is safe enough for me to go. I go to the bathroom and take the knife out. It turns out only the handle is red. The actual blade looked red from reflections in the room. I look around the bathroom, hoping nobody is there. Nobody is. All of a sudden, I hear the door open. I put the knife back in my pocket and put the bottom of my shirt over it. I end up seeing Uncle P. He says, "You all right?"

"Mhm," I reply. "I'll let you tell my mother about today," I add, scheming to save myself from getting into trouble. "You'll sound like such a brave person!"

"Wha-wait, what? She's *your* mother!"

I nod. "I know."

"Okay. I'm going to help more with all the cleaning," Uncle P tells me.

"Me too."

We both walk back and pick up more empty envelopes. I start to wonder if the Knife Thrower wants to somehow know me. I have a good feeling that John Bryans is the Knife Thrower. I'd always wondered if the mines had dry blood in them from when the teens were killed. John didn't own the mines, though. I want to open the envelope so badly, but I need to be alone, and it would seem weird going into the bathroom twice in the same ten minutes.

Once we finish cleaning up all the envelopes, Adam calls the police and once he hangs up, he says, "You guys are free to leave unless you would like to speak to the police."

I look at Uncle P nervously. "I'd like to just go home. I would feel safer."

Uncle P nods. "Okay, sorry I think we are going to head home."

"Have a safe day, folks," Adam says, waving.

We get into the car and it's completely silent. In the back seat, I take out the red-handled knife. I wonder what the letter inside the envelope says. It obviously has to do with the Knife Thrower. Or should I say, John.

I never went into the Mines of Murder. I would have been petrified. The Mines of Murder house was black and very big, but it seemed to be falling apart. Anytime I saw John he looked very suspicious. He looked like a detective because of his outfits. Some people suspect him of being the Knife Thrower, but otherwise, there are no other suspects.

I'm not sure what I am going to do today. I know that I am going to end up on the news because of the knife attack that just happened. I don't open the envelope because the ripping noise would draw my uncle and stepfather's attention.

When we get home, I plan to run upstairs to my bedroom, lock the door, and look inside the envelope. My parents have a key to unlock my room, but it's usually a struggle because my lock has been getting rusty, so I'd hear if they wanted to come in and I'd quickly hide what's in the envelope. I bet the knife attack that just happened is already on the news. My mother is probably going crazy. I bet Adam is getting interviewed right now. He doesn't know whether we are injured or not. I doubt that he's saying we are.

Life is going to be boring until the Knife Thrower is caught. I'm used to doing school all day. Sure, school can get a bit boring, but it at least keeps me busy.

Uncle P used to keep me company, but I think things are a bit odd between us now with the whole CIA thing and lying to my parents. I wonder if Uncle P will ever come clean to them. I still have to be careful in front of Jonah and my mother, because I can't say Uncle P. I have to stick with Uncle J. Otherwise they'll think he told me about him being in the FBI. Then Uncle P will have to come clean to everybody and I would have to act surprised. My mother doesn't need to know that I know about Uncle P's secret. It's just best for everyone.

Maybe he'll come clean tonight. I mean, after your family members were almost killed, a few hours later one of them wouldn't just ditch you to go to a friend's lake house. Or would they? I'm not sure. I'm thinking that Uncle P will somehow have to cancel his trip to Saudi Arabia, or if he's lucky his boss will cancel it. I was thinking earlier that it would be cool to do the kid CIA training session, although I figured it was more for high schoolers. If I were to do it, I don't think I would see many kids my age. Also, I'd probably be doing it until I'm eighteen. Then I'd have to go to college. If I were to do the classes, what would I learn? How to be sneaky? Smart? A good liar, for sure.

I start to think about the knife attack that just happened. The Knife Thrower for sure wanted to send me a message. I remember him throwing the envelope to me like a Frisbee. It had to be for me. It was also red—the envelope—so I would for sure notice it out of all the white ones. And, when he tossed me that red knife, it wasn't a throw to kill me but a toss. Hmm...very suspicious to me. I couldn't think of anyone who would specifically want me to know that they were the Knife Thrower. The only obvious answer to me was a family member. It for sure is not Uncle P or Jonah, because I was just with them when we almost got killed. And NO WAY it's my mother. I'd been with her when we watched live news about the Knife Thrower having just killed somebody.

I'm very anxious to get home. Not to open the envelope, but so I can calm down my mother before she tells me to get in the car and go to the hospital. I appreciate her being very protective. It shows that she cares for me.

But I'm also anxious to get home so I can open my envelope. There's most likely a letter in there. It would be cool if it contains hints on who the Knife Thrower is. Like in the movies. Although this is real life. I know I shouldn't get my hopes up that a letter is even in there.

All of a sudden I get a text message on my phone. It's from Uncle P. I bet it's about the CIA because he wouldn't say it out loud, and it is. It says, *Not going to Saudi Arabia. Got delayed till Tuesday*. Well, phew. I look out the window and see we are close to home. I put the red knife in my pocket. I think it is a hunting knife. Then we arrive home. I get out of the car and walk into the house. I see my mother.

"Are you okay?" she cries.

"I'm fine," I say gloomily.

"What about your uncle and Jonah?" she asks.

Right then, they walk in. "They're fine," I say.

My mother hugs me tightly and says, "I'm glad you're okay." I nod. "I just saw on the news a few minutes ago!" she exclaims.

"I think I'm going to go upstairs," I say.

My mother replies, "Do what you need to do!"

I nod and run upstairs to my bedroom as fast as a lightning bolt. I lock the door and plop onto my bed. I'm very nervous about what is in the envelope. I take a deep breath while closing my eyes. I take another deep breath and open my eyes. I slowly open the envelope. I feel something inside. There's a letter! Excitement, nervousness, and shock all shoot through me. I look at the letter. It's an old-looking piece of parchment. Although, it is very strange....

4

BQXOSNFQZOG MNSDR

XNT ZQD HM FQZUD CZMFDQ

BNLD SN ____ SGD LHMDR
NE LTQCDQ GNTRD
ZS LHCMHFGS HE XNT CNMS XNT VHKK
QDFQDS HS SGD RDBNMC ADENQD XNT
FDS
ZRRZRRHMZSDC FNNC KTBJ

I gasp! What is this? What does this mean? What is going on? I am shocked and bewildered. I quickly close my blinds, then get back to the letter.

I flip the letter over and shake my head. Did I look at it wrong? I slowly turn it back over and verify what I saw. I wonder what it could even mean. I flip over the slip of parchment and look around to make sure nobody's watching. I feel like I am being haunted right now.

It must be a code letter, I think. I don't even know how it's supposed to make sense. Before I figure out what the note is saying, I decide I won't tell anybody about it. I probably won't get much sleep tonight.

I pull out my red knife and survey the paper with it. Disorientation flows through my brain, which makes me feel like I am hallucinating. My stomach is getting queasy and I'm dizzy. I look at the knife, noticing the blurry reflection of myself on the blade. I look back at the note. I want to try to crack it, but how? Maybe if I get another letter like this, it might help me solve this.

I get out a piece of paper and open my laptop to look up codes. I am very anxious to learn. When they load, I write down what I see. I write down cypher code and Morse code. I've seen those codes written out before.

I know for sure that this letter isn't in those two codes, but I write them down anyway. I need as much information as I can get about codes. I don't really find any more information after that.

I am perplexed from staring at the bright screen. I then lower the brightness on my screen. I've only been researching for fifteen minutes, but I feel like I have a migraine. I don't know whether my life depends on solving this letter. I then think that there is no specific code used! It's a made-up one. I feel like an imbecile for not realizing that. Now I have to come up with my own codes and see if they match up with the letters. Maybe that doesn't make sense, but my mind is going crazy, so I don't blame myself.

My mom tells me whenever I feel like I have a headache, I should nap, draw, or exercise. Jonah enjoys all three, which was no surprise to me after I started to get to know him. Some of his drawings are very cool. He is actually a pretty good artist. Although when I stop to say hi while he is working, he acts as if the word "art" is a type of religion. In a way he seems to practice it anytime he paints. Yeah, I know, it makes no sense.

I then start to make up codes. Maybe it's something like A = Z and Z = A. To go on, B = Y and Y = B. That sort of pattern, where the farthest letters from each other in the alphabet equal each other. It actually might be it! I then look at the letter and write the new letters for it on another paper. Many words do not make sense, but maybe they mean something? I look at my paper and all I see is my handwriting, sloppy from writing so quickly. Nothing on the paper makes any sense at all.

I crumple it up in anger and chuck it on the ground. I accidently sit on the parchment with the secret notes on it, but as soon as I hear a noise, I jump up. I want to make sure the letter with all the code stuff doesn't get ripped. Sure, it does seem very wrinkled and old, but I don't want it getting any worse. I sigh in relief because the parchment is not ripped. I then feel very bothered. *Maybe I should lie down just for about five minutes or so*, I think. What harm can that do anyway?

I turn off the lights and lie down on the carpet in my room. I am too lazy to get back on my bed. I'm half asleep, and I pull out the red hunting knife from my pocket. I slowly turn it around without even having any thoughts about it. I just peer at it with a loose mind. My mind is filled with bemusement, nervous feelings, and shock. Adrenaline starts pumping in my chest. I put the hunting knife back in my pocket, so if anyone were to walk in on me napping, they wouldn't see me holding a knife. Then I close my eyes.

When I wake up, I feel much better. I take a deep breath. It feels great getting up. I turn on the lights and look at my clock. It's four o'clock! I'd slept for almost two hours! My mind feels fresh, although it is weird because of everything that has happened today. It feels like Uncle P told me about being in the CIA years ago….

School feels like decades ago. But the Knife Thrower attack, that seems recent. Which it was. I'm not completely awake yet, so I've forgotten what I was doing before I took my nap. I sigh and see the letter on my bed, then I remember that I was trying to solve the note. That was it! I can't think of anything to do next and start to get very antsy. I'm a very impatient person. I pull out a few pieces of paper from my drawer, along with a red marker.

I look at the letter code I am trying to crack. Then I have an idea! Not for a type of code, though. To buy the Code Detector 2000! It's just come out, and it can sense the meaning of a code. It's often used by people who needed to learn Morse code, cypher, and probably many others. Unfortunately, it cost $2,000, and I don't have that kind of money. I probably have about 35 percent of that. I need to borrow some money, but from who? And if the adult asks what I want the money for, I can't think of something I'd want that would be so pricey. Except for the Code Detector 2000, of course, but then the person would ask what I would need it for. And no way I would steal it! That is a *big no* for me. Maybe I could buy some lottery tickets? Actually, that idea is pretty stupid because my odds of winning the lottery are not so good. Maybe I could go to Uncle P? Or sell the 4TX…

No, I can't do that. I would feel horrible, and Uncle P would be very sad. I stare at the ceiling. It's how I think. Maybe I could just ask Uncle P for money, although he probably wouldn't get me any birthday presents for the next four years. If I told him I needed the Code Detector and he asked why, would he respect that I didn't want to tell him? I mean, hey, he didn't tell me about being in the CIA. I'm also in a situation that might mean life or death. Still, it would be awkward to walk up to your uncle and ask, *Oh, can you please give me two thousand dollars? I can't say why.* That would sound pretty weird.

I think of how I'm going to ask him. I think I'll just ask for the money and then hope there are no follow-up questions. I know there will be, but I'm just being optimistic, which is never a bad thing. I also need to make sure nobody is around him. My mother and stepfather aren't so chill in these cases. Sure, Uncle P would be confused about the insane amount of money I need, but he likes helping out.

I walk downstairs. I see him sitting on the couch sipping a cup of coffee. He's also watching TV at the same time. I walk over to him, but before I can say something, he turns off the TV and says, "Oh, hey bud! You disappeared after we came home!" I'm about to say something, but he cuts me off and says, "And since my trip to Saudi Arabia is delayed we can hang out! Sound fun?"

"Um, yeah, it does." I then casually ask, "By any chance can I borrow around two thousand dollars?"

"Whoa!" he shouts. "That's a whole lotta money! What do you need it for anyway?"

Yup, he knows something is up. I reply, "I prefer not to say why."

Uncle P remains silent while I am hoping that he will say yes. He then says, "Fine." As I expected, he adds, "But this counts as your next four birthday presents."

"That's fair," I reply. "Oh, and can you not tell my parents about this?"

He nods. I jolt with happiness. Now, I have to figure out how to get out of the house and buy the Code Detector 2000, because it isn't safe to leave the house with the Knife Thrower out there, or maybe I am a little too nervous due to my interaction with him at the ax throwing place. I can only go if I'm with an adult. I change my mind about sort of telling the truth to Uncle P. I turn around and say, "Well, I need to buy the Code Detector 2000." He looks at me. He seems very abashed and I don't know why. He's about to say something, but I say, "Please don't ask why."

"Okaaaaaaaaay," he says, with confusion. "Where are we going to buy it?"

"We'll go to the Superstore," I suggest.

"Okay," Uncle P agrees. "Let's go."

We hop in the car and drive there in silence. I'm hoping that our trip will be quick and that we do not encounter the Knife Thrower again. My mother would go crazy if we did. I think that this Code Detector 2000 will help. It doesn't just detect types of codes; it also detects patterns. It has a mini screen on it and a button. What you do is wave the device over something, then a word will pop up on the mini screen such as *cypher*, *Morse*, even *rainbow*! Any pattern that is found. It's usually one simple word, but sometimes not. I wonder if this gadget is used by the CIA. The people working there are probably trained to use a code language, but it wouldn't hurt to try something new. This is probably one of the most high-end pieces of technology. Or at least in my opinion. That was probably because I found it very interesting.

We are very close to arriving at the store. It starts to rain cats and dogs, and ironically, on the road I see a lot of cats and dogs in people's cars. I wonder if the Knife Thrower will ever get caught. He's quick, clever, and seemed pretty strong when climbing that rope at the ax throwing place earlier. I am flabbergasted that there is still a knife range. I'm wondering where I would be now if I'd went on with building my own knife range. Uncle P's lecture about not building it and practicing throwing knives was long and boring, but it was good enough to convince me.

I look out the window. There are not many cars because few people are out. I think people being in cars is fine. I feel safe right now. Very safe, in fact. If my uncle saw the Knife Thrower on the side of the road waiting to kill someone, he would run that killer right over. So would I, but I don't have a driver's license.

Drops of rain hit the car windows. Before I know it, we are in the parking lot of Superstore. We walk over the puddles of rainwater. If the Knife Thrower saw us now, we would be his next victims. All of a sudden, I realize I have my red knife in my pocket, so we'll be safe if the Knife Thrower happens to be around and my uncle and I see him first.

We walk into the store, and the temperature compared to outside makes me feel like I'd just touched the sun.

"So, you wanna get your thing and we'll meet up at the checkout line?" Uncle P asks.

"Sure," I agree.

I dash over to the technology section of the store. I get many stares for being alone and young, especially at this time in our town. I quickly grab the Code Detector 2000, then speed-walk to the checkout line so I can avoid all the stares. I see Uncle P.

"You have it?" he asks. I nod. We then check out. There is actually a twenty-five percent discount for it. My uncle then whispers to me, "Like I said, no presents for four birthdays."

I chuckle and nod a bit. If this Code Detector 2000 helps me find out who the Knife Thrower is, my uncle, mother, and stepfather will be furious that I didn't tell them about the notes. But they'll still be nice because they'd find out what I had been going through, which truthfully, is kind of fun. It's like I'm in a murder mystery movie. The thing I do not like is that it's *real*. I could possibly die.

We get back in the car. I hear sirens and see police cars! The Knife Thrower probably just killed somebody. Maybe. I hope not. If so, I don't even want to hear about it. I've been through a lot already today: I found out Jonah was once falsely accused of murder; I found out that my uncle is in the CIA; I almost got killed by the Knife Thrower; and I got a code letter that is most likely from the Knife Thrower. Today has been full of chaos.

* * *

It is about 4:30 p.m. Hopefully my mother didn't realize we were gone. She was probably a bit paranoid about Jonah. Every Friday, he has an art class from four to five o'clock. About two months ago there was a robbery there and now with the Knife Thrower at large my mom doesn't like the feeling of Jonah there. I think that his art classes seem boring. To me, it's an unusual thing for an adult to do, because I haven't heard about many adults who take art classes. Mom has probably realized that me and Uncle P are gone by now, but she probably thinks we're safe. If at least two of the four of us in the family are together and going out, she thinks that's fine. But one? That's meh. It depends on which person you're talking about, though. I'm the one who can't go out alone, but I don't mind. I don't usually go out at this time of season because I'm not doing any bike rides.

Finally, we arrive home. I quickly get out of the car. I barge into the house, dash upstairs, and grab the letter. I take the cellophane off the Code Detector 2000. I don't even bother to read the directions off the chrome-colored cellophane. I know how this thing works. I click the 'on' button. The word *ON* pops up on the mini screen for about a second. I then click a button that says scan. On the screen it says *STARTING SCAN IN 3 SECONDS.* I hold the Code Detector over the letter. I slowly move it so it can get every letter on there. I do that for about ten seconds. My hands are shaking, and I am so anxious. Then the little screen says *LOADING RESULTS.*

"Yes!" I whisper. The screen then says *NO PATTERN OR CODE HAS BEEN FOUND. PLEASE TRY AGAIN.*

What?! I exclaim in my head.

There has to be some mistake. I straighten the piece of parchment out so it's less wrinkled. Maybe that made it hard for the detector to scan? The parchment didn't straighten out so well, so I get a book its size and carefully put it on top of the letter. I press down on the book with all my strength. I feel my face going crimson. I let the book sit on it for a bit and pull out my knife. I look at it for a moment. I'm assuming it has to relate to the letter. I'm surprised that Uncle P and Jonah didn't see that red envelope—or even the knife—get tossed to me. It should've been so noticeable because of the color. They were probably busy trying to throw a weapon at the Knife Thrower. They were behind me when the whole knife attack happened.

After about fifteen minutes I take the book off the letter, and it's straightened out. I grab the Code Detector and click the scan button. On the mini screen it reads *STARTING SCAN IN 3 SECONDS.* When three seconds pass, I scan the letter. It takes around ten seconds to do so. The mini screen then says *LOADING RESULTS.* I'm very anxious to see the results. My heart is beating fast, so I take a big deep breath.

On the mini screen are the words *NO PATTERN OR CODE HAS BEEN FOUND. PLEASE TRY AGAIN.*

"Argh!" I shout. I'm exasperated now. Why isn't this working? Is it too hard for the detector to solve? I believe that that's the issue. Now I'll never find out what the letter says, no matter how hard I try. I am in a very ominous situation. If technology can't do it, I for sure cannot. I know people say to have an optimistic mind, but in my case it's hard to. I sigh with frustration. Annoyance and anger rush through my body. From my toes, to my feet, to my thighs, through my hips, up my ribs, through my stomach, to my chest, up my neck, and to my head, making it very red.

I seem very calm right now, but in my mind I'm not. I shake my head a few times quickly, thinking it will refresh my brain. It doesn't. I could really use some help with this, but I'm not sure if I should be telling anyone about it. I don't even know if I'm supposed to be able to solve this code. It would be a heck of lot easier if the Knife Thrower just got caught by the police.

I know there has to be a reason why the Code Detector 2000 cannot detect a code or a pattern in the letter. I write everything on a new piece of paper, because the real letter still looks very wrinkled.

No luck...

This is so aggravating! I'd rather listen to Jonah's thoughts while painting. Also, the fact that the Code Detector didn't help at all makes me feel horrible that my uncle got it for me. I'll have to just figure it out. It will be complicated knowing that one letter means another letter. I want help, but I have no clue whether I should ask someone.

This situation is probably only about me and the person who gave me this letter, who I know is the Knife Thrower. Maybe I should go to the police station. But what if the Knife Thrower is watching me? I flinch when I imagine the Knife Thrower right in front of me. I then quickly turn around, thinking that he may be right behind me. This feels like torture, but maybe that's because I'm making myself feel like that. I want to ignore the letter, but solving it is so tempting. Would you be able to keep your hands off a secret code letter from a serial killer who hasn't been identified? I don't think so.

Maybe going to Uncle P is my best option. He wouldn't go to the police if I told him not to. Actually, maybe he would. This is a very serious situation. Of course he would go to the police! What am I thinking? I still don't know whether it's the right thing to say anything about the letter.

I think of what I will do. I won't tell anybody about the letter, at least until I find out what it says. I could really use some advice, but it would be very weird if I walked up to some kid in my class and asked, *What would you do if you were getting code letters from a serial killer? Because I am.* Yeah, that would be very unusual. Especially when said out loud.

I get up and slowly pace around my room like I'm a tiger ready to fight in its tiny cage. I'm trying to think, but I can't. I also need to figure out where to hide my hunting knife and letter. I stare down at the ground, and from behind me it looks like I just got handcuffed. No code ideas come to my mind. I am a lot calmer now, though. I think about going downstairs to talk to everyone. Take a break from all my frustration.

I walk downstairs. I see my mother, Jonah, and Uncle P chatting. Right when they see me, they stop talking.

"Hello, Andrew," my mother says, then takes a sip of coffee.

"What's going on?" I say with confusion. They were obviously talking about me. The looks on their faces seems suspicious.

"Nothing," Jonah replies.

"What's for dinner?" I wonder.

"I'm going to be making chicken pot pie," my mother tells me. I shoot up with excitement. I love chicken pot pie. There is one word that describes it. *Perfect*. My mother continues, "We will also not be ordering food from any restaurant."

"Why not?" I ask, even though I don't feel hungry for dinner yet.

"The Knife Thrower." She pauses. "I don't know how he did this, but he hacked into a restaurant's phone and pretended to be an employee there. The restaurant got an order. He answered the call. He then obviously got the person's address. He showed up at their house and executed them," she says quietly.

"What?!" I shout. "That is crazy!"

"It is," my mother responds. "There are some things we adults need to discuss, so would you mind going back to your room?"

I nod, then walk back upstairs, feeling very annoyed. I wish life could be normal. I pick up the letter and stare at it. I don't even think about codes. I just stare. I'm like a lion eyeing a wildebeest for dinner.

I wonder if this is all a dream. But it's not. I realized that after I hit myself in the head. When the Knife Thrower gets caught, I won't just be excited to have a normal life again. I'll be excited to find out who the killer is.

My suspects are John Bryans and Carlos Bills. I haven't mentioned Carlos Bills yet, but he is another very shady man. He shows himself as very kind, respectful, and caring. But anytime he smiles it looks like a devil's smile in my eyes. I see him as a barbaric person with his green, shining eyes. It's because I see a smirk in his smile. An *evil* smirk. He lives two houses down from my house. Coincidentally, I saw him out my window running to his house shortly after somebody was killed by the Knife Thrower. Although, before the murders even began, I always saw him running around. I think that John is for sure more suspicious than Carlos.

I wonder if Carlos ever went in the Mines of Murder. He didn't own that underground land. People could legally go into the Mines of Murder, but nobody has. I bet John has been down there a few times. I never see John at stores, malls, or other places around town, but he has a balcony at the very top of his scary house. He's usually sitting up there reading a book. I see his house every day whenever a family member and I drive somewhere, because there is one way in and one way out of my neighborhood.

I haven't seen my father in a few weeks. The reason my parents got a divorce was not because they fought a lot...they just didn't love each other anymore. I was eight years old when they got divorced. My dad lives all the way in Trenton. He lives in an apartment. I used to see him every weekend, but with the Knife Thrower around, I don't. My father is great—the opposite of Jonah. But the one thing that's the same about them is their kindness.

My dad's brother, my Uncle Frank, is in rehab. He has a drinking problem. My father tells me that growing up with Frank was hard. He never listened, and in high school, was out past his curfew. He says that my grandparents did everything they could to help him, but now nobody does because my dad's side of the family has tried for so many years. It honestly sounds depressing.

I look at the letter from the Knife Thrower, trying to crack the code. Once again, I have no luck. I look at the red knife with the big black A on it. I don't know if it's supposed to represent my name, Andrew. That'd be my only guess. I try the Code Detector again, but it doesn't work.

All of a sudden, I have a realization. I think to myself, *you need to crack this code! Get to work or you will be executed by the Knife Thrower!*

Suddenly I am full of energy. I try the Code Detector multiple times while doing research on my computer. I then think that maybe the letters are mixed up and I have to solve each word. I mix them up in many ways. Nothing works, but I keep going. Confidence rushes through my brain. Ideas come, then go. It has been a few hours of research, and I have no new leads.

It's 8:00 p.m. now. My face is very red. I spend some time just looking at the note, trying to identify what it means. I haven't found very many patterns in the note. I just study it. I don't want to be working on this until 11:00. That will be too long. I get a bit hungry, so I go downstairs to have a small bowl of chicken pot pie, and then head back to my room.

My eyes start to hurt from staring at my computer for so long. It's almost out of battery too. I shut it and rub my sore eyes. It's 8:45 p.m.

now. I plan on getting a good night's sleep, so I want to go to bed around nine o'clock. After fifteen minutes I get in bed. I shut my exhausted eyes shut and sleep.

* * *

When I wake up, my clock displays 9:30 a.m. Wow, I slept over twelve hours! How tired was I? I don't really remember. I walk downstairs and smell amazing pancakes. Only my mother and Jonah are around. "Oh, good morning, honey," my mother says, and I smile. "Oh, by the way, you got a letter in the mail. It doesn't say where it's from." She twitches her head for a moment.

I grab the letter. *Uh-oh!* I'm very nervous! The envelope is red, just like the other one. My heart jolts as I dash up the stairs. I jump on my bed, then take a deep breath. Did the Knife Thrower send me another letter? I am shaking. I feel hopeless. I open it and read…

VGX CHC XNT MNS BNLD?
BNLD SNMHFGS ZS LHCMHFGS. HE XNT CN
MNS BLND AX STDRCZX MHFGS
H LHFGS ZR VDKK GZUD SN JHCMZO
XNT

What is going on? This is just crazy. I have no clue what this means! I have to crack this code! Who knows? I might die if I do not figure this out! I need to, and fast! But right now I'm starving, so I'm going to go eat. I go back downstairs to the kitchen.

"Who was it from?" my mother asks me.

"Oh, um…just a letter from a friend," I say, forced to lie.

"Who?" she asks.

"Oh, someone from overnight camp."

"Okay!"

She believes me. *Phew!* I slowly eat my pancakes. My stomach gets queasy. The syrup doesn't sit well with my stomach, but I don't bother to talk at all. Everyone sits down but no one is speaking. Then I say, "I'm done," thanks to the gross taste that was just in my mouth.

I walk up to my room. I look at both letters I've received and see what things are similar. For example, they both have the same peculiar words, which gets me thinking. I don't think there is really anything I'm going to do on this dull and rainy Saturday. The only thing that is distracting me is the loud raindrops.

Maybe I could bake, or cook? I will most likely be up all night trying to figure these letters out. I try my Code Detector a few times, but nothing works. I then start to think about what some of the letters could say.

At first, I think that they both start with *dear*, but that doesn't make sense because both letters start with a three-letter word. I need help, but I can't get any. Otherwise, I would look suspicious and the person who I asked for help would know that I'm hiding something. I'd seem suspicious. I feel discombobulated about these letters. I look very closely at the red knife. I measure it. It's about six inches long. What is very distinctive is the black A on it. My name starts with an A. Andrew. The A is not written in a Sharpie or marker; it's engraved on the red handle. I cajole myself to not look at the knife or the letters; it gets me worried and frustrated. I feel very happy doing nothing. I then put the letters and knife away. All of a sudden, my mother comes into my room.

"I haven't seen you since breakfast. What have you been doing?" she questions kindly.

"Nothing," I reply.

"What do you want to do?" she asks.

"I don't know." I seem unemotional. Especially while I lie on my floor, staring at my ceiling with a plain face.

"Do you want to play a board game?"

I shrug. "I'm just tired," I say.

"Okay. Well, I'll see you later then."

"See you," I say.

My mother leaves my room. I look out my window at the lousy weather—the pouring and pouring and pouring rain. My stomach grumbles, but I don't bother to eat. Maybe me not finding out what the letters mean is a good thing. I decide I won't look at them for the rest of my life. The Knife Thrower will be caught someday and then I won't need to figure out the letters.

Then I start to think of a way to manipulate my uncle into figuring out the letters. It's a very odd thing to all of a sudden think about, but it works. I chose him because he's smart, and he's in the CIA. He's probably used many codes before. What I'll do is tell him that I created a code and he'll have to figure it out. Once he does, I'll find out what the letters are saying! He might recognize this one or easily figure it out.

I walk downstairs to the kitchen holding the first letter I got. At the table, my uncle is rapidly typing on a computer, probably doing something that has to do with the CIA. I say, "Hey, do you have a minute?"

"Yeah, what's up?" he asks.

"Well, I've created a secret code you have to figure out!" I say with excitement.

"What is it?" Uncle P asks.

I put the letter in front of him. "Try to figure this out." I tap on the paper. He seems very confused. "Oh c'mon!" I say jokingly. "It'll be fun!"

"Seems hard," he replies, seeming bored.

I sigh, which is something I do occasionally. By "occasionally" I mean all day, every day. "Please?" I ask kindly.

"Sure...but what is this for anyway?" Uncle P asks.

I shrug. "I don't know...just something fun you can do," I suggest.

"Huh?" He seems very confused. "Well, okay, then. I'll look at it."

Excitement rushes through my body. I see him study the letter. Do I feel bad for manipulating him into trying to figure out something that seems impossible to me? Yes. But do I feel happy because I might find out what these letters are saying? Yes, I do. I'm not meaning to be rude or mischievous, but him solving that code would help me a lot. Plus, maybe this could also help my uncle. What if he needs to figure out some codes and it's the same as this?

It then seems like he is starting to get it! On another piece of paper, he's writing down many things very quickly! I think he is solving it! *Yes!* I think. I watch him as he figures it out. But then he sighs. He gets annoyed and so do I.

"Can you give me a hint?" he asks.

I don't know what to do then. Maybe going to Uncle P wasn't the best idea. "How about we do this later," I say. "Tell me some more about you being in the CIA," I add, trying to change the subject.

"Well, as you know, I'm leaving Tuesday night," he replies, "and I'm saying that I'm going to a friend's lake house. I was considering confessing about my job, but it is too secretive. And because of some emails from earlier I will be coming back Monday night, the next week. Also, do you want to see a piece of technology I'm going to be using?" I nod. "It's called a watchet." He pulls out something from his pocket that looks like a watch, except where the clock is supposed to be, there's a screen.

"What does it do?" I ask.

"It tells me how far another human is away from me. That's how I know when I need to get out of somewhere in case somebody is by me." He taps on the watch. A few things pop up, but one says: *THE NEAREST PERSON IS 2 FEET 1 7/12 INCH AWAY.*

"Wow, that is cool," I say. "I wonder how hard things were back in your generation when there was no technology like this. Being in the CIA, that would be a pretty hard job."

"Well, in thirty years, *your* nephew might call this generation's technology bad. No matter how good technology gets, the CIA will always be a hard job...and dangerous, of course."

I nod. "I've never thought of it that way." I tilt my head, look up at the ceiling, tap my index finger on my chin, and bite my lip at the same time.

Since our conversation has ended, I take the letter and walk upstairs to my room. I exhale loudly. I try the Code Detector yet again, but it obviously doesn't work. Annoyed and mad about my circumstances, I think about ripping up the letter…but I don't. But I do crumple up the letter and throw it. *This is so stupid!* I think. Maybe the Knife Thrower just wanted to drive me nuts. I almost did kill him, but that knife didn't hit him that hard. It was obviously hard enough to make him bleed and fall, though. Maybe it caused him to break an ankle or a leg. I pull out the red knife, hoping that the Knife Thrower comes to me now. If he does, I'll be ready to stab him and find out who he is.

I'm cognizant that maybe the Knife Thrower will send several letters to me, make me go to the police, and then I could get in trouble. If I say I got the first letter at the knife range when he attacked us, the police won't believe me because Uncle P and Jonah might chime in and say that they never saw him throw a letter or a knife at me. I would seem like a liar. I could get into serious trouble with the police and at home. Well, with the police maybe things wouldn't be *too* serious; it's not like they would send me to jail. Maybe my family would have to pay a fine? Either way, it'd be somewhat serious, because it would sound like I'm lying about something that has to do with a killer. If my family knew about the letters and heard my crazy thought that the Knife Thrower just wanted to get me in trouble with the police, they would probably disagree with my theory. Now that I fully comprehend the situation with the letters, I realize how foolish I've been.

I don't think that I'll get any letters later today. Hopefully. Are the letters a trap? I grab the red knife with the engraved A on it. It's very unique and somewhat strange. I survey the letter with my knife, as if I'm planning on plunging the blade into the piece of thin parchment. Staring at both letters has bemused me. *The code letters…*

I then want to practice throwing knives, even though yesterday my uncle told me not to. I'm thinking of going back to the knife and ax range I went to yesterday, but I'll need to ask an adult. If I snuck out, my mother would find out. I then think of asking Jonah, since he would be pleased to spend time with his stepson. I need to develop skills with a weapon. Something may happen to me if I can't solve the letters.

I walk downstairs to see him painting. "Sooooo what are ya doing?" I say.

"Nothing much. You?" he asks.

"Same here. By the way, that painting looks super good." I start coaxing him into a good mood so there is a better chance of him letting me go to the ax and knife range.

"Thanks, it's uh—"

"Let's go to the knife and ax range we went to yesterday!" I say quickly. Before he can even reply, I shout, "Great! Let's have some fun!"

5

Spying

"Okay," Jonah responds, seeming bewildered.

I dash to the car, hoping he won't call me to come back. To my luck he doesn't. When we get in the car, I holler, "Whoo-hoo! We are going to have so much fun!"

"Yeah," he says happily.

I grin the whole time we are in the car and pat my thighs quickly to show how "excited" I am to hang out with him. We have mostly green lights, so we fly through the roads. All of a sudden, I feel famished due to barely eating breakfast.

Once we arrive, we see Adam at the front desk. "How've you two been?" he asks.

"Good!" Jonah replies, smiling sweetly.

"Where's the other one?" he asks, meaning Uncle P.

"Home," Jonah replies in a monotone.

Adam nods. Jonah hands him some money, and as we walk to the ranges Adam gives us a friendly wave. I hope that this time I won't get attacked.

As we walk in, I see the ax range, knife range, bows, and arrows. I see small scraps that I figured were from the envelopes yesterday. I even see small bloodstains on the fake grass. I jog to the knife range.

"Whoa, whoa, whoa, whoa!" Jonah runs toward me. "No knives!" he demands.

"Why?" I argue.

"Dangerous!"

"Just like your axes!" I shout.

"Fine," he says annoyedly.

Well, that was a relatively quick argument.

I walk over to the knife range. There are five knives. I pick one and I see the target. I look at the knife I chose. I look behind me, and I see Jonah throw an ax. The way he throws it seems like he is anguished. I then glance at the bows and arrows, wondering if maybe that'd be more fun.

Jonah seems to be worn out from throwing the ax with such energy. I look at my target and throw the knife without hesitation. It sticks about eight inches away from the red bull's-eye. My knife-throwing skills already seem terrible. I look behind me. Jonah is gaping at me. "Show me what you've really got," he says encouragingly. I'm slightly baffled that he is giving me such confidence when yesterday we had some competition with each other. I grin at him.

I grab a knife and throw it! It darts into the bull's-eye with a big thud! I look behind me. Based on Jonah's face, it seems like he was expecting me to miss. He says nothing. After a moment of silence, he says, "Pretty good." He repeats that multiple times, murmuring.

I smile to show I'm appreciative of his cordial compliments. I keep practicing. It takes a lot of energy to throw a knife. I practice in many ways. Sometimes before I throw, I do a quick duck, then a quick throw. This is because if I ever need to throw a knife at somebody, it will most likely be because they are trying to attack me. I move my body around quickly as if someone is throwing a knife at me and I need to dodge it. A second later I throw a knife. It's hard to throw right at the bull's-eye when

I am ducking and dodging because I have to throw a knife in that position. It's challenging. Jonah does his ax throwing.

Next, I walk to the archery set. Most of my shots at the target are bad. Archery is not my strength. It turns out I really did have luck yesterday with the archery, which is unfortunate. It built some confidence in me that just fell apart, but I really shouldn't complain about it. Who cares? At least I can defend myself with a knife. Using a bow and arrow at close range could be hard. Getting a good aim could be hard. Or maybe that would just be for me, not for professional archers. It's more likely for me to find a knife than a bow and arrow if I ever needed to defend myself. When I say 'defend myself,' I mean from the Knife Thrower, because something might happen because of those letters.

I'm back at the knife range now and I throw a few more knives. I find it very peculiar that out of all the people in this town, the Knife Thrower sent me the letters.

My town is small, and the Knife Thrower is probably Carlos Bills or John Bryans. I have to admit, though, they're doing a good job if they are the serial killer. They haven't been caught, nor have they left any clues showing they're the culprit. A few people have seen the Knife Thrower after he killed somebody, and pictures have been taken. As you know I have seen him live, and I have seen the pictures on the news.

Some look like Carlos: medium height and a little plump. Maybe Carlos and John are in on this together? Maybe they've both been the Knife Thrower? People have told me that they are close friends. Was this true?

All of a sudden, I hear a bell ring. Someone must've walked in. I then see Carlos and John! I realize that they probably practice knife throwing here! They smirk at each other. My heart beats quickly. Both Carlos and John stare at my petrified face. John cordially says, "Hello, young man, how are you?"

"Um, uh-uh-uh, hello." I stumble on my words because of how scared I am. "I'm g-good. How are you?" I take a step back.

"We are quite fine," John says, speaking for both of them.

And that's it. I become aware that I might have just had a conversation with two serial killers. I look at them so I can study their knife-throwing skills. John is a master. I see him close his eyes for a few of his throws. Carlos really shows himself as the Knife Thrower with all his crazy ways of throwing a knife. Both of them hit the bull's-eye almost every single time. My heart thumps loudly when they throw a knife so quickly. They look over at me. I have to show them how good I am at knife throwing so they know who they might try to kill tonight. I then throw a knife with my right hand. Bull's-eye!

They both jump a bit. They gasp and then whisper—probably talking about my knife-throwing skills. Jonah and I make eye contact. I gnaw on my lip. He signals me with a wave to come to him. I walk over, but I can't get my eyes off those serial killers. I want to call the police, but I have no proof of them being the Knife Thrower, nor would a police officer believe that some little kid like me has any idea what they're talking about. I say, "Yeah?" to Jonah.

"Is it just me, or do you think one of those guys is the Knife Thrower?" he whispers.

"I was thinking the same thing," I reply.

"With the knife-throwing skills they have, it would make total sense," Jonah says.

"I agree," I answer. I then say, "I want to call the police and we'll explain what we think." I pause. I think about how Jonah and I are building a good relationship together by solving a murder mystery. Sure, that's odd, but still. It would help us. "It's just...we have no stupid proof!" I clench a fist. I don't know why I should be angry right now, when I should feel very scared, but I am very angry.

"Yeah," Jonah says, annoyed. He then mutters a curse word. My eyes widen. "Sorry," he apologizes.

I roll my eyes. "Anyway, we need to find a way to prove that one or both of them is the Knife Thrower."

"What do you mean both?" Jonah asks.

I exhale. "I've had some thoughts."

"Maybe we should follow them," Jonah suggests.

"Really? That doesn't sound like the best idea," I say nervously, then squint.

"What's the worst that could happen?" he asks.

"Um, they see us and then kill us," I reply with annoyance.

"We can bring weapons," he suggests. My eyes widen. "Only for self-defense!" he states. "Otherwise, we don't use them," he says, while pointing at me to show he is being serious.

"When are we doing this?" I ask.

"Once they leave this place, we'll follow," Jonah says mysteriously. I nod. "But first we need weapons. I'll go and ask Adam if we can buy some. Go outside for now." He then walks away, and I go outside.

I cannot believe what is happening! It is very shocking. Jonah used to seem like a nice guy, but now he is not necessarily mean, but just…different. Like Uncle P. He first seemed like a lazy, happy person, but then all of a sudden, I hear that he is in the CIA and very wealthy. If my mother found out what Jonah and I are about to do, she'd go nuts. She would be furious. Uncle P would be all *I'm not mad, I'm just disappointed.* I hate it when my mother, Jonah, or Uncle P say that. It makes me feel horrible, but knowing that this time Jonah is in on this "bad" thing with me, my mother would be madder at him. On the other hand, I highly doubt that she would find out about Jonah and me spying on two people who could be serial killers.

I feel wind fly into my face, and I see trees wrestling each other. Looking at nature, it seems like today will be a beautiful day. Even though it will be unpleasant soon. I am a little upset, though, because I wanted to spy on that teacher—the one who let the Knife Thrower get into the Zoom class—at the police station. Well, I could at least probably hear updates on the news about suspects. I usually never watch the news, but now I have been because I find this whole Knife Thrower mystery fascinating.

Not in a good way, though. Not when someone is killed. I just always find murder mystery movies entertaining. And now that I'm practically living in one, it is truthfully a very entertaining life. Also, very scary, of course. It bewilders me that nobody was killed last night. Maybe tonight, though...

Since I can't solve the letters and I have no clue what they really say, that is the part that scares me. Whatever the Knife Thrower is trying to say in the letter might be time-sensitive and dangerous. I need to find out. I wait and wait for Jonah to come back. When I think about two people who could be murderers in the same building I'm in, I feel quite frightened. I stare at the sun. I've always wondered how it could be raining for a long time, but then in such little time the sun comes out. I notice a rainbow as well. The end of it seems about fifty yards away from me. However, it's really millions of yards away. I wonder what my mother would think if she knew not just that Jonah and I will be spying on people, but also that I'm standing alone in public. She would freak out. I can't blame her, though. The Knife Thrower is on the loose.

Jonah then comes out. "You got the weapons?" I ask.

"Yeah," he whispers. He unzips a big bag. There is an ax, a bow, and arrows. "Here you go." He hands me the bow and a quiver with twelve golden arrows.

I say, "You know that I stink with the bow!"

"Um, you looked pretty good with it yesterday," he protests.

"But I am much better with a knife," I correct.

"It's fine. Who knows if we'll need them anyway?" Jonah responds.

I roll my eyes. "Fine."

"Now let's go behind this corner." He points to the side of the building. I nod.

We walk back there. I have my steel bow with a quiver of golden arrows, and Jonah has a dark red ax, which reminds me of the knife I got from the Knife Thrower. We press our backs on the side of the building. We turn our heads and wait for them to come out.

"What if they're not the Knife Thrower?" I ask.

Jonah shrugs. "Today, we either find out nothing or we find out if they're the Knife Thrower. Plus, most of victims get assassinated at night. It's day, but if they're telling each other secrets we might hear some." I nod. "Also, when they walked in, they didn't seem scared of anything. Like when we go to places, we know there's a chance that something might happen to us. They seemed fine. And they shouldn't be scared of killing themselves. You get what I mean?" Jonah asks.

"Yep," I reply. My heart beats quickly. I'm nervous, but also somewhat excited. Twenty-five minutes go by, and they haven't come out yet. "Ugh," I say annoyedly. "When are they coming?"

"Shhh," Jonah says.

I then see Carlos and John walk out of the building. Jonah and I are silent. I'm ready to shoot them with my golden arrows if they attack us. We follow them, walking slowly. It is kind of weird. We seem to be stalking them, which is odd, but we are for sure spying on them. Jonah seems like he is ready to throw his ax. They walk down strange streets, where nobody is around. We follow them into an alley. Jonah and I stare at each other with confusion. Then they start to talk.

"No one is around," Carlos says.

"We'll be waiting for him," John adds.

"He better have that money," Carlos says roughly.

"Money?" I whisper to Jonah. He shrugs.

"If he doesn't arrive, we're going right to his house!" John says solidly. "He's already twenty minutes late. Chris should for sure be here right now!"

I wonder who this Chris guy is.

Carlos shakes his head. "Guy's an idiot," he adds.

"A crackpot too," John snarls.

"He probably doesn't have that two hundred dollars!" Carlos says hotly.

Jonah then steps on a twig. Carlos and John hear the noise. Quickly, we hide behind a dumpster, which reeks.

"You hear that?" John asks.

Carlos walks slowly. I can hear his footsteps coming toward us! He says, "Nothing. Hmm?"

I breathe with relief. I really thought that Carlos was going to see Jonah and me, but if neither John nor Carlos is the Knife Thrower, they would be very perplexed to see us spying on them. John says, "What is taking so long for Chris to arrive?!"

"Dunno," Carlos replies.

I see John's face build up with anger. I wonder what's going on. Maybe Carlos and John have been doing illegal things. Selling bad things to this Chris guy. When I saw them walk into the range together, they seemed like very good friends. Other than that, I never pictured them as friends when people told me that they were. It confuses me when I think of them both being the Knife Thrower. I don't think that a lot of known murders involve two people. If Carlos and John are working together as the Knife Thrower, it is probably because if one gets caught, he'll go to jail while the other person can continue their dirty work.

To be honest, I hope that John or Carlos is the Knife Thrower, because then Jonah and I would catch both of them, or one of them, and turn them in. Then all the kids in my town would be in school, no one would be scared, and people would feel comfortable going to a lot more places. People would meet up more, people would go on walks, people would feel free. It sounds very sad when I think those words in my head, but they are true. Sometimes I wish I were a bird at this time. Then I would feel freer. But now everything is abhorrent, abominable, and ominous....

I hear John say, "Carlos, you sure nothing is there? I thought I heard something."

I hear Carlos walk over here again, getting closer and closer. I need to get his attention away from Jonah and me, so I shoot an arrow at a tree a little behind John to draw their attention away from us. Boom!

"What was that?" Carlos asks, seeming nervous, while Jonah seems shocked.

"Who's there?" John grouches.

I then shoot another arrow at another tree. "Run!" Carlos shouts.

I see the two start running, so Jonah and I run after them. John and Carlos scream. We run and run. We turn down alleys and then run through a mini forest, we jump over logs, and duck our heads when a branch is low. As we run, Jonah whispers, "That was smart."

"Thanks," I say quickly. We run faster and faster. As we're about to get out of an alley Carlos and John all of a sudden disappear! "Ugh, where'd they go?" I ask.

"Over there!" Jonah shouts. He points to the left, and I see Carlos and John running.

We're out of breath but we run after them. They end up running to a park. No one is around. Once I see their heads turn around, I turn my head back and Jonah and I are now behind a thick tree. Suddenly, I hear a crash, my eyes widen on instinct. They slip in the mud, and I see another man. "Where have you been!" John shouts to the man as he wipes mud off of his pants. Jonah and I squat behind a tree and listen to the three argue.

"I'm so sorry," the man says.

"Well, Chris," Carlos starts off with, "you better have that two hundred dollars!"

"Here!" Chris cries. "Here! Here's the money!" He then hands Carlos some money.

Carlos mutters numbers as he counts the money. "This is one eighty!" he shouts.

"Where is the rest?" John barks.

"I'm so sorry!" Chris cries. "I know! I know it's not enough!"

"We told you that this was your last chance to get us that money!" John growls. "And you didn't get it all for us!"

Chris puts his hands back like he is getting arrested. "Please don't hurt me!" he begs. "I'm sorry."

"We're not going to hurt you," John says, annoyed.

"You aren't?" Chris says wistfully.

"We aren't?" Carlos asks.

"No," John says firmly.

"Thank you!" Chris says gratefully.

"You give us a few beers and we're good," John announces.

"Okay," Chris sniffles. "We'll go to my place."

"No!" Carlos shouts. "You're getting the beating you deserve!"

"Stop," John says. "It's fine." Carlos rolls his eyes. "All right. Take us to your place," John says.

Chris then says, "Really, though. Thank you. It's just—"

"Take us to your place," John orders.

Chris nods. Jonah and I follow the three as they walk. We try to talk to each other by mouthing things, but it is unsuccessful. Chris looks down at the concrete gloomily. John and Carlos are obviously arguing when they lightly shove each other and whisper, while Jonah and I are just confused. I now suspect that neither John nor Carlos is the Knife Thrower. They just seem like some rude guys—not crazy killers. Maybe John, Carlos, and Chris are in a gang? As we follow them, my eyebrows go low when we pass dumpsters because of the gross smell.

All of a sudden, in front of me is not just Carlos, Chris, and John, but a small house. Once the three walk in, Jonah and I stay outside and look through windows to spy on them. "Wow," says Jonah. "They seemed like enemies, but now they're in a business meeting."

"Yeah," I agree.

The house is less than a story high. It looks like a pigsty. It's grotesque. I see the three men have some beer. All of a sudden, I make eye contact with John! I hear him shouting. Jonah and I don't know what to do. We hear big footsteps. The three men walk outside, but they don't see Jonah and me. They look around and see no sign of us. That is because we climbed up the brick siding to the roof of Chris's house!

"I swear I saw somebody," John says. He looks like an idiot looking around for me.

Then Carlos shouts, "Up there!" He points to Jonah and me.

We spring off the house. I feel like I twisted my ankle when I made my rough landing. We run as fast as we can to get to the ranges so we can grab the car and go. "Stop right there!" John shouts.

I look behind me for a second, and there is no sign of Chris. I then look forward and run with Jonah. I turn around for a split second to shoot an arrow. Carlos dodges it the second before the arrow hits him in the chest. I keep running and running. I wonder what would have happened if I had hit Carlos. Would I have killed him? Would I have injured him badly? What would John have done? We jump over logs and rocks. I breathe quickly. It looks like I'm trying to whistle. I then look behind me. No sign of John or Carlos.

I shout, "Jonah! They're gone."

"Phew," he says. "Are you okay?"

"Yeah," I respond.

"Good."

"By the way, when my mother finds out about this, she is divorcing you."

"W-wait…what!?" Jonah shouts.

"The interesting part about what I just said is that I'm not even kidding," I say.

"Okay, so what are we telling your mother?" he asks.

"Nothing, I guess."

"Why? Well, I…I mean I know you said that she'd divorce me, but still."

"Well, what do you think we should do?" I ask.

"I guess we have to come clean. Maybe even tell the police," Jonah suggests.

"No!" I shout.

"Why?" Jonah argues.

"Because…I shot a few arrows at them. They may have missed, but it is an attempt at violence. Also, if you think about it, Carlos and John never did anything to indicate that they would hurt us. So, technically they are victims in this situation. Actually, they *are* the victims." Jonah looks at me with disdain. "We spied on them! Looked into Chris's home, which is his property, and we went on his property without permission!" I exclaim.

"That is true." Thank God Jonah agrees. "I guess we have to stay away from the police. Although we could report their actions with Chris."

"But they didn't do anything illegal!" I protest. "Well, unless…"

"Unless what?" Jonah asks quickly.

"Unless the three of them were selling or trading drugs." Jonah shakes his head. "You heard how much money Carlos and John wanted from him…*two hundred dollars*!" I holler. "And they were going to meet up at a random place where nobody goes."

"Makes sense, but we have no proof," Jonah says, annoyed.

"How about we do nothing and tell no one," I say.

"Maybe we could tell my brother?" Jonah suggests.

"What would he do?"

"Oh, um, uh, uh…never mind, go on," he says quickly.

I then realize that Jonah wanted to tell Uncle P because he is in the FBI. I want to share my secret that I know Uncle P is actually in the CIA, but I can't. I never can, and never will, but will never stop wanting to. Instead, I say, "I guess we should go home now."

"Well, we've got to go back to that ax throwing place first. That's where our car is," Jonah says.

"Okay," I reply. We walk and walk. "To be honest, it was pretty cool spying on John and Carlos. It was very interesting."

"I guess," Jonah says carelessly.

My legs get very tired. I could fall down and sleep for hours. "So, what are we doing the rest of the day?"

Jonah shrugs. "Should we spy on them to make sure they don't go to the police?" Then, for some reason, he then acts like everything that happened was my fault. I try not to listen, but I fail. "Why did you shoot the arrows?" he asks. He asks again in many different ways. I'm pretty sure he is doing this so I sound like the bad guy if my mother finds out what we've done. "And why did you come up with the idea to spy on Carlos and John?"

"Whoa, whoa, whoa!" I exclaim. "It was your idea to spy!"

"Was not!"

"Was so!"

"Was not!"

"Was so!"

We argue back and forth like we're little kids. I know that I am right. I remember his words: *Maybe we should follow them.*

"*Was not!*" Jonah roars.

"You told me at the ax throwing pl—that place…!" I'm so outraged that I can't even speak. I exhale, showing how angry I am. "You said we should follow them."

Jonah looks down with guilt. "Oh," he says.

We then walk in silence. I feel a gust of wind across my cheeks. I hope that I don't get attacked by the Knife Thrower before we get to the car. Yesterday had been horrible. I don't remember seeing Uncle P or Jonah much during the attack because I was busy trying to kill the Knife Thrower. It confuses me that Jonah doesn't seem so nervous about me. We used to be in an okay spot in our relationship. Now we're in a bad one. I think that many things will change once the Knife Thrower is caught. Friendships will return, school will resume, and lives will be much better for everyone in town. Except for the Knife Thrower, who will rot in prison. Maybe he'll even get a death sentence. I've heard that you get around twenty, twenty-five years in prison for murdering somebody. And the Knife Thrower has killed enough people that his time in prison would add up to a few centuries.

I have also been thinking that I would like it if Uncle P came clean to everyone. No more lies, no more secrets, which were the two things my mother hated! My mother is always honest. Not once do I remember her lying to me. When I think about my parents, I realize I have the best mom and dad in the world, but stepfather? Meh…

I wish I lived with my dad during this time so I wouldn't have to be worried about getting murdered. Jonah and I finally get to the car and drive home. Whenever we make eye contact, you can tell we've been arguing. There's silence the whole time.

Once we arrive home, I say hi to Uncle P and my mother. Then I drag myself to my room. I look at the letters and try to figure out the codes. I have my red knife too. What's very frustrating about solving the letters is that I can't even come up with codes, which is annoying. If I did, and they were all unsuccessful, fine, but *this*? Ugh, I hate it!

I regret opening those letters. No doubt it was the worst decision ever! But now I'm eager to solve them. I stare and stare and think about crumpling them up. I finally think of a code for the letters! One letter in the alphabet equals the letter before it! As in A = Z, B = A, C = B, D = C, and so on and so forth! I try them out! I did try this code, but in reverse, how did I not think of this? I do lots of erasing and singing the alphabet in my head. When I think I've figured the first letter out, I look at my handwriting and I see:

> *You are in grave danger come to the Mines of Murder house at midnight if you don't you will regret it the second before you get assassinated good luck.*

Oh my God! This has to be from John! He's the only person who it could be from! After Jonah and I had that chase with him and Carlos earlier I figured he was just a gangster, but his house is above the Mines of Murder! Why would anyone besides him go in there? I then figure out the second letter. It says:

> *Why did you not come? Come tonight at midnight. If you do not come by Tuesday night I might as well have to kidnap you.*

6

The Mines of Murder

I need to go to that Mines of Murder house tonight! If I don't, I'll have nightmares! Never mind, I always have nightmares. John Bryans is going to kill me if I don't. I crumple up the papers I wrote out the letters on so they will never be found. I will need to bring my knife tonight. That might come in handy. I breathe heavily. I might get kidnapped tonight. Who knows what the Knife Thrower will do!

The day drags on. I have lunch and I try to avoid everyone in my family for now. My mother and I have some interactions. I don't talk much with Jonah or Uncle P. I also think about how surprised I am that I actually broke the code in those letters. I wonder what my visit will be like at the Mines of Murder house. I might have to go into the mines. Should I go? Maybe if I don't, I'll get executed. Maybe yesterday that wasn't really the Knife Thrower. Maybe it was someone trying to send me a message by giving me the letters. But if so, that would be very peculiar because they tried to kill me. It was very perplexing. It astounds me that I didn't die yesterday, nor did I get hurt by John and Carlos. Hopefully they aren't talking to the police.

When I think about how I had almost hit Carlos earlier it makes me feel very guilty. It was attempted murder. So, I would not be surprised if John was talking to the police. With the amount of time I've spent practicing knife throwing, I know I could survive tonight. I also think John sent me those letters because why would a random person want to have a meeting with someone or execute them under another person's house? That would be scary and weird. I might need to bring multiple knives tonight, because one may not be enough.

If my mother caught me sneaking out at 11:45 p.m. I would be busted. I also hope that I don't get kidnapped. Maybe the Knife Thrower didn't send me the letters? Maybe the person who sent me the letters thinks that the Knife Thrower is targeting me. But if so, they could've just given me a call or talked to me in person instead of giving me code letters and trying to kill me.

As the day goes on, I get more and more bored. I have dinner and then my mother tucks me in for bed at 10:00 p.m., only one hour and forty-five minutes until I have to leave the house to go to the Mines of Murder. I lie in bed for a bit. I grab my knife and a flashlight. I then go to the kitchen and grab a few more knives. As time goes on, I get more tired. It is now 10:30 p.m. and I have to leave the house in one hour and fifteen minutes. I exhale, then stare down, hoping this is a nightmare. I go to the fridge and take a big sip of Coca-Cola to get some energy. I have to admit sugar gets me hyper. So does carbon dioxide. Then one sip turns into a whole can. I predict that my dentist won't like me much when I go for my next visit.

I hope my meeting tonight with whoever will be brief. I mean, that person must know that I have to get home before my mom, Jonah, and Uncle P realize I am gone. Wondering what will happen, I hope it doesn't lead to me needing to go on a mission. One, I wouldn't have an excuse to leave the house. Two, I'll feel stupid for opening the letters, which I already have. And most of all, three, I could die.

Due to my stupidity, I am in this annoying situation. My paradigm has changed so many times about so many things. I have many perspectives.

The thought of going to that horrid house creeps me out—although I am very curious about what it's like there, at the Mines of Murder. Hopefully, there are no skulls waiting to turn me into one of them. I remember yesterday when I was excited to open the letters. Everything has been chaotic. Finding out my uncle is in the CIA, getting attacked by a serial killer, getting code letters, and spying on two people! After tonight I need to start policing my actions and calm down. I need to be more aware of my decisions.

Should I really go to the Mines of Murder tonight? Or will that cause more chaos? Eventually, I coax myself into going. Maybe I'll find out who the Knife Thrower is. Maybe I'll get an award from the police. On the bad side, my mother, Jonah, and Uncle P will be furious with me. I can see Uncle P being a little excited for me. My mother would then always be checking on me to make sure I'm not traumatized from my experience. And Jonah. Jonah and I would be at a more awkward stage in our relationship than we are now. We were fine before the whole knife attack and spying, which I feel guilty joining in. Yesterday, I should not have gone to the knife throwing place. That led to getting attacked by the Knife Thrower, the code letters, and probably way more things coming up in the near future.

As time goes by, it becomes 11:40. Although I'm still not leaving for another five minutes, I realize that I should ride my bike so it's easier to get away from the killer.

When I stare at the clock in the kitchen, I hallucinate for a moment. I see different times on the clock and get pretty sleepy. I blink a few times quickly, and things go back to normal. Only seconds go by when it feels like hours. Then finally it becomes 11:45 p.m. I exhale and I'm very nervous. I walk to the garage. Without making any noise, I bring my bike into the house and out the front door, because opening the garage would draw attention. I get on my bike, put my knives in my pocket, and put my flashlight in my water holder so I can see better.

I start riding in the cold through the deep puddles. No cars pass by me, which isn't surprising at this time of night. I feel like I'm going to fall off my bike because I'm so tired. I think I'm half asleep until an obnoxious truck comes by and shoots out a long and loud honk. Well, *that* woke me up. I shake my head quickly and then focus my eyes back on the road. I'm happy with myself because I brought a flashlight. It's pitch-black outside.

I have arrived at the house. The trees swaying around it kind of scare me. The door is wide open. I walk in and say, "Hello…is anyone here?"

No response. I look down and I see a broad gap. I see a cart on a track by the edge of the gap. I can't see the bottom of the gap. There is a sign on the cart that says Ride.

I slowly get on the cart, and it starts moving. There are loud screeches coming from the cart. I go *down*, *down*, *down*, until I can no longer see where I'd gotten onto the cart. I take a knife from my pocket knowing I might encounter the Knife Thrower once this cart stops moving. I can now tell that I'm in the mines. I see a few skulls and a stream of adrenaline goes through me. The next thing I see is the end of the track. Once I get to the end, I climb out of the cart. I notice a sign pointing to go right. I do, and then I see a table. Sitting there are two people who look like detectives. They are wearing black sunglasses, black hats, and fancy coats. There's one man, one woman.

"Who are you?" I ask.

"I'm George," the man says.

"And I'm Grace," the woman adds.

"What am I here for?" I ask.

"For us," Grace responds. I'm a little perplexed. "Well, I'm pretty sure that you figured out those code letters. Didn't you?"

"So, you guys have both been the Knife Thrower," I whisper. I then throw a knife at George. It spins in the air while getting closer and closer to him. He catches it with one hand.

"Calm down, kid," George says. He then gives me back my knife. "We're not the Knife Thrower. We sent you those letters—"

"But at the ranges—" I break in.

"Was not the real Knife Thrower. It was me," George interrupts.

"Why'd you try to kill me, then?" I ask anxiously.

"I knew you could dodge them. Grace and I gave coded letters to fifteen other kids in town. Or pictures or some indication to come meet us. Some around your age, and some way older than you."

"George and I chose you and those other children because you are the most clever and brave children in town."

I stare at them with confusion. George finally says, "You will come back here Tuesday night and meet your fellow Contestants."

"For what?" I ask.

"The MMR," he says proudly.

"What's that?" I ask.

"The Murder Mystery Race. We host it every year."

I'm confused, because I don't know whether I should know about this.

"What's it about?" I ask.

Grace says, "George and I carefully study all children around town. Then every March we think about who is the most clever and brave. We send them code letters, pictures, and other things. But that's not the point. Once all sixteen children figure them out, they come to us. You were the last one to figure out your code item," she pauses after that, and I sink in a feeling that the other Contestants are much smarter than me. "Anyway, George and I always find a town where murders are occurring. Luckily, this year it was this town—because we live here. Well, obviously not here-here in the Mines of Murder, but in a house. The Knife Thrower is going on a cruise. You and the other fifteen Contestants will go on the cruise, which will be nine days long. The first one of you to find the Knife Thrower gets one million dollars. We know who the Knife Thrower is, but there is a reason why we cannot say who it is. We only can once he's in prison. There are also four well-experienced Contestants."

"What do you mean—'well-experienced'?" I ask.

"They are all teenagers, but the way they got in again was because one of them won this whole thing last year. The winner of the most recent MMR gets to automatically be in the next MMR, unless they are eighteen when they win. They also get to choose three Contestants and let them automatically participate in the next MMR. The winner usually chooses the weakest of all Contestants so they are guaranteed to have less challenging competitors, but the winner last time picked their three friends. George and I have taken care of all the plane tickets and stuff to get on the cruise. When you come back here Tuesday night, you will meet the other fifteen Contestants. Then George and I will take all of you on a private plane to Florida where the cruise will begin."

"What happens if nobody finds out who the Knife Thrower is?" I ask.

"Trust us," George says. "Someone will."

"I don't know how I'll get out of my house, though," I say gloomily.

"We've been spying on you for a while, and we can hack into phones. Maybe you could ask your uncle to cover for you. Go to your uncle's friend's lake house," Grace suggests slyly. And I can tell she knows that Uncle P is in the CIA based on how she said that.

"Smart," I reply. "He'll cover for me. I can say that I want to go on a camping trip and I could ask if he'll lie for me."

"Smart boy," George says.

"Thank you," I reply.

"I think that the MMR will be very interesting this year," Grace adds. "Things like this cruise hardly happen. Usually, we just tell the kids that they have nine days to just be around a town to find out who the murderer is."

"How'd you guys know that the Knife Thrower is going on a cruise?" I ask.

"Well, with all the spying Grace and I have done, we overheard him telling someone. He also said he'll start killing people." George becomes subdued.

"He's working with someone else?" I exclaim.

"Yes, the two help plan the kills," George replies.

"Interesting," I say.

I think this is all crazy! I do feel honored, though, that I get to go on this…quest, maybe you'd call it. If I win, I could give Uncle P $2,000. If so, I'll have to tell everyone in the end how I went on the cruise. Grace then says, "Do you have any questions?"

"No," I say, still engaged in the conversation.

"Then you may leave," she says.

"Well, what about the cart?" I ask.

"Oh, sorry," George apologizes. He then picks up the cart from the track and turns it around. "There ya go."

"Thanks," I say.

"See you Tuesday night." Grace waves goodbye.

"At what time?" I ask.

"Eight thirty," she says.

I nod and get on the cart. It starts moving up. I then shout, "Goodbye!"

Grace and George wave. As the cart moves up the track, I hear a voice. It's Grace. "George and I would like to do a Zoom meeting with you today at 9:30 a.m."

"Sounds good," I say.

George then adds, "We know your email. We'll send the information." I nod. "And get home safely. Be quiet. I suspect that at 12:20 a.m. your parents are sleeping." I chuckle.

The cart arrives at the first floor of the house. I wonder whether John built the coaster. I walk out of the house and get on my bike. I don't remember Grace's voice much, but it sounded like she had a French accent. I'm not sure, though. This MMR sounds very interesting. I'm now very glad that I solved the letters. I would love to compete in this. And if I win it, I'll then be in the next one.

The MMR was surprisingly easy to understand. Grace and George explained it very well. Although I wasn't excited to compete with the four teens. They were probably arrogant, obnoxious, and annoying. I'm actually very excited to meet the other Contestants, which is a shock to me because I'm trying to win a million dollars against them. I have been selected as one of the most clever and brave kids in town. Maybe I could trick some of the Contestants, but they're also supposed to be very smart so they would recognize a trick.

It sounds like Grace and George have been doing this for a while. It also sounds like there is no age range. Well, you have to be under the age of eighteen. So, really, a five-year-old can get picked. Although I wouldn't think so. Maybe I shouldn't be thinking that, because hearing that there are teens competing against me, and that I'm only ten, shows that I could be the youngest Contestant. Twelve of the sixteen Contestants are from my town, while the other four are from a different town because one of them won last year's MMR and chose three Contestants to be in this year's MMR.

A fraction of the four people who have already been in an MMR could have been in it for the past five years. It kind of stinks that it has to be the teens who are the four well-trained Contestants. I bet that if one of the four finds out who the Knife Thrower is, they'll all split the money.

I wonder if Grace and George will be on the cruise. Probably not. I bet when I meet the Contestants on Tuesday night, George and Grace might have to put some sort of camera or tracker on our bodies to make sure we're okay. At least while I'm on the cruise everybody in town will be safe from the Knife Thrower. My mother and Jonah will be too, because they'll think I am at a lake house with Uncle P, safe and sound, but I won't be there. Nor will Uncle P. He'll be facing potentially deadly situations just like me, which is unfortunate. If I win this thing, my mother will find out about everything because I'll have to come clean.

I suspect that life will change after this MMR. As I ride home, excitement rushes through my body. I'm excited for the MMR. I wonder if people in town will be on the cruise. Maybe they *advertised* the cruise to people in town? Who knows what Grace and George are up to! What really confuses me is why George and Grace can't say who the Knife

Thrower is, but they know. There had to be some reason why, but it makes me feel like an imbecile for not figuring it out.

I bet that I can cajole Uncle P into covering for me. I could say I want to go on a camping trip and my mom won't let me go, and then he'll say that I'm coming with him to his friend's lake house.

I think they'll tell me on the Zoom that I'm going to need to bring my knife on the cruise. All Contestants probably have their signature weapon. It could be an ax, bow and arrow, a knife, or even a spear.

I need to make deals and alliances with my Contestants. So, even if I don't catch the Knife Thrower, I might get a portion of the $1 million and maybe get chosen for next year's MMR.

Grace and George must make lots of money yearly if they can afford to give a kid $1 million every year. I also wonder how long they have been doing this for. Ten years, maybe? That seems accurate. George and Grace seem like…not necessarily old people, or young people. Sort of middle-aged, I guess.

It bewilders me that the Knife Thrower is going on a cruise to start a bunch of murders. It would be very easy to get caught unless he were to jump off the boat. The Knife Thrower is a crazy killer. People have seen him, and he always gets away. He does crazy stuff. If anything, I bet the Contestants and I will have big confrontations with him. There will be lots of chasing, and lots of weapons used.

Maybe when I'm an adult and George and Grace get old, they could hand the privilege of taking care of the whole MMR thing to me. That'd be fun. Lots of planning would have to be done.

I don't think I'll die, nor will any of the Contestants because we're all supposed to be the most clever and brave people in town. I bet when all the Contestants meet, many of them will underestimate kids my age. I'd be surprised if not.

I wonder how deaths will be reported on the cruise. The captain will probably make an announcement. I predict that there will be a point when everyone on the ship is required to stay in their room, or maybe not. I've never been on a cruise where murders occurred.

I lift my shoulders a few times quickly because I'm excited for the MMR.

After riding my bike through a rainy night, I finally get home. I bring my bike inside the house and to the garage. Again, I can't open the garage because that'll wake everyone up. When I get back inside, I clean up the wet and dirty floor from my bike wheels. I take off my coat, go upstairs, put my pajamas on, and finally lie down on my bed. It's easy to fall asleep.

* * *

My eyes open. My clock displays 9:01 a.m. Twenty-nine minutes until my Zoom with George and Grace. I open my computer. I'd won it at a raffle, which is cool. It doesn't work very well, but I'm happy. I check my email. I have a message from "Flardin, Grace." I open it. It has the meeting ID and passcode for the Zoom.

It's crazy to think that Zoom was around for roughly two years when my parents were kids. Not just for them, but for people all over the world

I go downstairs, quickly eat breakfast, and go back to my room. It's only 9:20, so I have ten minutes until my Zoom with Grace and George. I'm very excited about being on the cruise in a few days. I think I might get caught up in a fun activity. I don't think people will be looking for the Knife Thrower the entire time. I mean, come on. This cruise has *got* to be fun.

I also need to ask Uncle P if he'll cover for me. I walk back downstairs, and to my luck, he's there. "Good morning," I say.

"Morning," he replies.

"So, on Tuesday night I want to meet up with a few friends and go on a camping trip. One of the kids' dad will be there," I say. "It'll be nine days."

"Okay. So, what's the problem?" he asks.

"Mom won't let me go. So, I was wondering if when you announce that you're going to a friend's lake house you could say I'm coming with you. Even though I'm going to really be on the camping trip."

"No can do. When I'm in Saudi Arabia," he whispers, "I'll be gone for ten days. Then you'll have to find somewhere to stay."

"That's fine," I say. "Absolutely fine. So, you'll cover for me?"

"Give me twenty dollars," he says excitedly. "I really need to pay Jonah back for something and I can't find my wallet. I promise I'll pay you back."

"No."

"Then I'm not covering for you."

I sigh and then drag myself upstairs to my room and grab a twenty-dollar bill. I come back downstairs and slam it on the table. "There!" I shout.

"Thank you. Now, I'll cover for you," Uncle P says.

"Good," I reply gruffly.

I stomp upstairs feeling somewhat mad because I had to give my uncle money so he would help me. But if he really knew what I was doing he'd call Grace and George and yell at them for not including him in the MMR. Even though he isn't under the age of eighteen, he would still be mad.

I'm thinking that for the MMR I need to be an ally to everyone. Therefore, if I don't win, the person who wins might pick me for next year's MMR. I'm determined to make friends. I then look at the time. I realize I have my Zoom with George and Grace now, so I log in. They are already on.

"Hello, Andrew," George says.

"Hi," I say.

"Hello," Grace replies. "How are you?"

"I'm good."

"How'd you sleep?" George asks.

"All right," I reply.

Grace begins, "So, we were wondering if you have that red knife we gave you. Do you have it?"

"Yes," I say.

"Good. You'll bring that on the cruise. Now we need to go over everything you'll need." I nod. "You'll need clothes, of course. Maybe bathing suits. I'd bring them just in case. Also, you might want to bring about one hundred and fifty dollars. Probably more. You'll need it to buy yourself meals. That is it."

Geez, $150 is crazy, but I think I have enough.

"Any questions on packing?" she asks.

"No," I reply.

George then says, "Are you excited?"

"Yes."

"Good," he says. "By the way, Tuesday night when you meet your fellow Contestants, everyone will receive a Quillix."

"What's that?" I ask.

"It's a phone that you can only call Grace and me on. You call us if you find out who the Knife Thrower is. If not, you will not earn the million dollars, because then we won't know if you found out who he is in the time from getting off the cruise to coming back to the Mines of Murder."

I'm a bit confused because I never heard about going back to the Mines of Murder after the cruise. George reads my face, then says, "We'll all meet back at the Mines of Murder to congratulate the winner of the Murder Mystery Race." I nod. "Do you have any questions so far?"

I ask, "Why can't you say who the Knife Thrower is?" Even though my question isn't a type of question he thought he'd hear, I still said it.

He sighs. "I told you that I cannot say why until the Knife Thrower is caught."

"I know, but what would happen?" I ask, but I get no response.

"Okay, let's get back to talking about the cruise," he says instead. "I'm going to give you strategies on how to find the Knife Thrower. First, try to get on the cruise before anyone else. Then watch everyone come on.

It will be a while, but you will see people from this town. Also, look for spots on the boat. It's probably stained blood from a person who recently got killed by the Knife Thrower. If you find blood and it's not dry, run away to a high height in zigzags and duck multiple times, because the Knife Thrower could throw knives behind you. Also make sure you are always armed with multiple weapons. Grace and I gave you one, but I bet you could easily steal a sharp knife from a restaurant. If you do see the Knife Thrower, get behind him; if he sees you, he could easily stab you. On the other hand, if you're behind him you could stab him or give him a deep cut. I bet the police prefer him alive when turned in so they can get answers. Only kill the Knife Thrower if you have to. If you're going to knock him out, make sure you have other Contestants with you in case you do not succeed. Therefore, if the Knife Thrower tries to fight back someone will save you."

I then ask, "Has any Contestant ever died?"

"About every three or four MMRs someone unfortunately doesn't make it back. After the first time it happened, Grace and I always focused on making sure we picked the smartest kids, so they're smart enough to not do something that would get them killed. I know that you will not die. I tested your survival skills at the ax throwing place the other day, right?" I nod. "So, you don't need to worry."

I then say, "Out of the sixteen Contestants, where would I rank as a fighter?" I wasn't being very specific, so George looks curious, based on his expression. I then say, "Meaning one is the best fighter, two is the second best fighter, and—"

"Oh, so you're asking what place you'd be in for the best fighter?" George asks.

"Yes," I say.

"You probably are the fifth best fighter. Maybe sixth," George answers.

"Who are the top four?" I ask.

"The four Contestants who were in it last year," he replies. Of course, that's true.

"How old are they?" I ask.

"There are two boys and two girls. One boy is sixteen. His name is Jack. Another girl is sixteen too; her name is Elena. The other two are both seventeen. Their names are Tiberius and Diana."

"What weapons are they best with?" I ask. I might want to steal their weapons. I know it's cruel, but it could help me win the MMR.

"Well, I think Jack uses a knife like you; Diana uses a bow and arrow; Tiberius uses a spear; and Elena uses a slingshot," George answers.

"What does Elena shoot with?"

Grace says, "Do you know how there is a sharp-looking knife at the front of a gun that people in war use when they are close together? They use it to stab each other. Do you know what it's called?"

"No," I say with perplexity.

"It's a bayonet. She uses a saw to cut the bayonet off rifles and then slingshots that."

Well, I think that is crazy, but everyone has their own weapon. "Hmm," I say, curious how everyone would be getting on the cruise with weapons. Security is usually very good on cruise ships. I wonder if Grace and George will say how.

I do not think I'll die. I bet that if Tiberius, Diana, Elena, and Jack were to see the Knife Thrower, they would fight over who gets to be the one to knock him out. Whoever does will be the person who found out who he is and will get the $1 million. If I win the $1 million, I would pay for my own college tuition. Even though that bill won't occur for another eight years, my mother would be very proud. So would Jonah, Uncle P, and most of all, me.

Grace then says, "That is all."

"Thank you," I say. And to be nicer I say, "I'm excited for the Quillix."

Both of them chuckle a bit, then I leave the Zoom. I wonder what the Quillix will look like. It is an odd word. Quillix. I think it will be a very interesting gadget. I then start packing all the stuff needed for the trip. I put everything in a backpack. It feels like seven pounds on my back, which isn't too bad. I look at the code letters I solved. I'm annoyed with myself that I didn't solve them sooner. I scrutinize them, wondering why I couldn't solve them. I give myself no answer.

I really like George and Grace. They are very nice people. I feel like George is a bit like Uncle P. I'm not sure who I can relate Grace to.

I don't only hope I win the Murder Mystery Race so I can get $1 million, but I also want to win it so I can participate in next year's MMR. I really like George's idea of waiting to see everyone coming on the boat so I can narrow down my suspicions of who the Knife Thrower may be. I also know that the Knife Thrower is a male. I remember Grace's words: *We can only say once HE is in prison.* I'm not sure whether they realized they said that or not. My guess is not.

I also remember when my mom told me that the Knife Thrower had hacked into a Zoom class. I recall her telling me that the students and teacher in that class thought the Knife Thrower was a male because of the voice they heard.

I wonder how George and Grace came up with the MMR. To me, it sounds like it's different every year.

I think that the police must have found out about the MMR whenever a killer is identified by a Contestant. Then all the Contestants, George, and Grace would have lots of lying to do. I find it odd that George and Grace feel okay offering $1 million to a bunch of kids to find out who a killer is. They're putting kids in danger, but I remember them saying the kids they pick are brave and clever, which makes it sound like they're safe.

George and Grace may be nice, but they are a bit mystifying. I just don't understand why they cannot report who the Knife Thrower is to the police! It doesn't make sense at all. Maybe they are working as the Knife Thrower together? Maybe they frame innocent people into being a killer every MMR?

I find it very peculiar that the police haven't found out about this secret MMR that George and Grace have been doing yearly. I remember them telling me that sometimes a Contestant perishes in the MMR. I bet they feel horrible whenever a Contestant is killed, although I don't think it happens very often.

I go downstairs to say hi to my mother and Jonah. "Good morning," Jonah says.

"Morning," I reply.

"Would you like any breakfast?" my mother asks.

"I've already had some," I say.

I see Jonah staring at the newspaper. "Ugh," he snarls. "This town is horrible!" I have to agree with Jonah. In the town I live in, Wayverlyn, it is horrible because of the Knife Thrower.

"Did someone get killed by the Knife Thrower?" my mother asks.

"Yeah," Jonah says. "There are thirteen suspects of who he may be."

"Do we know any of them?" my mother asks.

"Not that I recognize," Jonah says while skimming the list of names. "The thirteen people are going to be questioned at the police station today." Jonah then takes a sip of coffee and licks his lips. "I wonder when the Knife Thrower will get caught. It's been almost two weeks of murders around town." I shrug, not knowing what to say. "Abhorrent," he mutters while staring deeply into the newspaper. I try to not think about yesterday when Jonah and I spied on John and Carlos, which was *Jonah's* idea.

I sometimes can't comprehend Jonah, his hobbies, his personality, and almost everything about him. Sometimes he is subdued, while other times he is garrulous. He bewilders and annoys me.

My mother says, "So, what's everybody's plan for the day?"

Jonah says, "Nothing, but I have a few work calls."

I shrug and respond, "Nothing."

Sundays are always boring, as everyone's schedule is usually open. Only two more days until Tuesday when I go back to the Mines of Murder and meet the other Contestants. I'm very annoyed because I have nothing to do until Tuesday night. Unless being anxious counts.

I'm pretty sure that I won't have trouble deciding who I want to have an alliance with when I meet all the Contestants. I, for sure, know that everyone is very smart, and they probably have all the things I would want in someone if they were to work with me to find out who a murderer is. I'm also confused about how I got into this MMR thing.

Today would be a good day to see my father, but it's a long drive from Wayverlyn to Trenton. I guess I could sleep over tonight and tomorrow night and then come home so I can get to the Mines of Murder. I then say to my mother, "Hey, Mom, can I go to Dad's tonight and sleep over there for two days?" I glance at Jonah, and he seems annoyed. Anytime I bring up my father in front of him he gets annoyed.

"I'm afraid not," my mother says.

"Why?"

"I don't want you around him much anymore."

"Why?" I ask again, tensing up.

My mother clears her throat, "Well…" She doesn't finish her words.

"What?" I ask, with confusion.

"Well, I have a thought about your father." I stare at her with disdain. "An ominous thought," she says calmly. She then takes a deep breath. "I think that your father might be the Knife Thrower."

7

The Contestants

"WHAT!" I shout. "Are you crazy?!"

Jonah's eyes widen as he drops a mug of coffee. It shatters to the floor and miraculously doesn't get my mother's attention.

"I'm not crazy," my mom says calmly. "I just have an opinion on who I think might be the Knife Thrower."

"Yeah, and you suspect that a man who you raised a child with is a killer! Who tried to kill Jonah, Uncle J, and me?" I shout. Even though I know it was George at the range, not the Knife Thrower.

"Yes," my mother responds calmly again.

"Why?" I say with perplexity.

"Your father is a shady man," she says, as if it's a fact.

"No, he's not!" I correct. "Why don't you think Carlos Bills or John Bryans is the Knife Thrower? They're shady! You're only framing Dad because you hate him. Also, he lives all the way in Trenton! Why would he come all the way here to murder people?"

"Your father is unpredictable," she argues.

"And you're a liar!" I roar.

"Um, excuse me, mister!" she says sternly. "You don't talk to me in such a tone!"

"Then tell me!" I shout. "Tell me why you think Dad would kill tons of innocent people!"

"I…I…I just—"

"Exactly!" I yell. "You just hate him."

"Hey!" Jonah chimes in. "Don't talk to your mom like that!"

"Well, then tell her to not accuse my innocent father of killing innocent people!"

Everybody becomes silent. Finally, my mom says, "I'm sorry."

Sorry? I think. She accused my father of killing people because she doesn't like him? That's like me walking up to a rude kid in my grade and saying, *I think you killed tons of people because I don't like you.* That sounds ridiculous. But I say, "I'm sorry too."

For a brief moment, I consider that maybe it was my father's fault they separated and I wasn't told, but then I just go back to being irritated about what my mom said.

My mother walks away, and it is just me and Jonah. "Hey, buddy. So…how ya doing?"

I shrug. "I'm fine."

Jonah nods. "Good."

"Is there a secret my mom is keeping from me about my father?" I ask.

"Not that I know of, but maybe. I think that she just hates him and that's why she's accusing him," Jonah suggests.

"Maybe, but I doubt that."

"Also, I know having divorced parents is hard for you," he says.

"How would you know?" I ask.

"Because when I was your age, my parents got divorced and everything has been hard since."

"Really?"

"Yes, and that is why I'm trying to be the best stepfather to you as possible. It's because I hated mine."

And at that moment I felt horrible. I found Jonah annoying, but he was only acting that way so I could experience an amazing second father. I don't think that I could have felt worse.

"Oh. I'm so sorry," I say, feeling guilty.

"It's okay. It's just while I was dating your mom and she told me about you, I knew that I wanted to be the best I could be to you. Even if I didn't marry your mom, I still wanted to be a nice person to you."

"Well, I'm sorry your parents got a divorce," I say.

"It's okay, it's not your fault."

Our conversation then ends, and I walk up to my room. The whole time he was just trying to be an amazing stepfather. Well, no kidding—I don't think all his kindness was to be mean. That wouldn't make sense.

I want to get my mind off anything that has to do with family. That leaves me with the Murder Mystery Race. Going on the cruise will be a wild experience. I'll possibly see torture, fighting, and death. I wonder what the Contestants will think of me. I also wonder something about what George and Grace said. They told me that the winner usually picks the weakest Contestants for the MMR. But why is that? If I were to win, I would pick randomly, unless a friend is in the MMR.

The days go on…

* * *

Finally, it's Tuesday morning. Tonight, I will meet my fellow Contestants, the people I will compete against in the Murder Mystery Race to find out who a killer is. I will fly on a plane to some city in Florida, then go on a cruise. The past few days were all right. I'm just annoyed that my mother thinks my father is the Knife Thrower. Could he be? I don't think so.

The day goes on and on. I have breakfast, lunch, and dinner. Now it's 7:30 p.m., forty-five minutes until I say I'm going along with Uncle P to his friend's lake house. I'm in my room and all of a sudden Uncle P comes in. He says, "Are you ready to leave? You'll go on your camping trip and I'll go to Saudi Arabia?"

"Um, yeah," I say. Although I realize I'll have to find somewhere to hide for a little while until I go to the Mines of Murder.

"Okay, let's go downstairs to say goodbye," he suggests.

I nod and bring my backpack that I'll need for the cruise. Yesterday, I got my mom's approval to go to the 'lake house.' Jonah did not like the idea because my bond with Uncle P is getting better, while mine and his isn't really changing. When we get downstairs, I see Jonah and my mother in the living room. "Hello," my mom says.

Jonah gives a vacant smile.

Uncle P then says, "Andrew and I are going to leave now. We've got our luggage and we are ready!"

"Goodbye! I'll miss you guys so much," my mom says enthusiastically.

Jonah says the same. There is a long, monotonous goodbye. Uncle P and I walk out of the house.

"Okay," he says. "I'm about to drive to the airport. You go wherever you need to go."

We say goodbye and then I walk to the Mines of Murder. So what if I'm thirty minutes early? I walk and walk and finally I arrive at the Mines of Murder house. I take a deep breath and go to the same area I did a few days ago. There I see sixteen tracks, but only twelve have carts on them. Four people must've arrived really early.

I take my red-handled knife out of my backpack and just hold it. I then get on a cart and I start to go down and turn a few times. The track is very narrow. I am in the mines, and I see four carts at the bottom of the other tracks. I walk to the area where I last met up with Grace and George.

I see Grace and George sitting at a table. Four teens are standing nearby, two boys and two girls. One girl holds a bow and arrow. She has a sticker on her shirt that says "Diana 17." The other girl is holding a slingshot and has small, modern bayonets sticking out of her pocket. She has a sticker that says "Elena 16." Elena has shining emerald-green eyes that stand out. I look over at one boy. He is holding a black-handled knife and has a sticker on him that says "Jack 16." I look at the other boy. He is holding a few spears and has a sticker that says "Tiberius 17." I assume the number is supposed to mean a Contestant's age.

"You're very early," Grace says.

"So are they." I point to the two boys and two girls.

"They're supposed to be, but anyway, come grab a sticker. Write your name on it and put it on," Grace says.

I walk over to the table, and George hands me a sticker and a Sharpie. I write my age and name on it. The teenagers stare at me with disgust, judging me because of how small I am compared to them. "How old are you?" Elena snarls.

"Elena!" Grace shouts. "He's ten. Be more kind."

She rolls her eyes and I after that first impression I can tell she is sassy. The boy Tiberius then says rudely, "How did you even get in this? Y-you're literally ten."

I don't say anything. Grace then says, "Hey! Just 'cause he's ten, that doesn't mean he isn't as smart as you guys, so don't flatter yourselves now."

The four roll their eyes and continue to silently judge me. I ask, "Which one of you guys won this thing last year?"

"I did," says Tiberius.

Afterward, we all wait for everyone to show up. I see some kids holding knives, bows and arrows, spears, and some axes. The second youngest is a boy named Austin, who is eleven. I see him holding a metallic gold bow with a quiver strapped on his back that holds sharp, golden arrows.

The most common age out of all Contestants is between fourteen and sixteen.

Grace says cheerfully, "Welcome, everybody, to the Murder Mystery Race! Before I explain everything, I would like Tiberius to come up." Tiberius smiles and walks to Grace proudly. They shake hands.

"Tiberius won last year's Murder Mystery Race. George and I are nothing but proud of that. Congratulations." Tiberius then walks back to what feels like a crowd of kids. "As you know, this year's Murder Mystery Race is different. All sixteen of you clever and brave children will go on a nine-day cruise that the Knife Thrower will be on. The first one of you to find the Knife Thrower will get the reward of one million dollars." Everybody smirks. "I know," Grace says while chuckling. "A coveted prize, isn't it? Now, George and I will hand you guys a Quillix. Those of you who participated in last year's Murder Mystery Race are very familiar with it."

George and Grace pass out Quillixes. George hands me one. It's bigger than a phone but smaller than an iPad. "All you have to do is tap the screen and you should see the time and our names." I do as I'm told, and I see the time and two squares. Each has George and Grace's name on it. "Everybody see it?" Grace asks, and everyone nods. "Now if any of you guys get into danger or if you would like any hints about the Knife Thrower, call one of us by clicking our name."

Some kids gasp, obviously not knowing that Grace and George already know the Knife Thrower's identity. "Something weird is that this year we know who the Knife Thrower is," Grace continues. "But we cannot say how we know until he is in prison. George and I have also suggested to many people in town to come on the cruise. This is so you can have many suspects. The Knife Thrower also knows about the Murder Mystery Race."

Everyone gasps, including me. "Yes, I know, very shocking. George and I also have camera lids for you. Those of you who participated in last year's Murder Mystery Race know what this is. It is like contact lenses that some people wear. They have a clear camera on them. This is so George and I can watch you all to make sure you're doing okay on the cruise. We will pass them out now. Put them on."

Grace hands me a pair. They look exactly like contacts. I struggle to put them in my eyes, but when I do, I blink a few times to adjust to the camera lids. It is a little complicated to put them in without a mirror. For the first few seconds of them in it is a little blurry, but after I see clearly, everybody's eyes seem sea blue, which is very strange. Grace continues, "This may lightly affect your color vision of what you see. It won't be that bad, though. Tonight, we will fly to Palm Beach, Florida. Then you will get on the cruise, and that is when the Murder Mystery Race will begin. For now, I will give everyone fifteen minutes to get to know each other; then we're out of here and getting on the plane."

I hear loud voices. The eleven-year-old boy, Austin, walks over to me. "Hi," he says.

"Hi," I say. "I'm Andrew."

"I'm Austin. It's nice to meet you." We shake hands. "Do you want to work in an alliance? We could work together to find the Knife Thrower, and if one of us wins we split the money."

"Deal!" I say quickly. We shake on it. "What are your strengths?" I ask.

"I have good aim and I shoot very well when it comes to the bow and arrow. And I'm cunning," he answers.

"Interesting," I say.

"What about you?"

"I know how to throw a knife," I say.

"Cool. Are you smart?"

"I guess I'm smart enough to get into this thing."

"Do you know what smart actually means in the Murder Mystery Race?" I shake my head. "It doesn't mean you're good at school. It means you're cunning."

"Who told you that?" I ask.

"George."

"How did George and Grace get you to the Mines of Murder? They gave me code letters," I say.

"Oh, I actually participated in the MMR two years ago—I did not win, but this year Grace and George gave me a call and asked if I wanted to participate. I'm not sure why they chose me," Austin tells me.

I lightly shrug, not sure what to say. "Did you meet any other Contestants earlier?" I ask.

"No," Austin says gloomily. "I don't have interest in being friends with a lot of people. Grace and George told me about you. They said the two of us would make a phenomenal alliance. I'm sure they told you the same, right?"

"No," I say with confusion. "No, they did not tell me that."

"Huh? That's weird. Tell me about your family."

"Well, I live with my mother, stepfather, and his brother. I recently found out about my step-uncle is in the CIA." I then tell Austin about my mother and Jonah thinking Uncle P is in the FBI and that situation. "Tell me about your family," I say.

"I live with my dad and mom. I also have a sister who is fourteen. Nothing interesting about them."

"Do they know about the whole MMR thing?" I ask.

"Oh, yeah. Does your family know about it?"

"No. I lied to them. My stepfather and mother think I'm going to my step-uncle's friend's lake house. Even though he lied and he's really going to Saudi Arabia. He said he'd cover for me because I told him that I was going on a camping trip with a few of my friends."

"Really?" he exclaims. Austin then looks at me with disdain. "If you're the one who finds the Knife Thrower, you'll have to tell them about the Murder Mystery Race!"

"I know," I say bluntly. "I haven't figured out a plan for that yet."

"Well, you'll have to," Austin says seriously.

I shrug. "Are you allowed to shoot arrows here?"

"I guess," he responds. "Do you want me to show you how I do?"

"Yes," I reply.

"Make an O with your hands and hold it above your head," he orders.

"What!?" I shout.

"Do it," he says with annoyance.

I make an O with my hands. "If you hit me, you are paying for my hospital bills." He aims for a few seconds, then *boom*! The arrow flies right through the O!

"How did you do that?" I ask, flabbergasted.

"Practice."

A lot of the Contestants look over; then I see them murmuring things about Austin.

"All right!" I hear George say happily. "Let's get out of these mines and get on the plane!"

We all ride our carts out of the mines. There is a big bus in the street. "That's our bus," Grace says. All the Contestants seem scared for some reason, and so am I.

"Get on the bus!" Grace yells. I've never seen her yell. She's such a nice person.

We all do as we're told. Austin and I sit next to each other on the bus. The bus is fancy—it's a navy-blue color and modern looking. Surprisingly, when I go to the bathroom the toilet doesn't look grotesque. The bus is very clean.

We ride and ride. "Who do you think will win the Murder Mystery Race?" I ask Austin.

"I hope you or me. Either way I'd get $500,000. If not us, then Jack. He was in the MMR last year, but he did not win. I heard that last year Jack found the killer, but Tiberius injured Jack and then took the killer and was announced winner."

"Who told you that?" I ask.

"Elena," Austin answers.

"Hmm. Why do you think Tiberius picked Jack to be in this Murder Mystery Race, then?"

"I'm not sure. I didn't hear many details," he says.

"Have you met the four teens who were in it last year?" I ask.

"The Administrators?" Austin asks.

"The what?" I say with perplexity.

"The four Contestants who were in the Murder Mystery Race last year are known as Administrators. That's how it always works."

"How do you know all this?" I ask.

"Remember what I told you a few minutes ago? How I had already been in the MMR?"

"Right," I say, feeling like I'm an idiot. "That's cool that you've already been in an MMR," I say. "George and Grace must've thought even though you did not win, that you are still smart and a good fighter."

"Yeah," he agrees quietly, probably not to sound arrogant. "I wish the Administrators this year were nice, because then I would go to make an alliance with them. But Tiberius, Diana, Jack, and Elena have always been so rude in the MMR that sometimes it feels like they cheat in it."

"What do you mean?" I wonder.

"Well, two years ago when I was in it, Diana stole all my arrows in my pack. After that, I didn't have much courage to find the killer because then I'd get killed. But this year I'm going to steal her arrows. One by one. I might use one of my arrows to shoot the bow out of her hands. Diana doesn't have good aim and she's not a good fighter. She just kisses up to Elena and awkwardly flirts with Tiberius so she can get picked for next year's MMR. She's a really weird person. Well, maybe I think that because I'm eleven. You're ten, right?"

"Yes," I say. "Can I see your arrows?"

"Sure," he says. He takes his quiver off his back and shows me them. Now that I see his arrows up close I can see them shining. They are covered in glitter—you can tell they were painted carefully. There are a few white feathers at the end. Overall, there are eighteen arrows.

"Cool," I say. He smiles. "What are we going to do when we land in Florida? I doubt the cruise starts boarding at midnight."

"I don't know. Ask Grace or George."

I get out of my seat and go to George and Grace, who are sitting in the front of the bus. "What are we doing once we land in Florida?" I ask.

"Well, the original plan was to send you to a hotel and then in the morning you will all board the ship. But there has been a slight change to that. Once we land, you and all the Contestants will go off on your own. We'll tell you where you'll board the ship, but over the night and early morning you'll have to take care of yourselves. Grace and I will hand you your tickets to get on the cruise."

I nod, then walk back to my seat.

"What'd they say?" Austin asks.

"They said once we land we'll get our tickets to get on the cruise and be told where to board the ship, but since we'll land very late we all have to take care of ourselves for the night," I say annoyedly.

"What!" Austin shouts. "We'll have to find shelter and food, then."

"Yup," I say.

There is silence for a while until I hear Grace's voice. "Here we are!" she says dreamily, letting a grin slide across her face.

I look out my window and see a few planes. One is marked g & g.

I hear lots of wows echoing throughout the bus. "Settle down," George says. I don't think I'm now the biggest fan of George and Grace due to them just kicking us off the plane and expecting us to fend for ourselves for nine hours. The bus stops and George says. "Get off the bus!"

Everyone holds their bag and weapon and gets off the bus. We walk in a big mob. I feel gusts of wind all over my body. Austin then asks me, "Do you think the plane looks cool?"

"Yeah," I say quickly. "Let's make sure we get seats next to each other."

He nods.

Everyone boards the plane. The Administrators take a while to board because they're busy kissing up to Grace and George talking about how lovely their plane is. I guess I just find that annoying, because they are really rude people in reality.

Once I get on, I sit down in a seat. The aisle is also very big. The seats are a beige color and are very clean. There is also a tray in front of me.

Once Austin comes by, I say, "Hey. Open seat right there." I point to the seat next to me.

"Thanks," he says.

I unzip my backpack hoping there is some food in there that I might have forgotten about before I packed up for the MMR. I find a chocolate chip cookie in a plastic bag. I break it in half and hand a piece to Austin. "Here," I say. "I bet it's good."

He grabs the cookie from my hand, quickly takes a bite, and spits it out right away. "Yuck! Frankly, that was disgusting and stale."

I take a bite of my half and I agree with him. "Blech! These really *aren't* good," I admit.

The plane then takes off and I feel the bumps from the runway. I wonder what Jonah and my mother are doing right now. Uncle P is probably not even halfway through his flight to Saudi Arabia. That'd make sense. The Administrators act like they deserve the respect and service a monarch gets, and order some of the Contestants to grab them drinks. I ask Austin, "Who do you think the Knife Thrower is?"

"I don't know. I don't even live in Wayverlyn, remember?" he says.

"Right," I say, "but there are three guys who I'm pretty sure could be the Knife Thrower."

"Who?" Austin asks anxiously. He grabs a notepad and pen from his backpack to write down the suspects' names.

I say, "John Bryans." Austin writes slowly. "Carlos Bills. And some guy named Chris."

The girl across the aisle says, "Really?" as if I'm the weirdest person ever. "You actually think one of those three guys is the Knife Thrower?" She starts laughing and swings around an ax.

Austin and I look at each other with confusion while she keeps laughing. "Yeah, and what's wrong with that?" I say.

"Um, well, many things," she says in an obvious tone. She swings her ax around, as if the large lethal weapon in her hand is just a little fidget.

"I'm Albie, by the way, and something I know for sure is that the Knife Thrower is not John Bryans."

"Why?" I ask.

"You shouldn't have to ask why. Realize 'why' yourself," Albie says annoyedly.

"Just tell me," I say.

She rolls her eyes. "First, an obvious suspect is never the killer. Second, you really think he has the guts to kill people?"

"I mean, I guess I don't really know if he has the guts to kill people," I say, feeling disoriented. "But I did see him threaten to beat up a guy, and I think he's selling drugs."

"Oh, well who am I kidding…it's not like you even know him." She doesn't even have a response to my answer. "John is my uncle, so I know him. Is he cunning, a weirdo, kind of scary, and barbaric? Yeah. But he's not the Knife Thrower," Albie says, like she's resolute about her opinion of her Uncle John.

I'm shocked that one of the Contestants is blood-related to John. Coming from my point of view, I'm sure he is the Knife Thrower. I then say in a slow and peculiar voice, "Okay, then."

"What's your relationship with your uncle like?" Austin asks her.

"Uncle J is what I call him," Albie remarks, which reminds me of what I used to call Uncle P. "And I would say it was a little weird going through his home to get to the mines to meet Grace and George. Anyway, our relationship is fine. A little awkward, I'd say, due to his lack of social skills, but he's an okay guy. He's always reading murder mystery books, which for some reason scares me. Maybe it's the covers of the books, but I don't know. He's nice and a bit of a wimp, if I'm being honest with you. The guy screams like a little kid when I scare him. And what you were saying about him earlier that he sells drugs? Well, that's true, unfortunately. I once saw him smoking… well you know—he was very tired and dizzy that day." She stops talking and starts to sob a little, but does a poor job of hiding it.

Austin and I exchange looks of disappointment and sorrow. I wonder if Albie lives with John considering she said she "caught him." I now think Austin, Albie, and I all have slightly more of an advantage to winning the Murder Mystery Race because it doesn't sound like John is the Knife Thrower, but he could be. My point is, many people are probably sure about him being the Knife Thrower while Austin, Albie, and I think that he most likely is not. Well…I used to think he was the Knife Thrower, but not anymore.

There is silence for a little while. I have my eye on Jack and his knife. I will steal it on the cruise, just because of circumstances. He seems rude; he could have helped Diana steal Austin's arrows two years ago. Most of all, stealing his knife would help me. If I encounter the Knife Thrower and I miss a throw at him, then I'll have a second knife to throw. I could also easily steal one or two at a restaurant on the cruise.

Maybe on the cruise I can take pictures of people. Then at the end of the day I can look at them and see which one has a body that looks like the Knife Thrower. I have seen him on television several times. Just like how everybody else has, but I think taking pictures of people is a good idea. Every night, I think I'll eat at a restaurant. I'll do this because the Knife Thrower wouldn't come into an open area and kill people or he'd get caught, or get stabbed, because that would be a human's reaction when encountering a serial killer. If I were to be in my room, the Knife Thrower could easily overpower me. That is why I won't order room service.

I wonder if anyone I specifically know from my town will be on the cruise. It's possible. It will be a little confusing when I first see them. What if I were to run into a person I know? I mean, they would obviously call my parents. Unless I say my parents are somewhere else on the cruise.

I then have an idea and take Austin's notepad to write it down.

I think that John could possibly be the Knife Thrower and Albie knows it. Now, what she is doing is trying to convince people that John is *not* the Knife Thrower so he won't get caught.

I write down my thoughts. My handwriting is sloppy because of how anxious I am for Austin to read my theory. Once I finish writing, I tear the piece of paper out of the notepad. I then fold it two times and hand the note to him. After about five seconds of reading his eyes widen. Austin then looks at Albie with a face that shows that he is thinking something negative and very strange about her.

Albie seems to be in a state of bewilderment, which I do not blame her for. "What?" she says.

"Albie," Austin says, as if he's a detective. "Is there anything you would like to share with us?"

Albie looks at me with confusion and says, "What's he talking about?" as if Austin isn't there.

I shrug and look at Austin with confusion to show Albie I have no clue what he is talking about, even though he's just going to say what I think.

"Do you?" Austin asks.

"No," Albie replies slowly. She doesn't seem honest, though, which Austin can tell. That's probably what makes him keep their conversation going.

"Are you sure?" he says, very slowly.

"Why don't you just say what you want me to say?" Albie says, with annoyance.

"Um, uh-uh-um…" Austin keeps stuttering for a long time, unsure of what to say.

Finally, Albie says, "Whatever."

But right before Albie turns around, Austin quickly says, "Andrew and I think that your weird uncle is the Knife Thrower." He then looks down and seems to feel bad.

I click my tongue and look around, hoping that that's the last of this conversation. But it's not….

"Why?" she says with confusion.

"Well, to add on to what I said about your uncle being the Knife Thrower, we think that you know," Austin says.

"First of all, you're saying that as if my uncle is the Knife Thrower. *He is not*," she says firmly. "Second of all, don't you think that someone smart like me who got into the Murder Mystery Race would go to the police if I found out my uncle is a killer? Are you inferring that I'm stupid?"

Now Austin is on the defensive. "Um, uh-uh-uh no," he says, seeming scared. Albie turns away but doesn't even look upset at all.

"Nice going," Austin says with annoyance.

"Me?!" I shout. "What did I do? You were the one telling her everything!"

"Because of your stupid thought!" he argues.

Then I hear a voice from the seat behind me. It's Tiberius.

"Shut it, you little squares," he says. Next to him is Jack, and Elena and Diana are in the two seats across the aisle from them.

Austin and I don't know what to say. I feel like I'm in a slight dilemma. "Seriously," Jack says, agreeing with Tiberius. Then, in surprise, he says, "Hey!" which I can tell is directed to Austin. "What are you doing back here?"

Austin says, "George and Grace gave me a call to participate in this year's Murder Mystery Race."

"Well, all that did was just help everyone else get a better chance of winning this thing due to your stupidity," Diana says. They all laugh, except for Elena. Jack sort of does, but I can tell that he knows what he and his friends have said was rude to Austin.

Austin and I turn away. "They're just jerks," I tell him.

"No kidding," he says dejectedly.

"Yeah, well, it's not like they'll win anyway," I say.

"How do you know?" he asks, but I don't know how to respond to that.

After a long time, I can feel the plane touch down on the runway. We have landed in Palm Beach, Florida. Once the plane slows down, I hear

Grace's happy voice. "We have landed!" she squeals. "Now, as you get off, George and I will hand each of you a map and your ticket to get on the cruise. Currently it is 12:30 a.m. You can board the boat between 9:30 a.m. and 3:00 p.m."

Everyone looks very annoyed. How will we all find shelter for nine hours? It's also the middle of the night and everyone is getting kicked off the plane, which George and Grace seem to think is normal. Everyone groans—not just because they're annoyed but because they're tired.

"Oh, calm down, everyone," George says calmly. "This isn't the biggest deal ever! This is to teach you survival skills."

"Survival skills," Diana blurts out. "We're going on a cruise, not into the wild," she snarls.

"Hey!" George shouts. "Keep that attitude up, young lady, and I will shred your ticket to get on that cruise into pieces!"

Diana rolls her eyes.

"Now, everyone, you may get off the plane," George says.

He opens the door. Grace walks out holding sixteen maps and sixteen tickets to board the cruise. She acts like a model by the way she walks down the stairs and seems very excited for the Murder Mystery Race to begin. As everyone gets off the plane she says, "Have fun," even though there is a chance someone might die on that cruise.

Once I get down the stairs, Grace hands me a map of Palm Beach and my ticket to the cruise. It says my name, and there is a logo that says *Convivial Cruise.*

8

The Convivial Cruise

"Hmm," I mutter, looking at the ticket. I'm thinking of the pandemonium it will lead me to once I am on board.

Grace then whispers to me, "Just so you know, I'm rooting for you."

I smile. "Thank you," I say, even though she probably said that to every other Contestant so far.

"And you," she says to Austin, who's behind me. "You too. You guys are together in an alliance, which is perfect."

"Friends too," Austin adds.

"Yeah," I agree happily.

Grace chuckles. "Well, you make a dynamic duo."

I look behind me and I see Albie, who seems to be jealous. "Bye," I say.

"Bye," Grace says.

"Bye," Austin says gloomily.

Austin and I walk through the very tiny airport. I see many lights from buildings and cars. It looks very pretty. "So," I say slowly, "what's the plan?"

Austin exhales. "Well, let's open the map to see where the cruise is."

He opens the folded map. I then spot a place on the map that says "PPA." In parentheses it says "Private Plane Airport South East." I point there and say, "That must be where we are right now," feeling smart that I noticed it so quickly.

"Good eye," Austin says.

"Do you know where the cruise might start boarding?" I say with bemusement.

"Hmm," he says. Austin then looks east. I follow his eyes. Then I see a gigantic ship that displays *Convivial Cruise* on its side.

"Wow," I say, flabbergasted.

"That is really awesome," Austin says joyfully.

"Well, I guess we found where the cruise is," I say happily.

"Yeah," he agrees.

"Well," I say, then exhale. "Where are we going to stay overnight?"

"Don't know," Austin says while gaping at the boat.

I get exasperated due to his little worry about where we will spend the night. "Any ideas?" I wonder.

"Hmm." I can tell that when his eyes look up at the sky he's thinking. "I don't know. Maybe, at least for shelter or to find some food, we could go into a casino?"

"Yeah," I say, annoyed. "But don't you think it would look weird seeing two boys about eleven years old wandering around a casino in the middle of the night without an adult?"

"I guess that's true," he admits.

"So, I guess we just sleep on the streets," I suggest.

"How about on the sand. It's not concrete. We just have to be very far back from the waves."

"We also need to buy blankets to stay warm," I say.

"Good point," he says, while pointing to me. "There's got to be some store around here that sells blankets."

"Yeah," I agree.

"Andrew," Austin says.

"What?"

"Do you think one of us might die on that cruise?"

I think about it, and then say, "My answer is not a yes or a no. It's maybe, because you never know."

"Hmm," he says. "Okay, now let's go get blankets."

"Okay," I say.

We go to many stores, but apparently, we didn't realize that stores are usually closed at 12:30 a.m. I guess tonight will be a cold one....

Austin and I lie on the soft sand on the beach. I feel big gusts of wind all over my body. I would say, though, that when we walked to the beach it was not so bad because it was very humid outside, making it barely cold.

I lift up my head and see Austin sound asleep. I'm tired, but for some reason I can't sleep.

I wonder who will be on the cruise. Based on the cruise liner I saw earlier, it seemed humongous. I wonder how all the murders will start. How bodies will be found and much more. I just know a lot of chaos and assassinations will happen. I wonder what strategies the Contestants have. I bet the Administrators know what they're doing. Including Austin, because he was in the Murder Mystery Race two years ago. Maybe I'll ask him in the morning about what the Murder Mystery was about when he was in it.

I'm thinking that if one of the Administrators wins, I am not going back to the MMR next year, but I for sure am if Austin finds the Knife Thrower himself. If Albie wins, she might pick me for next year's Murder Mystery Race, even though we left off on a bad note during the flight. If anyone else wins, I might cajole them by saying that I would be a great ally for next year's Murder Mystery Race, although lots of other Contestants would probably do that.

I wonder where everybody is right now. I bet that because all the Administrators have about $1 million, they're staying at some fancy hotel suite. Then I hear a voice, and it's one that I recognize.

"Andrew?" I look up and I see Albie.

"Oh, hi," I say wearily.

"What are you doing here?" she asks.

"Just trying to stay safe during the night," I answer. "You?"

"Nothing really. I was actually practicing throwing axes at trees."

"Hmm," I say. "You have that much energy to throw an ax right now?"

"I have ADHD." She doesn't say anything for a while. "Hey," she eventually says.

"What?"

"Wanna throw an ax?"

"No, not really," I say in a way to show I'm very tired.

"Well, I want you to try."

"Okay," I say, feeling befuddled. I slowly get up.

"Here," she says, then tosses me an ax carelessly. I hesitate for a second and catch the sharp ax before it plunges into my chest.

"What was that for?" I ask.

She shrugs. The ax she gave me is very small—more like a hatchet. It's about one foot long. Albie is holding another ax just like the one she gave me. There's also another one, and it's very big. All the Contestants were given good weapons from Grace and George. Getting a knife isn't bad, but I would like more than one.

Albie says, "What are you waiting for? Throw it!" she shouts.

"Where?" I exclaim.

"At that tree." She points to a palm tree. "Just chuck it at the tree."

"Okay," I say. I focus for a moment to get a good aim.

"Throw it!" Albie yells. She doesn't even give me a second when she rips the ax out of my hand and throws it herself. It sticks right into the tree.

Feeling disoriented, I don't know what to say except for, "Nice throw."

"Thank you," she replies, sounding surly. Albie then pulls the ax out of the tree. "Bye. I'm going to find somewhere to stay tonight."

"Bye," I say.

I'm exhausted. I fall to the ground and close my eyes…

* * *

My eyes open. The sun is beaming down into my pupils. "AGH!" I shout.

Austin is gaping down at me, squinting. He is also holding his gold bow and has a quiver of arrows strapped on him. "You okay?" he asks.

"No, not really," I say with exhaustion. "What time is it?"

"Ten," he responds. "You were out for a while."

"Hmm," I say, because I don't know how else to respond. I shrug. After about five minutes or so I say, "Hey. When do you want to board the cruise?"

"Whenever you're ready," he says. "Also, I don't wanna go to some restaurant for breakfast. I just want to get on the ship and we'll find something to eat there."

"Sounds good to me," I say.

"Well, let's go, then."

I slowly get up and stretch my arms. The weather is very nice. A little humid, but the wind feels refreshing.

There is silence. People give Austin peculiar stares because they see him holding a bow and he also has sharp arrows in a pack strapped around him. Luckily, I have my knife in my pocket. If someone saw me holding a knife, they would call the police. I am actually very shocked that no cops have approached Austin, because you'd think when a person sees a young kid without an adult holding a weapon, they would call the police. I guess not, though. I hear whispers that I'm sure are about Austin and me.

I want to pacify my relationship with the Administrators, but my hypothesis is that I will fail to do so. They are narcissistic and selfish. I even wonder how arrogant people get along with one another. It's confusing to think about.

I think that Elena and Jack follow along with Tiberius and Diana. They remind me of the leaders of a pack.

I look around and see crowds of people. A lot of families with suitcases are going on the *Convivial Cruise* while I'm just bringing a knife and a backpack with a few items in it. Besides, I bet the Contestants and I are the only ones in Palm Beach with Quillixes. I feel like Grace and George invented it, but maybe not. That would take a long time and they are probably always busy with whatever goes on in their mysterious lives.

"Andrew," Austin says.

"What?"

"There's going to be security to go through before we enter the cruise," he says nervously.

"And?" I say with confusion. "What's wrong with that?"

"We'll get caught with weapons."

"Ooh. I haven't thought of that," I say with embarrassment.

"Yeah," he says nervously.

We stop walking and stare down, trying to find a solution to our dilemma. "Have you thought of anything yet?" I say wistfully.

"Nope," Austin says. I wonder what all the other Contestants are doing about this. "Hey," he says. "Why don't we call Grace and George on our Quillixes?"

"Good idea," I say happily.

Austin unzips his backpack and takes out his Quillix. He turns it on and calls George.

"Ah, Austin. How are you?"

Austin ignores George's question and says, "George, how do we get through security without getting caught with our weapons?"

"Well, the Administrators know what they're doing to get through security. One moment, I am going to check to see where they are and what they're doing. Oooh," he says. "You've got to catch up with them."

"What? Where are they?" Austin asks anxiously.

"Go to the boarding area and you'll find them." George then hangs up.

"What does he mean?" Austin asks.

"You heard him! Find the Administrators," I say.

We start running to the boarding area. Fast. I breathe heavily while the wind tries to push me back. After a little while, I start to develop cramps. My throat gets very dry, and my stomach is rumbling. I guess I am getting good exercise right now. Austin seems to be fatigued just like I am.

Finally, we arrive at the boarding area. We pant for about fifteen seconds until Austin says, "Look! There are the Administrators." He points to them. "C'mon."

We jog over to them. "Hi," I say.

"Um, hi," Tiberius says, seeming confused.

"We need your help," Austin says.

Elena, Jack, Tiberius, and Diana all have a conversation with the movement of their eyes. "Fine," Tiberius says firmly. "What do you want?"

"Well, according to Grace and George, you guys know how to get on the cruise without getting caught with your weapons," I say.

"And?" Elena asks.

"How?" I say without hesitation.

"Well," Jack says, "the plan is that we tie a rope around several arrows. Then Diana will shoot that onto the boat. The sharp points of the arrows will stick onto something. Then we'll climb the rope onto the boat."

"Don't you think that will draw a lot of attention?" Austin asks.

"That's why we rented a mini boat that we'll drive around the other side of the cruise ship without anyone noticing," Jack says.

"That's very clever," I say, surprised.

"Yes, it is," Diana agrees.

"C'mon," Jack orders.

Austin and I follow them, shrugging because who knew that the Administrators would help us. It seems a little odd that young kids like

Austin and I follow teenagers around like puppies. I'm starting to wonder what the other Contestants are doing to get through security. I don't really think that any of them have thought about what the Administrators are going to do.

We all walk to the beach in silence. "Here we are," says Tiberius. Right in front of us is a small dock with a very tiny boat tied to it. "Hop on."

Everyone jumps on. Tiberius goes to the driver's seat. The wheel is shiny and metallic. We untie the lines, and Tiberius starts driving the boat very fast. Whenever little waves hit the boat, splashes of water sprinkle on everyone.

We're now behind the cruise ship. I don't even see land anymore. "All right," Diana says, "let's do this." She grabs a rope that seems to be hundreds of feet long that is all bunched together. She then takes six arrows from a quiver strapped around her. Next, she ties the thick rope around them.

Diana aims the arrows at a point a little higher on the boat. She pulls back on the bowstring. For some reason about one minute goes by and she still hasn't let go. I inquire slowly, "When will you let go?"

"Shhh," she responds quickly.

Jack whispers to me, "She holds it so the arrows will go a farther distance. The longer she pulls it back the farther they will go."

I nod. Suddenly, Diana lets go! It startles me for a second. The six arrows whiz into the sky after being released from the wobbling string. I see the arrows flying with the rope attached to them. After a few seconds the rope doesn't move anymore. The arrows have successfully stuck onto something on the boat. "Tug it to make sure they are attached somewhere," Elena suggests.

Diana does what Elena says. "It's good," she reassures.

"Now," Jack says, "when climbing the rope, it could be a life-or-death situation. If you're almost on the ship you're at a high height, right? Therefore, if you let go of the rope you will fall into the water and you will die. It will feel like concrete versus falling into water from seven feet in the air."

"I'll go first," Tiberius insists.

He ascends the rope like a monkey, moving his hands as he gets higher. After he is about a fifth of the way to the top he stops climbing. He takes a few seconds to breathe and to let his sweat drip into the ocean. I hear him grunting. He then resumes his climbing and successfully gets on the boat. Most of us cheer.

Next, Diana goes. She stops and takes a few good breaths as she climbs the rope. It takes her a little while to get on the boat, but she pulls through.

Next, Jack starts climbing. He quickly gets on the cruise ship without even taking a second to take a breath. He does seem very sweaty, though. It looks like he just dove into a pool and came out with water dripping all over him.

Then Elena successfully gets to the top and so does Austin. I'm last.

I take a deep breath and start climbing. My famished stomach doesn't help my energy. Once I'm almost to the top I get so tired that I feel like letting go, but I can't. Otherwise, it won't feel like falling into water. Like Jack said, it will feel like falling on concrete because I am at such a high height. I'm very scared. I get even more scared when I look down at the ocean. It has a nice turquoise color, which sort of calms me. I'm now only a few inches away from getting onto the ship. I finally board the *Convivial Cruise*.

I see Diana's six arrows stuck in the deck. She unties the rope from her arrows and throws it overboard into the ocean. She puts her arrows back in her pack. Austin and I thank them for their help.

We sneak into the line where people check in. "I was very shocked that they were willing to help us," I say.

"Yeah," Austin agrees. "Maybe they're nicer than they were two years ago when I met them."

"I guess," I say.

After Austin and I get checked in, we get our rooms. I'm on level 13, room 727. Austin's room is on level 13, room 704, so he's just down the hall from my room. We agreed to check out our rooms and then meet back at my room at 1:30 p.m. I use a card I got from a lady who helped me check in to open the door to my room. It is very nice. A little chilly, but the bed seems nice. White sheets and a beige cover. There is also a little desk with a pen, notepad, and a magazine. I open the magazine. It has many pictures of the cruise. Based on the pictures, the cruise has waterslides by the pool, laser tag, go-karting, mini golf, a small ropes course, and a casino that seems big. I then think that the Knife Thrower might be staying in the room next to mine, which creeps me out for a second. There is also a menu for room service.

I start to unpack my backpack. I put my clothes in one drawer, put my toothbrush in the bathroom, and I sort out all my other stuff. I take my red knife from my pocket. Finally, I lie down, which is very comforting.

In my opinion, I think the Administrators are nice. Even though they were jerks on the plane, they did help Austin and me. They did seem a bit annoyed with us, though, which, frankly, felt a little embarrassing. It's about 12:30 p.m., so I expect to meet back up with Austin in about one hour.

9

Lethal Laser Tag

I change my pants and shirt to shorts and a T-shirt. I might as well look around the ship. I leave my room and take the stairs to get to the pool. The pool looks very nice. I see a few young kids splashing each other in there. I look to my right and see the go-karting. The track goes over the ocean! That is probably why there is a wall on that part of the track, so cars don't fall into the water. It looks awesome. I notice the ropes course. It looks very cool too. There are many things to walk across. Next to the ropes course is mini golf. There are many features such as loops, animals with open mouths to hit the ball into, and tiny rocket ships that make the ball come out of some random hole. A few people are playing mini golf.

I walk around for a little bit. As time goes by it, becomes 1:20. I start heading back to my room. and get on the elevator. There are three people on it with me: Chris, John Bryans, and Carlos Bills. My heart stops for a second! What are they doing here? I don't know what it is, but John is holding a slip of paper. I can't tell what it says because the side of the paper with the writing isn't facing me. John looks down at the paper. Carlos then says to John, "Hey, don't that kid look familiar to ya?"

They must remember me. A few days ago, I shot an arrow at them and they saw a glimpse of my face! "Huh," John says with confusion. He and I then make eye contact.

"I don't recognize you," I say with perplexity.

"Huh?" Carlos says. The elevator doors open. As I walk out, Carlos says, "Welp, have a good day!"

"You too!" I say cordially.

Well, I handled that well. Thank God they didn't realize that I was the kid who shot an arrow at them. I walk back to my room, feeling grateful that they didn't recognize me. I think it's a bit strange that Chris is with John and Carlos, especially after their quarrel about owing one another money. I'm also curious why they're on the cruise. If I'm being honest, they seem a bit sad? weird, and scary, so I don't feel like a cruise is a place for them, but what does it really matter?

I then remember what George and Grace told me. How they suggested to people in town that coming on this cruise would be fun—even though it was only to give all the Contestants more suspects as to who the Knife Thrower might be.

If anything, I bet my teacher Ms. Rolenstein is on this cruise. No doubt. She is always outgoing and is very excited to hear the news in town. When I was using Zoom for school, she was always asking if my classmates or I had any news—not as in, something personal you did over the weekend, but news about the Knife Thrower or something a lot of people are doing now. She sometimes tried to make sure she even had similar hobbies to her students. My point is, if someone told her about how lots of people in town are going on the *Convivial Cruise*, she would gladly go. Although she's not married, so if she is on this cruise, she's most likely with a friend.

Then there is my mother and Jonah. If they heard about this, they would 100 percent go on this cruise. No question. I'm very happy they're not, though, because if they were they would have told me and Uncle P.

Even if they wanted to keep it secret, they wouldn't be able to because they would be so excited and they have big mouths.

I hear a knock on my door. That must be Austin. I open it. For some reason Austin is just standing there and he seems petrified. He seems like he's been hypnotized or traumatized. He stares at me in discomfort. Worried, I snap in his face. "HELLO!" I shout. He doesn't even flinch. I wave in his face several times.

He then takes a letter out of his pocket. It's folded. He slowly hands it to me. I unfold the letter. It is confusing and scary at the same time, but above all, it is very creepy. I am bewildered. How…wh-what is this? Why US?! WHY?! NO! This can't be. How do they even know my name! This letter is j-just…I don't understand. It says…

Meet me at laser tag at 6:00 p.m.
Bring your little friends Albie and Andrew.
The worst is to come if you don't.
To all of you.
Yes you'd be shocked I know your names.
And you must not tell anyone.
I have eyes on you.
K. T.

"W-where did you even get this?" I ask anxiously.

Austin looks down and says, "I just heard a knock at my door. The letter slipped under my door. I opened the door, but by then nobody was there. This is for sure from the Knife Thrower. I'm pretty sure that is what 'K. T.' stands for."

"Well, first we have to find Albie, and I also have to find some knives. I can't only bring one," I say.

"Yeah," Austin agrees. His voice starts to get louder and faster. He doesn't seem so scared or traumatized anymore. "How about I'll find Albie and you find some more weapons?" he suggests.

"Got it," I say. I'm frankly excited for laser tag. It's fun. Even though I could possibly get killed.

"Meet back at my room," Austin tells me.

I nod. I start running around to find a staff member. I run upstairs to the sundeck. I run by the pool and the waterslides. I see lots of people holding ice cream, and everyone seems to be having fun while I'm certainly not. I mean, I wasn't told to go on this cruise to have fun. I was told to go on this cruise to find a murderer.

I then see some guy in navy shorts, and he's wearing a white T-shirt. He is holding a tray with a few margaritas and soft drinks. I run up to him. His name tag says Jacob.

"Whoa, kiddo, what's the rush?" Jacob says.

"I was wondering where the nearest restaurant is on this cruise."

"Well, what type of restaurant are ya lookin' for?" he asks me.

"I don't know." I shrug. "Um, maybe a fancy one." I indicate that I'm in a very big rush by getting antsy.

"Tenth floor," he responds with suspicion.

"Thank you," I say.

Before I start running again, he says, "Hey, kid."

"What?"

"Where are your parents?"

"Huh?" I say, even though I heard him.

"Where are your parents?" Jacob repeats.

"Oh, um, uh…uh, the casino," I reply.

"Hmm," he says, while squinting at me. "All right then, but you come to me if somethins' wrong. All right?"

"Yes, I will."

"Okay, because on the *Convivial Cruise* we always make sure that anyone under the age of eighteen has a parent or guardian with them!" he says happily.

"Ha-ha," I say vacantly, trying to forge a smile.

Next, I run to the elevator. I click the down button and the elevator doors open. I jump in and click the "10" button. The elevator doors close. A stop is made at floor twelve and an elderly couple gets on. Once the elevator gets to floor ten, I get out. Right to my left is a fancy-looking restaurant. There are no rooms on floor ten, just a bunch of stores. Lots of art and candy stores.

I jog to the restaurant. I see the hostess, and she says, "Hello, young man. How many for your table?"

I answer, "Four. The rest will be here soon," because that means four knives.

"Great," she says. "Follow me."

I follow her to a table of four. "Thank you," I say.

"You're welcome. Your waiter will be here in about five minutes."

The hostess then walks away. I grab four knives off the table and start walking out of the restaurant. I don't want to run. That'll seem suspicious. I then snag two knives off a table of eight.

Once I get out of the restaurant I start running. I get on the elevator and go to level 13, room 704. That's Austin's room. I then hear a ring from my Quillix: George's voice.

"Attention everyone! Attention!" he roars. "The Knife Thrower is now forcing his almost victims to commit murders too! His helpers will be wearing red masks. Remember: *red mask*. The original Knife Thrower wears a black mask!"

"Anyone copy?!" Grace shouts. "Anyone copy?!"

I yell into my Quillix, "Copy!"

I hear several voices yell that too. That is for sure very interesting. More people committing murders. I feel like I'm in a classic murder book or movie. A lot of people are trying to find the killers, and hopefully it'll end with the good guys winning.

I knock on Austin's door. "Hello," I say. "Is Albie here?"

"Yes. Did you hear about there being more killers working with the Knife Thrower?" Austin asks me.

"Yes."

I see Albie sitting in a chair. "Hi," she says.

"You saw the letter, right?" I check.

"Yes."

"Hey," I say. "I was just wondering—how did you get on the cruise without going through security? If you went through security, your axes would have been found."

"Well, when I got on, I told the lady working at security that I went through another security aisle and that I got separated from my family. Then, when she took me past security, I pointed to some random family that wasn't looking at us and told her that was my family. Then she walked away. It was really simple, honestly."

"Wow," Austin says. "And what was your plan if there was no family in that area?"

"Oh, c'mon," Albie says like he is an idiot. "Out of the maybe three thousand people on this cruise, you don't think that there could be one family on the sundeck?"

"I guess that's true," Austin says with embarrassment. His face turns partly crimson.

"Exactly," she says. "Now, laser tag is on the tenth floor. The arena is nine thousand square feet. There are three levels. Each one is three thousand square feet. You can only get to each one by a staircase and ropes. Now, let's look at pictures of laser tag in my magazine." Albie takes out her magazine of the cruise and looks at the table of contents. She skims it until she sees a line that says, "Laser Tag…46–49." Albie then flips to page 46.

"Here!" she exclaims. "Those are just some pictures of people. It also says here that there are usually sixty players during laser tag: twenty on the blue team, twenty on the red team, and twenty on the green team."

Albie then flips to page 48. "All right, this is a map." She studies the map for a little bit. "Be aware of mirrors. There is a total of 268 of them. Also, lasers bounce off mirrors, so don't get too frightened if where you're looking at seems like the Knife Thrower or anyone on his side is by you. Next, try to make sure you're on the third floor. Therefore, you'll get a view of almost the entire arena. Also, *do not play*! You're only there to find the Knife Thrower and people on his side. Finally, here is this." Albie hands Austin and me a Nerf-looking gun. It doesn't seem like any harm can be done with it.

"What is this?" Austin asks.

"A Satan Svare," Albie responds. "Well, that's actually a regular toy Nerf gun, but I filled it with a powder called Satan Svare. Satan Svare is not a drug necessarily, but when a human consumes it, they pass out. For thirty-five minutes, to be exact. So, don't put your Nerf gun upside down or the powder will spill. Just shoot a little at the people on the Knife Thrower's side. It takes about ten seconds for someone to pass out after breathing in the Satan Svare. Once they pass out, take off their mask, inspect them for weapons, and then call Grace and George. Also, make sure whoever you are targeting isn't running. You'll have a better chance of hitting them. And this is the most important rule. Right when someone on the Knife Thrower's side breathes in Satan Svare, don't run to them right away. If you do you could breathe in a little. Just wait about forty-five seconds after you shoot someone with the powder and by then it should have dissolved. Satan Svare dissolves quickly in the air. It has lots of power. If anyone who isn't the Knife Thrower or on his side comes by and they haven't heard of the Knife Thrower, tell them about him but try to hide your face because most likely that person will tell a staff member on the cruise, and you're not going to want to get stuck in that mess of being a witness in anything. That's the last thing we want—for someone who is not the Knife Thrower or on his side to see any of our faces. So, does this sound simple to everyone?"

"Yes," I say.

"Yes," Austin says.

"This is our time," Albie says with excitement. "This is our time to find out who the Knife Thrower is and split the million-dollar reward."

"Agreed," Austin says.

"Agreed," I say. I like that we work well together as a team and get along.

"Good," Albie says.

"So, what do you guys wanna do for the next four and a half hours?" I ask.

"I don't know," Austin says. "Maybe just sit around, I guess."

The Satan Svare powder seems exactly like a drug even though Albie said otherwise. I've never even heard of Satan Svare. I also wonder where Albie even got such a thing. She had to have been with an adult if she was going to buy a powder that makes people pass out. It's a little weird.

Over the next few hours, we all talk a little. Austin practices with his bow and arrow by aiming at some cups. Nothing that interesting happens. I'm starting to get a little nervous for laser tag. I might get killed, but with Satan Svare that lowers the chances, and of course with the knives I'll have even more protection.

Once it is about 5:50, Austin says, "I think we should go to laser tag now."

"All right," I say.

"Let's go to floor ten," Albie says. All of us hide our weapons by putting coats on before we leave the room. We all get up and walk to the elevator reluctantly. I click on the button for the tenth floor. Once we arrive, we start walking to laser tag.

Once we arrive, I see a man there. He says, "Welcome to the *Convivial Cruise*'s laser tag!" The man then opens a door for us. "Good thing you three just arrived. There are only three spots left to play. You guys will be on the blue team." There are three doors in front of us. One green, one red, and one blue. The man opens the blue door. "Here you are. Have fun."

"Thanks," I say.

Each of us picks up a laser gun. "So," Albie says. "In the three minutes before the game starts, look for anyone around here in a red mask."

"Don't you think they'll put it on once we get in the arena?" Austin asks.

"Good point," Albie says.

I look around for a few seconds. "I don't even see anyone who I recognize from Wayverlyn. The Knife Thrower and his side must all be on the same team. Red or green. At least, that would make sense," I say.

"And remember, guys—always be on the third floor," Albie says seriously.

"Got it," I say.

"Got it," Austin says.

Then I hear a voice. "The doors are about to open into the laser tag arena. You will be in there for forty-five minutes. In case of an emergency, you will see eight doors in the arena with an Exit sign on them. In the event of an emergency, go out one of those doors. Have fun."

A few doors open and everyone runs out. I start running around, trying to find the staircases to get to the third floor of the arena. Once I spot them, I start sprinting toward them, but—*boom*! I crash into a mirror. It's so hard to get up because I hurt my body so badly. I struggle to get up, feeling lightheaded.

When I turn around, I see the staircases, and then, a man with a red mask! Already? Right when the laser tag starts this happens! He's running toward me. I pull out one of my knives and throw it! The masked person blocks it with his knife! I then shoot some Satan Svare at the menacing person, but nothing happens because he is wearing a mask blocking lots of air. He's about to throw a knife at me, but all of a sudden, he's standing still! Then he falls forward. I see an ax in his back and one arrow. There I see Austin and Albie.

"C'mon!" Austin shouts. "We have no time to inspect this guy; others are after us!" Austin quickly pulls his arrow out of the guy, while Albie and I grab our weapons.

I get up and start following them. We don't run to a staircase; instead, we run to three ropes and start climbing. "Go up to the third level!" Albie shouts.

I look up and there is a floor connected to the wall, which is where I need to reach. I then look down and I see two men and two women all in red masks. They look like crocodiles and Albie, Austin, and I seem like their prey. "Keep climbing, everyone!" I shout.

We all keep climbing. Next to us are stairs, which are not far away. I see two masked men there, so I swing by them and shoot Satan Svare in their faces. They start to cough, and I then manage to get a good kick in one of their faces. "AGH!" he yells in pain.

I climb a little more. I look to where the two red-masked men were, and one is lying down. The other has already vanished. I'm almost at the top. Albie is already standing on the third floor. I spot a masked man behind her! "Albie!" I shout.

The man then pushes her! She screams, but she manages to grab onto a rope and she swings! She reaches to get her hands on the third floor on the other side, but her fingers slip. She's falling, but all of a sudden, she gets to the second floor to the right of me. She was able to quickly grab onto the edge of the floor. I'm trying to get to the third floor and so is Austin. I then get to floor three. Austin is up there with me, but now Albie is out of sight.

"Where is she?" Austin asks.

"I don't see her!" I shout. I look around the arena from my high height, but I still can't see her.

"I'm going to look around for mirrors," Austin says.

He then shoots at random places in the arena with his bow and arrows. "What are you doing?" I ask him.

"Well, my arrow will crash into somewhere, meaning there is a mirror," he responds.

"That's smart," I say. I look right in front of me and see a black-masked man. This one is the Knife Thrower.

"The Knife Thrower!" I shout. "He's right there!" I'm about to throw a knife, but as I lean forward ready to throw it makes a loud scratchy noise when the knife comes into contact with something. My knife scratches a mirror.

We both look around and no one's here. "I thought you said you saw him!" Austin says.

"Well, I did, but he must've gone away," I say with frustration. "Plus, these mirrors make it so much harder to see where someone actually is."

"Well, right now we need to go find Albie," Austin says seriously. "Albie!" he shouts.

"Down here!"

Austin and I look down, and we see Albie. She is holding a few axes. "Go down the stairs," Austin tells me.

"Got it."

We start going down the stairs, but when we get to the bottom there are two red-masked men. Austin and I run up to the second floor, but there is one masked woman standing there. I spray Satan Svare in her eyes. "*Ah!*" she shouts, and then she starts swearing like crazy. The other poor people in the arena are really confused.

When Austin and I run up many stairs to get to the third floor, there is a red-masked man there. We are trapped. I face the two that are behind us, and Austin points an arrow at the other guy in front of us. All five of us stand there cautiously. We're all hoping that in seconds no one kills anyone. Austin then shoots the guy in front of us right in his thigh.

"Nice shot!" I shout.

"Thanks," Austin says, out of breath.

We run up to the third floor while two masked men follow us. We run to the ropes and start to slide down. I'm starting to feel burning pain. I'm getting lots of rope burns. The two killers follow us, but they don't know what to do once they see us sliding down the ropes, so they cut the ropes with their knives!

"AHHHHH!" Austin and I both screech.

We are falling in midair from about fifteen feet. There is one red-masked guy waiting at the bottom. I lean my body out so I crash into him.

It's not the best landing, but it's a lot better than landing on the ground. That's where I see Austin, who shouts, "I twisted my ankle!"

I run to him, feeling thankful I knocked out the red-masked guy by landing my seventy-four-pound body on him.

I try to pull him up. Austin is doing very little to get up, which I don't blame him for because he is in serious pain. But we have to move. "C'mon!" I say.

"Andrew!" he cries, once he's finally on his feet. "I can't run anymore! What should I do?!"

"Hide somewhere! I'll find Albie!" I say, then I start to run around. I avoid everyone I see. I keep running around the laser tag arena, but then I stop. I notice a smudge that seems to be floating in the air. That is when I see an inch in front of me is a mirror. Phew, thank God I didn't run into that. I even take a second to take a deep breath. I then shout, "ALBIE?!"

"ANDREW?!" I hear.

"Where are you?!" I shout.

"Floor one!"

"Coming!" I shout.

I start running around, before remembering I need to be cautious about where mirrors are. Austin has already gotten hurt, and the laser tag is still going to go on for a while. I start to cautiously jog instead of run… until I step on someone.

I look down and see a dead body!

I feel their heart to see if they really are dead. Yep. Dead as a doornail. It's very sad seeing the body.

I had only seen a glimpse of the Knife Thrower in this broad area. That's all. A glimpse.

As I run around the arena, I encounter many mirrors. This place is like a maze. By now many of the players know that there are murders occurring around here. I run up a few stairs to get a good view of the arena. I assume Austin is okay, because I would have heard him yell if he got into trouble. I can't find Albie, though. Is she okay? Did something happen to her?

I'm on the second floor when I hear a thump behind me. A red-masked woman is charging at me! I'm right at the edge of the second floor. Right when she's coming to stab me, I duck. She plummets over me, then falls onto the hard floor off the second level. I grab onto the last rope that hasn't been cut yet and swing down to the first floor. I start running—then crash into two people. I'm lying on the ground when I see an ax falling down that might plunge right into my face. I roll over and then look up and there are Albie and Austin.

"Sorry!" Albie says. "I had no clue that I crashed into either of you. I just threw my ax without hesitation."

"Well, at least I was able to move in time," I say. I then ask, "Austin, I thought you twisted your ankle?"

"It feels better, I still wobble a bit when I move, but I can manage it," he says.

Albie then says, "Guys, I used Satan Svare on some guy. He got knocked out, but then another red-masked guy came. He said that he killed you guys. The next thing he knew my ax was sinking into his thigh. I don't think it killed him, but it caused serious damage. I started running around to find you guys. Let's go back to where the body is."

The three of us start running, and Albie leads us to a knocked-out body. A few yards beside it is another red-masked guy who is leaking blood, and it seems like he'll turn into another corpse. "Yuck," Austin says. "Well, this is the combination of goriness and grotesqueness."

Albie takes the mask off the guy who she used Satan Svare on. "Does anyone recognize this guy?" Albie asks as she stares at him as if she knows him.

"No," Austin and I say at the same time.

Albie reaches into the guy's pocket. She takes out three twenty-dollar bills. She hands one to me and one to Austin. "Here," she says. "Take this."

"What?" I say. I look at her in disdain. "Albie, we shouldn't be robbing people. Austin, you can have my twenty." I hand my bill to him.

"Serial killers deserve to get robbed," Albie argues.

"Technically, all three of us are killers. All of us have seriously injured a person in this arena, and maybe even killed," I point out.

"Our killing is self-defense," Austin points out. "But when someone just kills people that is a punishable crime."

"Okay," I say. "Whatever." Deep down, I would have liked to keep that twenty-dollar bill, but if there is a witness watching us right now all three of us would get into big trouble even though we killed serial killers in self-defense.

"Now, let's just snoop around the bodies for…I don't know, phones that might have secretive texts, or notes that'll give us hints," Albie suggests.

We all look in some more pockets. I look down at the unconscious, red-masked guy. He is a little plump and tall. I unzip his jacket and there are a few pockets in there. One pocket is big. It seems to be holding some square-shaped thing in it. I take it out and it is a navy-blue journal. I flip to the first page. It says,

Knife Thrower notes/plans for kills

"Oh, wow!" I say.

"What is it?" Austin asks.

"A journal. It has a bunch of notes about stuff that has to do with the Knife Thrower." I skim through the journal and see many notes.

"We have no time to look through that now," Albie says. "We'll look at everything when we get back to one of our rooms. For now, try to find more stuff."

I start taking a bunch of knives from the guys' pockets and shoving them into my pockets. I then say, "Guys, remember we for sure have been in this arena for over ten minutes, so don't use more Satan Svare. I know all the dead bodies will be found, but the less bodies the better. Only use the Satan Svare if you really have to."

"Got it," Austin says.

"Got it," Albie says.

Austin then says, "Look!" He pulls out a phone from one of the guy's jacket pockets.

"Nice. Now put it in your pocket so no one sees," Albie says. "You're still holding onto that journal, Andrew, right?"

"Yes," I answer.

We're all searching until someone on the Knife Thrower's side comes up behind us and grabs Austin! Probably because he is hobbling around. I don't even do anything for a second because I am so petrified. I'm about to throw my knife, but Albie says, "Stop! It's too risky. You could hit Austin."

"HELP!" Austin yells. The guy picks up Austin and throws him out of our sight, which I assume is because mirrors are blocking lots of space.

Albie and I start to run. Austin and the red-masked guy are out of sight. I run to my right and see the Knife Thrower. I start running toward him, getting ready to throw a knife, when suddenly I crash into a mirror. I look around and nobody is there. Not even Albie is by me, but then I look above me. Three people are staring down at me. Chris, Carlos Bills, and John Bryans. John looks down at me and we make eye contact. He says, "Wait a minute. You're the kid from the elevator. AND THE KID WHO SHOT AN ARROW AT US!"

I get up and start running. The three are chasing me! Hopefully Albie has saved Austin by now. Could Chris, John, and Carlos be on the Knife Thrower's side? Or is one of them the Knife Thrower? Right before they came by, I thought I saw the Knife Thrower. This place is so confusing with all these mirrors. I know Chris, Carlos, and John were not wearing masks, but maybe it was so people wouldn't think they're on the Knife Thrower's side.

I keep running and then turn around. Chris, John, and Carlos are already gone. Well, that was quick. I bet they got confused with all the mirrors.

I need to try and find Austin and Albie. I avoid all red-masked people I see, and I climb ropes and keep running around. Albie told us the place is nine thousand square meters, which is enormous.

I yell, "Austin!"

I then hear, "Andrew!"

"Meet me at the ropes!" I shout.

"OKAY!"

I run to the ropes, but Austin is still being held by that red-masked guy! He's covering Austin's mouth, but Austin is trying to slither out of the guy's arm. Austin moves the guy's hand off his mouth for a second and shouts, "*He* was talking to you! That was his voice just a few minutes ago!"

I sprint over there, worried I'll have to stab the guy, but when I get there, he kicks me in the stomach. He pulls out a knife and presses it against Austin's neck. "This is what the Knife Thrower said to do!" he scowls. "I will slowly dig a knife into your neck."

Austin bites the guy's finger, and I'm trying to figure out what to do. I can't throw a knife because I might hit Austin, and I can't run forward because the guy will stab me. Austin keeps biting the guy's finger and uses the heel of his foot to kick him in his shins. The man then says evilly, "Okay, let's kill you!"

Austin then pulls an arrow from his quiver and shoves it in the guy's chest. He picks up his shining gold bow from the ground and runs to me. "COME ON!" he shouts.

We run, but I look back for a second and I can tell that the guy isn't dead. In fact, he's still standing. Well, wobbling and moaning in pain. While we're running forward, there are two other masked men in front of us who both throw a knife. I duck. Austin does a somersault, then gets close to the guy and shoots him in the arm with an arrow. Austin's twisted ankle pain has definitely gone away. The other guy comes to pursue me, and I throw a knife that slices his cheek. I throw another knife that drives right into his heart.

There aren't that many people left on the Knife Thrower's side. Lots are dead, some are knocked about by Satan Svare (though maybe time has passed, and they are awake now), and others are seriously injured. I think about everyone I've already encountered—like that lady who charged at me, tried to stab me, but then I ducked, and she fell off the second floor. Or that guy who I kicked a while ago when I was swinging on the ropes. Then, of course, there is the Knife Thrower. The master killer.

"We need to find Albie," I say.

"Yeah," Austin agrees. We're both running out of breath.

"ALBIE!" Austin shouts.

Austin and I hear, "I'M ON THE THIRD FLOOR."

Neither Austin nor I say anything as we run to get to the third floor. BOOM! We run into a mirror. "AGH!" we both say.

"Ugh!" Austin yells. "I hate all these stupid mirrors!"

"Me too!"

Austin looks to his left. "This way," he says.

I follow him, but just a few inches in front of him is another mirror!

"Austin!" I shout. He jumps a little, almost crashing into the mirror. "To the right," I say, which turned out to be a successful way to go because now we're on the stairs.

Once we're on the third floor Austin shouts, "ALBIE!"

"AUSTIN? ANDREW?"

"WE'RE AT THE STAIRS!" Austin yells.

"COMING!" Albie then arrives at the stairs. "Hey, guys, are you okay?"

"Yes, even though Austin was almost slowly stabbed to death and a lot of other things happened.... But we're fine," I say. "Anything happen to you?"

"Nothing so bad, but I ran into the Administrators. I didn't even say anything to them. I just ran away. I also kept seeing little glimpses of the Knife Thrower. Mainly in mirrors."

"Me too," I say.

"Me too," Austin says. "I don't know why, but I don't think he's committing murders anymore," he adds with bewilderment.

I then say, "I think he's just using people to do his dirty work. I mean, the Knife Thrower *is* clever," I admit.

"I guess…but not cleverer than us," Albie says. "So, what are we going to do for the rest of this laser tag? I don't think we need to get into more trouble. We already have a journal and a phone."

"Well, then how do we get out of here?" I ask. "We can't go out the emergency exit; someone might come in to take everyone out of the arena. They'll then look around and see dead bodies."

"Well," Austin says, "they're finding those bodies no matter what. We just don't want to seem suspicious or something, as if we're trying to sneak out of the arena. We don't want to get framed for murder."

"Who would suspect that kids murdered and injured a lot of people?" Albie asks. "A fraction of the people on this cruise are from Wayverlyn, and they'd probably tell some staff members here about the Knife Thrower. Then they'll just assume that all those murders were committed by him."

"Except for the murders we committed to people on his side," I correct. "Why would he kill the people working for him? The only deaths people will assume were done by the Knife Thrower are the deaths of random people. The other deaths from the people on his side are mysterious."

"That's a good point," Austin admits. "Andrew's right. I also bet that the man who was at the front desk earlier would remember us coming into the arena around the time people were murdered. We'll be suspects, but so will many other people. I just think there'd be no obvious ones, because who would a suspect be? I doubt the guy working at the front desk was looking at people and thinking, *Ooh, that one looks like a murderer*. That would be odd, if so."

"I agree," I say. "I think that we should wait until the end of the laser tag session and then sneak out, in a way. Try not to be noticed. Stand in the crowd with others. Also, once we leave, let's not dash to the elevator. We can just walk. Oh, and by the way, I saw a few guys earlier."

"Who?" Albie asks.

"Well, I saw the guy named Chris who I was talking about on the plane last night, and the other guys were Carlos Bills and John Bryans." I take a deep breath.

"And?" Albie says defensively.

"And...they were chasing me for a little while."

"Why?" she says with befuddlement.

"Long story short, I shot an arrow at them a few days ago," I say quickly.

"You what?!" she roars.

"I told you, it's a long story," I say.

Austin then whispers, "Psst," and taps both Albie's and my back. He points about twenty yards in front of us.

There is the Knife Thrower, wearing his black mask. His scheming will be over in seconds, I think, when one of us kills him.

Austin stands up and says, "I will shoot him right in the head."

He aims for a while, taking many deep breaths. I know Austin has a perfect aim right now to kill the Knife Thrower. He's just being extra sure about it. Being 100 percent sure that his arrow will sink right into the Knife Thrower. Plus, the longer he holds it back the faster and farther the arrow will move. If I were Austin I would let go quickly, because if he wants the arrow to go fast it will kill the Knife Thrower right away. If it goes slower, it may not kill him right away; it will make him suffer before he dies, which he deserves.

"What's taking him so long?" Albie whispers to me.

I shrug. Eventually Austin says, "Okay. I'm about to let go," but Albie stands up and pushes Austin down.

"He's mine!" she shouts. Albie twists and levers her arms back and throws the ax. It spins through the air at what looks like fifty miles per hour, whistling through the arena. Then a red-masked guy pushes the Knife Thrower away.

"NO!" the masked man shouts. Albie's ax blade plunges into the guy's temple and blood shoots everywhere. The Knife Thrower then darts away, swerving around the menacing mirrors.

"NOOOOO!" Austin yells. He takes a deep breath angrily. "Maybe if you would have let me shoot my arrow, it would have gone so fast that the other guy wouldn't have had time to push the Knife Thrower!" he snarls.

"Shut up!" Albie hisses. "We both know all three of us wanted to kill him!"

"Yeah, well, only *one* of us could!" Austin yells.

"Guys!" I say, feeling annoyed. "Just calm down. You guys yelling isn't going to help at all. That'll just draw attention to other Knife Thrower people or whatever they're called."

Frankly, I'm on Austin's side. Albie shouldn't have interfered. An ax coming at someone is a lot more noticeable and slower than an arrow. Although I think there will be peace in this fight soon, Austin and Albie just made things worse. Well, honestly, Albie did. She should have just let Austin kill the Knife Thrower. Now there isn't a 100 percent chance we'll win the $1 million.

"Fine," Albie says rudely. "Let's just hide somewhere until the laser tag is over. Then we'll go back to someone's room to look at the phone and journal."

No one comes by us, but we do witness a few gory deaths. All the dead bodies look grotesque. We're hiding in the corner of the first floor. We all pace around a small area. There's only silence until one of us crashes into a mirror. As time goes on, things get more monotonous. We're all blankly staring at each other. Neither Albie nor Austin seems very mad anymore.

Both of them have guilty looks on their faces. I stare down at my shoes, not knowing what to do.

After a little while, I hear a voice saying, "I hope you had a great time at laser tag. Go back to where you entered the arena. Now, share your spectacular experience with others!"

"I guess I'll tell people how many times I was almost killed," Austin mumbles.

Albie and I stare at Austin. "Hide your weapons," Albie says.

I hide all my knives in my jacket pockets. I don't even pay attention to what Albie and Austin are doing. We walk out of the laser tag arena and out the door, which leads us to the room we were in before we went into the arena. "I guess we go back to one of our rooms," I say.

"You guys can come to mine," Austin offers.

We all get in the elevator, go to floor thirteen, and head to Austin's room. When we get in there, we all sigh at the same time. "All right," I say. "Let's look at the stuff we found."

"Well, I have the phone, but let's hold off on it for a little while because we'll have to find out the passcode. For now, we should look at the journal," Austin suggests.

"Okay," I say. I take out the journal from my pocket and flip to a page where there's writing.

"What does it say?" Albie asks.

I read what I see:

Day the cruise leaves.
—Kill the kids at laser tag.
—Torture them to death.
—Send them a letter to see magician at 9:00 p.m. Thursday.
—Figure out more things to do to them and the other Contestants. Then leave only Andrew for the Knife Thrower to kill at the end of the cruise.

"Wow," Albie says anxiously. "Read the next page."

I read what I see: "Kill the two older kids on Friday. Save the other kids to be killed the next day. Send pictures of the soon-to-be-assassinated children."

"Oh, wow," Austin says quietly. "That sounds a little gory and bizarre."

"No kidding," Albie says. "But I find it strange about which *two* older kids the note is talking about. There are many older teenagers here. Maybe two are being specifically targeted?"

"I'm not sure. There's a lot more stuff," I add. "But I guess tomorrow we're going to see some magician. We'll probably get another letter."

"I hope the magician doesn't choose one of us for his tricks," Austin says.

"Why?" I ask.

"Well, who knows whether or not the Knife Thrower is the magician. The magician might wear a mask or something just to entertain the audience, but if we're in one of this his tricks, he might make us disappear! Not literally, but he might take us backstage or something and kill us," he answers.

"Sounds like a little too much," I say. "You seem to be overthinking."

"Yeah, I agree," Austin admits while putting his palm to his forehead.

This Knife Thrower is very cunning, intelligent, and psycho, which just makes him harder to find. In my opinion, I think that Austin, Albie, or I might find him. We almost got him at laser tag. We might find him again. Maybe. I'm very confused about who the Knife Thrower could be. I guess my only two suspects are Carlos and John.

"So," Albie says. "Let's try to turn the phone on."

"Okay," I say.

Austin turns on the phone and then says, "Any idea what the password is?"

"Not a clue," I say. I then shrug. "But when you guess, don't click too fast because if you get the password right you probably won't remember it."

"That makes sense," Austin says.

Austin puts in random numbers. Albie and I look at each other in boredom. We shrug, honestly knowing he won't get the password to the phone, but nor would Albie or I anyway. After a little bit, Austin says, "Ugh, now I can't guess a password for another five minutes."

"Why?" asks Albie.

"If you keep getting the password wrong, the phone will think that it's been stolen, which this one was!" he points out. "By us."

"After twenty minutes go by, do you think I could try?" I ask.

"There's no point," Albie says with annoyance. "It's not like we'll get it anyway."

Austin and I make eye contact for a moment. "She's right," I admit.

"I guess," Austin says gloomily.

I then remember how Austin wants to steal all of Diana's arrows. Due to her and her friends' rudeness I've seen and experienced, I agree with what he wants to do. Although after the Administrators helped me and Austin sneak on the boat without having to go through security, it might not be the right thing to do.

All of a sudden, my Quillix rings. It's Grace. I answer. I see her face, which doesn't seem to have any type of emotion on it. "Hello," I say.

Austin, Albie, and I make three-way eye contact. "Hello," Grace says. "Because George and I put the cameras on your eyes, we see what you see. We saw how you saw the note about seeing a magician in that journal. I'm warning you to never go up to be in the magician's tricks. I highly suspect he would call on a child to participate. For all you know, it could be the Knife Thrower or someone on his side. Them *not* wearing a mask doesn't mean they're not the Knife Thrower. That's just my thinking. Also, you did a fabulous job in laser tag when it came to surviving. Now, goodbye."

She hung up even before I could respond. I don't bother to tell Albie or Austin what Grace just said because they heard her. Loud, clear, and specific.

No one really says anything for a while.

There's not much conversation, but when it gets late, Austin says, "Well, we'll all see each other tomorrow. You guys could leave now and go have dinner."

All three of us have a long goodbye, as if we are never going to see each other again.

I walk back to my room thinking about how harrowing it is to be here. It's just so ominous. I don't feel like I want to grab something at a restaurant for dinner. I'll just have some fruit that came in a big bowl for me. Maybe even some of the chocolate squares. I think there are also a few water bottles in there.

Once I get in my room, I make the lights a little dim. I then take a quick shower and get into my pajamas.

I drop down on my bed. It's very comfy. I stare at the ceiling and start to feel very tired.

I turn off the lights and go to sleep.

10

Silas, Kairos, and Ignatius

I wake up at 8:00 a.m. and don't even feel like I slept. It just felt like I blinked and *boom!* I'm up. Shockingly, I didn't have a nightmare about the Knife Thrower killing me. I had lots of nightmares like that back in Wayverlyn, but now that the Knife Thrower has found out who I am, it should be even more harrowing. I decide to find somewhere to go eat breakfast. Or should I knock on Austin's door to see if he's up? I get changed, brush my teeth, and go to the bathroom.

Before I leave my room, I eye something on my desk. Not knowing if I had put it there, my heart jolts. I slowly walk over to the desk. I close my eyes, pick up the piece of paper, and open my eyes. My heart beats quickly when I see the letter. What does this mean?

I have to show Austin and Albie this. I run out of room. I have no clue where Albie's room is, so I hurry to Austin's.

I knock on his door several times. He opens the door and says in a drowsy way, "People like to be able to sleep at this time of day."

He shuts the door, so I knock again, and as soon as he opens the door I say, "Look what I got!"

"What?" he hisses.

I take one last glimpse at the letter:

Come to the Escape Room at 9:00 p.m. Many other people will come. If you can't get out in the time you have, you'll be crushed to death. Oh...and make sure to bring some fellow Contestants with you. K. T.

I hand him the piece of paper and Austin reads it quickly. "Oh, my gosh!" he says.

"When I woke up, I found this was on my desk," I say, "even though I'm pretty sure I locked my door! It would make sense if the letter was slipped under my door, but this is creepy."

"Well, I guess it's true then," Austin says.

"What is true?" I ask.

"The Knife Thrower broke into your room during the dead of night while you were fast asleep."

"You think so?" I ask, my voice filled with nervousness. "Sounds really scary."

"The Knife Thrower kills people," Austin remarks. "He does scary things."

"Also," I say, feeling like a detective, "I thought we were seeing the magician tonight at nine."

"Oh yeah," Austin says with confusion. He looks around, and I can tell he's thinking hard by the way his head moves. He looks like he's disoriented. "That's true. According to that journal I thought we were seeing the magician."

"Me too," I say.

"Well, why don't we look in the cruise magazine and try to find the Escape Room. Maybe we'll find more information in the pictures?" Austin suggests.

"That sounds like a good idea," I say.

Austin grabs the magazine off his desk and flips through it. After a few seconds, he says, "I don't see any Escape Room here."

"Maybe that's because you haven't flipped through half of the magazine," I say, feeling a little bit annoyed.

"Oh, yeah, that's right," he says.

Austin does seem a little weary this morning. "You seem tired," I observe.

"Yeah, well, maybe that's because *someone* decided to knock on my door really early in the morning," he says angrily.

"Sorry," I say without even meaning it.

Austin had flipped through the whole magazine by then. "There's no Escape Room," he says. "I don't understand, though. I thought we have to meet the Knife Thrower there. If we don't go, the Knife Thrower will kill us. If we do go, we have a chance of surviving...but only if we escape the room."

"Well, we're not going to ever be escaping a room if there is no room," I say.

"But if there is, we do have a chance of living," Austin says, then changes the subject. "I'm getting hungry. Let's go for breakfast."

"Okay," I say.

Austin changes out of his pajamas, and we walk to a restaurant.

We're sitting at a table looking at the menu. "I'm just getting a hot chocolate," I say.

"Me too," Austin says, "and waffles."

We order our drinks and food and start talking. "So," I say, "who do you think might be the Knife Thrower?"

"First, Silas Betailu. He's about forty years old, has been in jail before for selling some illegal substances, and he is a surgeon. People have died during his surgeries, and some people say that it was on purpose...some of the people he performed surgery on were his ex-girlfriend and his father, who was an alcoholic. Silas is also brilliant. He's so smart, he's in the small percentage of people in Mensa—the society for people with high IQs. Silas took the test at the young age of eighteen."

"How do you know all of this?" I ask.

"A few days ago, I was sitting on a bench at the park by myself. Silas sat down. He gave me a weird look and then we started to chat things up. We got into a deep conversation. Honestly, I thought he seemed a little suspicious, as if he wanted to kidnap me. The way he dressed he seemed like a detective. Silas is a clever man."

"That's a bit odd that he sat down with you," I say, concerned.

Austin shrugs.

Who else?" I ask.

"Kairos Kartyule. He had four wives. He told me that before he got married to any of his wives, he was in debt. I think he used them all for their money. Kairos also told me that one of the four wives was killed. Her killer is unknown. She was shot right in the back of her head. Also, he was married to all the wives for exactly two years and two hundred and thirty-one days each. It's very coincidental."

"Wait a minute," I say.

"What?"

"The name Kairos meant 'time' to the ancient Greeks," I say.

"How would you know that?" Austin asks.

"Once, in the fourth grade, my teacher was reading a Greek mythology book to the class. One of the character's names was Kairos. She told the class that it meant 'time.'"

"Really?" Austin says.

"Do you think after every two years and two hundred and thirty-one days of marriage, he divorces his wives and steals their money?" I ask.

"Maybe," Austin says. "Then, I bet he spends all the money and marries another rich woman."

"That makes sense to me," I say.

Our waiter arrives with our hot chocolate. "Here you go," he says.

I take one sip of the hot chocolate. It is steaming hot. I blow on it for a few seconds.

"It could also just be a coincidence that Kairos happens to have a wife for a certain amount of time, and that his name means time," I point out.

"I guess," Austin says. "It's not like he would do that because of his name. Maybe it's just a coincidence."

"Now," I say, "we need to find them and spy on them. See what Silas or Kairos is up to."

"I wouldn't," Austin says.

"What? Why not?" I ask.

"I told you…they're smart. And if I didn't mention it earlier, they have good ears. They probably can hear their own heartbeat," Austin replies.

"Sounds like they have good ears," I say.

"No kidding," he says.

I take a few more sips of my sweet hot chocolate. There is silence for a moment. I then say, "Are you sure you still want to steal arrows from Diana?"

"Yes. Why wouldn't I?" Austin asks.

"Well, Diana, Tiberius, Jack, and Elena all helped us get on the ship," I say.

"I know, but trust me, they'll do something horrible to me either way!" he exclaims.

"Like what?" I ask.

"Like steal my arrows!" he shouts.

"Okay, but only steal Diana's arrows if she and the Administrators do something bad to you. Otherwise, you'll look like the bad guy."

"All right, *fine*," he agrees reluctantly.

"Okay, now is there anyone else who you think might be the Knife Thrower?"

"Oh, yes, one last guy. His name is Ignatius Balquere. That name means 'ignite,'" Austin says.

"Ignite?" I say, seeming discombobulated.

"It means to be set on fire," he says.

"Really?" I ask.

"Yes," he says.

"Now, tell me about Ignatius," I say curiously.

"Before I get to talking about Ignatius, I have to mention that Silas once lived in the forest."

"Really?" I say, not believing him.

"Yes, you could ask him," Austin says.

"Great idea, I can go ask someone who is presumed to be the Knife Thrower if they've lived in the forest," I say sarcastically.

"Now, about Ignatius. He is about forty-five years old. Fifteen years ago, he lived in a trailer in Tallahassee that was less than a mile away from a forest. In the forest, ashes of campers were found. Parts of bodies. Ignatius was only one mile away from the bodies eight minutes after they were burned. They were found a mile deep into the forest," Austin says hauntingly. "He also once was accused of murder in court. Someone else was found guilty."

"Do you notice how all these guys' names relate to themselves?" I say.

"What do you mean?" Austin asks.

"Well, the name Kairos means time. He has had four wives for the same amount of time. One of the four was murdered. Then, Silas. Silas means man of the forest. He lives in the forest. I know what I'm about to say is not relevant to a forest, but he could have purposely killed people in surgery, and he has sold drugs before. Then, Ignatius. Ignatius means set on fire. For all we know he could have set people on fire and killed them. Then, maybe he moved all the way from Tallahassee to Wayverlyn so he couldn't be a suspect."

"Well, the campers were burned," Austin remarks.

"So?" I say. "Why couldn't he have killed them?"

"Those people who were burned were *camping*. A lot of the time campers make fires to stay warm for the night or to make hot dogs or s'mores. My point is, something could have gone wrong with the fire if there was one," Austin says. "Also, that whole thing you went on about with their names is probably just a coincidence, right? Because, really, who would do things so horrible because of their name?"

"I don't know." I shrug. "It's still a possibility."

"Well, I do think it is possible that these guys are guilty of all the things they could have done. I just don't think that it had to do with their names," Austin says.

"Okay, but I'm a little curious, though. Are we seeing some magician tonight or going to the Escape Room?"

"I guess the Escape Room," Austin says while shrugging. "Neither of us got a letter to go see a magician. We just assumed it would happen after looking at the journal, which could be false."

"Well, Albie could have gotten a letter to go see a magician tonight," I point out.

"Maybe."

I finish my hot chocolate. Right then a waiter comes over, although it's not the one from earlier. She says, "*Avez-vous fini avec vos boissons*, gentlemen?"

I know that this woman is speaking French. I know the language. She was asking if Austin and I were done with our drinks.

"What?" Austin says.

"*Oui, merci*," I respond, which means "yes, thank you."

"*D'accord*," she responds, which means "okay." She then takes our empty hot chocolate mugs away.

"How did you understand her?" Austin says, perplexed.

"I know French," I say.

"Cool. I know Latin."

"Interesting," I say.

I do find it a little odd that the waiter wasn't speaking English, but maybe she just didn't have a strong English vocabulary. I did hear her say "gentlemen" in her sentence.

We pay the bill, leave the restaurant, and start heading back to Austin's room. On the way, we bump into three people.

"Oh, sorry," Austin says. "Oh, wait a minute. Hey! Silas, Kairos, and Ignatius!"

"Oh, hello, young man," one of the three guys says.

"Hello, Kairos," Austin says to the man.

"And Silas," Austin says to another one of them. "How are you?"

"I'm quite fine," Silas says.

I assume that the other guy is Ignatius. "Hello," he says.

"Hi," Austin says in a surly tone.

"And who is this friend of yours?" Silas asks.

"Andrew," I answer. "Andrew Mikaelson."

"Hmmm," Silas says suspiciously. Based on the way he looks at me, he seems to be scrutinizing me.

"Is there something wrong?" I ask.

"No," Silas says. "Nothing is wrong."

"How's your new wife, who you recently married, Kairos?" Austin asks firmly.

"We just got divorced," he answers.

"Let me guess—after two years and two hundred and thirty-one days?" I say. "You've had five wives now."

"And how would you know that, young man? I was talking to your friend about that a few days ago, not *you*," Kairos says.

I don't really know what to say, because it sounds like Kairos didn't want Austin to tell anyone about his wives. Austin and I look at each other, not knowing what to do.

I then say, "Well, we need to get somewhere," and everyone awkwardly says goodbye.

"That wasn't too bad," Austin says as we walk away. "Talking to them, I mean."

"I guess...it seemed a little odd," I admit.

"Let's go back to my room," he says, and then we walk to the elevator in silence.

Once we get to our floor, we see the Administrators by Austin's door. All four of them are laughing.

"I wonder what they're up to," Austin mumbles with confusion.

Once we're in his room, I say, "Now, what's the deal with going to the Escape Room? How could it not be in the cruise magazine?"

"Maybe the magazine was from a time when there was no Escape Room on the boat. You know, before it was built in," Austin suggests.

"Possible, but not probable," I reply. "You would think they would do that so lots of people come to their Escape Room."

"I guess that makes sense," he responds. I then see Austin look on his bed. He eyes his quiver of arrows for a moment. "Wait a minute! Why are there only two in there?! Last time I counted them I had fourteen!"

"You used a lot of them at laser tag," I say.

"I know, but I took the arrows out of their bodies afterward!" he protests.

"Well, you also shot at a lot of random spots to find mirrors."

"Yeah, maybe I lost a few…not *twelve*, though."

Nothing positive can come from this. Two arrows is not enough for Austin to survive the cruise, even though he'll for sure be careful to take arrows out of bodies now that he needs more. Assuming many people on the Knife Thrower's side will go after Austin, he'll need a few more arrows.

"Well, you could always steal knives from a restaurant," I suggest.

"I guess," he says with annoyance.

"At least I don't think you'll need arrows for the Escape Room. It sounds like the Knife Thrower won't be in there. We'll just have to find hints to get out."

"That's true, but many more things will happen on the cruise that I will need arrows for," he says, his face worried.

Being frank, I say, "I guess so," but in a gloomy way.

11

The Escape Room

"Let's maybe walk around the cruise ship and try to find the Escape Room," I suggest.

"Sure," Austin says. I can tell he's angry since he doesn't have all his arrows anymore.

We leave his room and I say, "Why don't we go to floor ten? That's where all the activities are. Besides the mini golf course and ropes course, which are on the sundeck."

"That's good to know," Austin says.

We walk to the elevator and get in. We press the button for the tenth floor, and I can feel the elevator ascending slowly from floor 7.

Once we arrive on floor ten, I say, "Let's start looking around for this Escape Room."

We walk past the laser tag area with the big LASER TAG sign above the door. There is yellow tape blocking the door that says CLOSED, which draws our attention, so we walk back there. There is a staff member from the cruise standing by the entrance area.

"Why is laser tag closed?" I ask.

"Believe it or not, dead bodies were found," the guy responds. "And knives, arrows, and axes!"

I realize that laser tag is closed because of the Knife Thrower and all the murders he committed there. And the ones that Albie, Austin, and I committed. "Oh, wow," I say. "That's crazy."

"I know, right? I've heard rumors that some serial killer is on board. I think his name is the Knife Killer or the Throwing Knife? Something like that," the guy says with confusion.

"That sounds brutal," I say, trying to act surprised.

"Yes, it's very upsetting that some people are dead," Austin says.

"Yeah," the guy agrees. "Very depressing. Very sad. Sad, sad, sad," he repeats.

"Well, we hope laser tag reopens soon, because we really want to play," Austin says wistfully.

"I know," the guy says regretfully. "Sorry, fellas."

The guy then clicks his tongue. "Well, I hope you boys stay safe. Don't get into any trouble."

"We won't," I lie.

"Have a good day!" He gives us a dismissive wave.

"You too," Austin says.

Once we're out of earshot, I whisper, "Where do you think the Knife Thrower might be now?"

"I have no clue," Austin says. "He could be walking around without wearing a mask. It's not like you would just see him and think he's the Knife Thrower, because he wouldn't be wearing a mask in the middle of the cruise. It's possibly we could have just walked past him."

I look behind me, startled for a moment.

"Or, maybe he's staying in some room plotting with other guys about more murders," Austin says.

"Maybe."

"I wonder where the Escape Room is," Austin says. "Actually, why don't we go find Albie?"

"Good idea," I say.

"I know where her room is, but she may be somewhere getting breakfast." We walk past the entrance of the casino, and there is a sign that says Age Free!

"Age free?" Austin says. "What does that mean?"

"I think it means that anyone can gamble. It doesn't matter what their age is," I guess.

"That's weird."

When we get to the elevator, Austin clicks on level fourteen. "I hope she's awake," he says. "Albie told me that she likes to sleep in, but now it's late morning."

"Okay," I say.

"Her room is 1404," Austin adds.

Once we arrive on floor fourteen, we walk down a hall. When we get to room 1404, I knock.

Albie opens the doors, "Oh, hey guys," she says. "Come on in."

As we walk in, she asks, "So, any news about the Knife Thrower?"

"Yes," I say. "Laser tag is closed. All the dead bodies were found. Also, we're going to an Escape Room tonight at nine…not seeing a magician."

"How do you know?" Albie asks.

"Well, when I woke up, there was a letter on my desk saying to go to the Escape Room. Austin and I assume that the Knife Thrower broke into my room last night."

"Really?"

"Yes, unfortunately that is probably true," I say.

"Sounds scary. Didn't you put the deadbolt on your door?" Albie asks.

"I thought so, but obviously I didn't," I say with annoyance. "He must have stolen a key from the maid to open the door. If I had locked the deadbolt then he wouldn't have gotten in."

"Oh, and how do you know that we might not be going to see the magician tonight?" she asks.

"Well, we just assumed that, after reading a journal we weren't meant to read," I say.

"That's a good point," she admits.

"But Austin and I were looking through the magazine of the cruise, and there was no section about an Escape Room," I say.

"Did you consider asking a staff member? Or anyone, even?" Albie asks.

"No," I say.

"Let me grab my magazine. I'm sure that the Escape Room is in there," Albie says confidently. "It has to be, because why would the cruise not put a fun activity like an Escape Room in their magazine?"

Austin and I look at each other, knowing that she won't find the Escape Room. "Besides, what will we be doing in the Escape Room?" she says.

"We'll have one hour to escape," I say somberly. "If we can't escape in that time, we'll be killed."

"Yikes," Albie says. "At least it doesn't sound like people will be trying to kill us while we're trying to escape. And we have one hour."

"I bet it will be hard," Austin says nervously. "The Knife Thrower expected us to die in the laser tag arena. He must have really made the Escape Room hard, because he wants us to be executed."

Albie reads all the words and looks at the pictures carefully in the magazine. She seems a little embarrassed not finding anything about an Escape Room. "C'mon, c'mon, c'mon," she keeps saying. "Where could it be in this magazine?! I've read everything carefully, slowly, and twice!"

"TWICE?" Austin shouts. "I can't even read that whole magazine once in thirty minutes."

Albie gives me her most condescending how-can-a-person-read-so-slowly look. I shrug, figuring it would probably take me as long to read it as it takes Austin.

"So, how will we find the Escape Room?" I ask.

"Let's just go ask a staff member," Albie suggests. "I don't know why you guys haven't already."

"Hey!" Austin says defensively. "We didn't think that it would be so complex to find where an activity is on this cruise!"

I give Austin a look showing that I agree with him.

"Let's go," Albie says, seeming embarrassed.

We walk out of her room and over to the elevator. When we get in I press on the button for floor fifteen. Once we're on level fifteen the elevator doors slide open. We get out and we're on the sundeck. I see kids playing in the pools and people going down waterslides, having breakfast, and relaxing. When we see the nearest staff member, Albie says, "Excuse me, hi. We were wondering where the Escape Room is."

"Excuse me?" the staff member says.

"You know," Albie says, "the Escape Room."

"I don't follow," she says.

"THE ESCAPE ROOM!" Albie yells.

"Dear, I heard you. I'm just not familiar with any Escape Room on this cruise."

"Huh?" Albie says.

"There is no Escape Room on this cruise."

"What?" Albie says.

"Well, not that I know of. I only started working here a couple of days ago, but I would assume that my boss would have mentioned an Escape Room when telling me about the cruise." The staff member seems a little bewildered by our question.

Austin, Albie, and I all give each other glares of confusion. "That's weird," Austin says.

"How so?" she asks.

"Nothing," Austin says quickly.

"I'm sorry that we have no Escape Room on this cruise for you and your friends," the staff member says. "Although, what is a little weird is that I did hear a few kids—some who looked about your guys' age and older—saying that they were going to an Escape Room. I'm not sure, but I must've misheard them because there is no Escape Room on this cruise."

I exchange a look of interest with Albie and Austin. "Thank you for your time," I say.

"You're welcome. Have a good day, kiddos."

Once we walk away, I say, "I bet other kids in the MMR are trying to find the Escape Room."

"Why do you think that?" Austin asks.

"Because that lady was saying how she thought that she might have heard other kids talking about going to an Escape Room," I respond. "My guess is that those were Contestants in the MMR."

"Oh," Albie says. "That's an interesting thought."

"Well, I'm not sure about what we'll do now, because we don't know where the Escape Room is," Austin says.

"I guess we won't go, then," Albie adds.

"'*Don't go?*'" I exclaim. "Then we'll all get hunted down one by one and our hearts will be stabbed!"

"I don't know what we're supposed to do, then," Albie says, annoyed.

"Me either," Austin adds.

We're all standing in silence, pondering our next move, when Albie all of a sudden says, "Ouch!"

"Are you okay?" I ask.

"No," she hisses. "Something just hit my back!"

I look behind her. "It's a piece of paper!"

"A what?" Albie and Austin both say.

"A piece of paper," I repeat.

I grab it off Albie's back. It says, *Laser Tag 9 pm k.t.* All three of us read it.

"What?" Austin says. "The Knife Thrower must've just walked past us!"

"Let's get out of here, then," Albie says. "How'd he even get away so fast?"

"I don't know," I say. "First, we thought we were seeing a magician; then we thought that we were going to an Escape Room; and now, we're going back to laser tag?"

"That is a little weird," Albie says.

"Wait a minute," Austin says. "What if the Knife Thrower built the Escape Room in the laser tag arena? No one is there because it's closed. He must've snuck in!"

"That makes sense," I say.

"I agree," Albie says.

"Oh, and…!" I shout. "We're going to be on this cruise for nine days, right? Maybe the magician is next Thursday on the sixteenth of March. Then the next day, Friday, will be our last night on the cruise."

"That makes lots of sense," Austin says.

"Good thinking," Albie compliments.

"Thank you," I respond.

"Okay, let me get this straight. We are going to the laser tag arena tonight because the Knife Thrower built an Escape Room in there, and we are going to see the magician a week from today?" Albie asks.

"Correct," Austin says. "Now, I guess we just wait until nine to go back to the laser tag arena."

"How about we all do whatever we need to do for the rest of the day and we can meet back at my room around 8:45?" Albie asks.

"Sounds good to me," I say.

I walk out of Albie's room happily because I feel like a genius, which gives me lots of confidence that the three of us will break out of the Escape Room. I'm very shocked that the Knife Thrower was able to build an Escape Room in such little time. I bet, during the middle of the night when no one was really walking around the ship, he snuck into the laser tag arena and made the Escape Room. I'm also shocked that he came up with ideas for how to escape it.

I assume that the only people who will be in the Escape Room will be Austin, Albie, me, and the other people who the staff member said she heard talking about an Escape Room earlier. If the Knife Thrower gave letters to other people, they might realize that the Escape Room is in the laser tag arena.

There is honestly no point in thinking about how to get out, because who knows what will be in that creepy, dark room. I just hope that it will be easier than I think it is. But who am I kidding? It will be very hard to get out of that room. Probably rigged, even. Nothing will make any sense in an Escape Room the Knife Thrower designed. There will probably just be random numbers, pictures, and useless items. Who knows if you need a code to get out or not. Maybe there will be items we'll need to use to open boxes and locks to find more and more hints to get out of the room. I sigh and hope for the best, knowing it will never come.

When I get to my room I hop on my bed. I start to roll around my bed for some strange reason. Maybe because I'm stressed? Scared? Confused? Shocked? Angry? Everything is just confusing and frustrating. I'm a word that describes being confused and stressed combined, which unfortunately I do not know a word for. Why would I care about that right now? I tell myself, I'm not in a reading or English class!

I wonder what Uncle P is doing right now. What if he's being killed right now by a Cartwixziz, that weapon that shoots bullets and grenades? He could have already fallen from a rope and plummeted to his death, wishing that he had told Jonah and my mother the truth about being in the CIA. I would definitely have to speak up then and say how he told me everything about being in the CIA and how he lied to my parents. That is the worst thing to imagine at the moment.

What are my mother and Jonah doing right now? Probably thinking that Uncle P and I are at his friend's lake house, tubing or waterskiing, having a complete blast. Instead, we both might be dead in the next eight days. Although Uncle P right now thinks I am on a camping trip with my friends, having the time of my life, while really, I am on this cruise in a life-or-death situation. With all the lying going around in our family right now, I'm the mastermind. I know everyone's secrets and who is lying to who and who would be mad at who for lying or telling the truth to another. I know everything.

I hope that my mom hasn't called Uncle P yet. She would probably ask to speak to me then. I bet Uncle P would just say that I'm in the shower and come up with a big lie. He is clever, although most people would be able to come up with a lie easily like that. Also, if my mother wanted to talk to me she would just call me. Why would she call Uncle P instead of me? Not to sound rude, but obviously she loves me more than her second husband's brother who started living in her house.

I have noticed that my mother doesn't really seem to care for him. She thinks he's some idiotic alcoholic. Well, Uncle P does drink a lot, but he's not a grumpy alcoholic. He's always outgoing and happy, but in a drunken way, unfortunately. She just acts like she thinks of him like that in front of me, when in reality, she and Jonah think he's in the FBI. Of course, in real, real reality he is in the CIA. I've thought over that whole situation about a million times.

It's confusing and honestly a little stressful for someone to keep such a big secret. Like that one time I messed up a few days ago when I told my mom that Uncle P was on a call for the CIA. Thankfully, she believed me when I said that we always imagine him in the CIA. Something like that *is* what I said. Fortunately, the letters F-B-I didn't slip out of my mouth. I mean, I don't know how I possibly would have said that, but then my mom would know that Uncle P told me. Also, I'm happy that I never called him Uncle P in front of Jonah and my mom. They might think I just mixed up my letters, but that would seem a little, not suspicious… but awkward, in a *slightly* suspicious way.

Later in the day I have lunch with Austin and Albie, which is fun. Afterward I just walk around the ship looking for any signs of the Knife Thrower, which I unfortunately do not find, but who knows? I might find out who he is at the Escape Room. I also thought that before I went to laser tag, and look where I am now.

It's about 8:30 p.m. right now, so shortly I will need to go to Albie's room, which I remember Austin saying is 1404. I put all my knives in my pants pockets and the few pockets I have in my jacket. I know it's weird wearing a jacket on a boat when it's very hot outside, but there are a few pockets inside the jacket that I filled with knives.

Next, I will go to a restaurant... Then I will go to Albie's room. But before I go, I look out the window on this vessel with many people, including the Knife Thrower.

I think again about how I need to catch the Knife Thrower. I want to win that million dollars and be known as the kid who caught a serial killer. Of course, I would split the money with Albie and Austin. I bet, though, that all three of us will catch the Knife Thrower together, and we'll all take pride in catching him. If one of us for some reason catches him alone, it would be annoying, because all three of us are taking credit no matter who does. Who knows if we even will, though. Maybe the Administrators will win and then be in the Murder Mystery Race again next year.

Any Contestant could win, but I hope it's me, just like everyone else does. I think most Contestants have allies, although maybe two or three don't. Maybe they're arrogant and they think they're the best. Or they just don't want an ally.

I walk out of my room and start walking to room 1404. I feel nervous shivers going through my body because I'm going to the Escape Room soon. When I get to Albie's room I knock on the door. Albie opens it up and says, "Come on in," so I walk in, and notice Austin is already there.

"So, does everyone have weapons?" Albie asks, while exhaling.

"Yes," I answer.

"Hardly," Austin mutters.

"Huh?" Albie says.

"I have two arrows," he says, still seeming very annoyed about his missing arrows.

"Why?" Albie hisses.

I shake my head to Albie, meaning, *Don't ask.*

Austin doesn't respond.

"Okay, then," Albie says. "Let's head to the Escape Room."

We walk out of her room and go to the elevator. We go to the tenth floor, and when we walk to the laser tag area no one is guarding it. "Hurry, quick!" I say. "Before anyone sees!"

We slide under the yellow tape and get into the laser tag arena. "What level should we go on?" Albie asks.

I notice a sign that says:

FLOOR 3
K. T.

"The third," I say while pointing to the sign.

We take the stairs to the third floor, but when we get there, we find a set of doors in front of us. I can see how a fraction of the third level is the Escape Room. The doors open automatically, and when all three of us step into the room, the doors close. I jump a little. It's dark and I can't see anyone, but I hear others talking. It's not just me, Albie, and Austin. There are other people here. Adults, in fact. I can tell by their deep voices.

I then hear a voice. It says, "This is the Knife Thrower. The ceiling will move down to the floor as time goes on. If the hour goes by and no one has found their way out of this room, you will have all been crushed to death. At certain points depending on your height, you may have to bend because the ceiling is moving down to the floor every second. *Slowly*. Also, many things will hit you here. A knife might be thrown at you, a spear might be thrown at you, and you might get shot with an arrow. By the way, I am in this room. I will leave out a secret door that you cannot see. Use your time wisely. Your time starts now."

There is a bunch of talking going on. Things glow around the room. Numbers, pictures of weapons, and letters. Over the rumble of voices, I say, "Guys, let's look at the door and see if there is a lock that needs numbers or letters to be unlocked."

"Good idea," Austin says.

Not seeing where Austin or Albie are, due to the darkness, but remembering where the door is, I turn and walk. I put my hand out and I feel a handle. Above it, a light suddenly shines. A screen has just turned on. It has eleven small horizontal lines and a big space between lines five and six. It seems like I can type in numbers, letters, or small pictures of a weapon. "Hello?" I say, wondering where Austin and Albie are.

"Here!" I hear two people shout.

In the sliver of light from the small screen, I see an arrow flying at me. I turn left, then throw my knife. "AGH!" I hear someone yell.

I run toward the yell, and I find a man with a mask on. He's holding a bow. A knife is in his shoulder—my knife. He seems dead. I grab his quiver and shout, "Austin!"

Austin and Albie jog up to me. "Yeah?" Austin says, seeming anxious.

"I just took these arrows from a red-masked guy," I say. "Here." I hand the quiver to him.

Austin admires the silver quiver of arrows.

"Okay, so did you find where the door is and what the lock is like?" Albie asks.

I lead them to where I think the door is. I then hear a voice again. "This is the Knife Thrower. Your first hint is 'northeast.'"

"What?" I say, completely perplexed. "What does that mean?"

"We'll discuss it in a minute. First tell us how the lock works," Albie says.

I show Austin and Albie how to work the lock on the screen. You can type in numbers and letters, after you hit the word enter on the screen.

"Now," Austin says. "What does 'northeast' mean?"

"I think it means that we have to go to a corner, probably in this room, pointing northeast," I say.

"Well, no kidding," Austin says.

"Wait," Albie says. All of a sudden, lights turn on in the Escape Room. Albie then says, "This way!" and Austin and I follow her to a corner.

Now that the lights are on, I look around. I see Carlos, John, Silas, Ignatius, and Kairos. I whisper to Austin, "Hey, it is *so* time to get out of here."

"We can't!" he says, not seeing the five of them.

"Look around for a second."

He does and gasps. "Okay, then. I would like to get out of here."

The three of us are in the corner looking for something, not seeing what is behind us. There's a screen in front of me that all of a sudden turns on. Albie and Austin don't see it because they are looking at the numbers, letters, and mysterious pictures on the wall. Then some words display on the screen: *Hello, Andrew.* The letters fade and new ones appear. *What do you remember?*

What do I remember? I don't know. The words fade away and new ones display. *From the beginning of the Knife Thrower.* I think about it. I remember the day when my mother was watching the news. She seemed frightened. It was about 9:00 p.m. on a Wednesday night. A man witnessed another man getting a knife thrown into his stomach right in front of Quain's Bakery. That was the beginning of the Knife Thrower's murder spree.

I whisper that to myself, which I cannot deny is very weird, but the creepiness that I feel from the screen gives me the chills. The words fade away and new ones are displayed. *Ah, I see, so you remember that Quain's Bakery was where I committed my first murder?*

How did the screen just hear me whisper? And how is the Knife Thrower making words appear on the screen that respond to me? Those words fade and new ones display: *You gave yourself your first hint… now goodbye.*

I look up and I see the ceiling moving down. The last thing I want is to be crushed to death, but I have no idea why remembering something about the Knife Thrower might be the way to get out of here. I hear a tap behind my shoulder. I turn around and Carlos, John, Kairos, Silas, and

Ignatius are surrounding me, murmuring things. John then says, "*Puer interficere*," in a language I do not understand.

"Yes," Kairos says deeply. "We've been listening in on your conversation. Now, stop gossiping about me and my friends. You should know that a fish with its mouth closed never gets caught. But you already have been. *And I am the hook!*"

Confused, I hear Austin yell from across the room. "They're going to kill us!"

Kairos pulls a bronze knife from his pocket and tosses it to Silas. Silas throws the knife up in the air and the heavy metallic knife spins. Silas grabs the knife by the blade, then throws the knife at me! I duck and roll under Ignatius's legs. At the same time, I draw a knife and throw it into his calf. The blade sinks into his flesh. He can't be dead—legs aren't a vital part of the body—but it still makes me nervous. I see Austin and Albie looking worried while the other people in the Escape Room are lying down. They don't seem dead, though, and there's no blood. Maybe they've been knocked out?

I turn and see Ignatius fall to the ground, moaning in pain. The other four look at me, shock on their faces, and I can tell they're about to charge me. Could one of these five be the Knife Thrower? All of them might be working together. John runs toward me. I throw a knife at him, but he ducks his head and gets ready to tackle me to the ground. But right when he leaps, I move just in time before he grabs my body. He seems to be hurt badly. Albie turns her head to see her uncle lying on the floor. She now realizes that he is the Knife Thrower or likely working for him since he isn't wearing a mask. I can see a pool of tears rise in her eyes.

Carlos, Silas, and Kairos start running toward me. Albie and Austin can't use a weapon on them because they are running so quickly, so they start to chase the three who are chasing me. I duck down, and all three of the men trip over me.

"Are you okay?" Albie asks.

"Yeah, I'm fine," I say. "We have to figure out how to get out of here."

I then see Ignatius crawling his way to the door. He quickly punches in a code, and something appears on the screen for the passcode. It says, *Part 2*. He puts in another code that I can't see.

"Hey!" I shout.

The door opens and Ignatius crawls out. I try to get to the door in time to get out, but it slams shut. Ignatius has escaped.

"Ugh!" I shout.

I look down at the four men whimpering in pain, waiting for the pain to go away.

"Did you find any hints about the lock?" Austin asks.

"Sort of," I say. I then think for a moment. What…what if the code is Quain's Bakery? I dash over to the lock screen and type in "Quain's Bakery."

"I got it!" I shout.

I look behind me and see Austin and Albie holding down Kairos, Silas, Carlos, and John on the ground. "Really?" Albie says, but she quickly turns back, and I see her quietly say to John, "*I can't believe you. You are no longer family to me.*"

"Yep," I say proudly.

Albie lets go of Silas and Carlos and says, "You stay right there! Move one inch and I'll kill you!"

I jump a bit, even though Albie's scary order wasn't directed toward me.

Austin just gives Kairos and John a nasty look. "So, what was the code?" he asks.

I whisper quietly so the other guys can't hear, even though they may know the code to the lock already. Ignatius did, after all. "It was Quain's Bakery."

"How'd you figure that out?" Albie asks.

"Well, it asked me what I had remembered from the beginning of the Knife Thrower, and—"

"Wait, what asked you what?" she asks.

"To unlock the door, you type the code into a screen. On the screen, words appeared asking me questions," I answer. "Anyway, the screen asked me what I remember from the beginning of the Knife Thrower's crimes, which was the first murder by Quain's Bakery!"

"Okay," Albie says, "So, maybe this 'Part 2' will be what happens last?" she guesses.

"Maybe," I say. "That's probably true!"

We all get excited and jump, but when we do, we feel the ceiling getting closer to our heads.

"*Ow!*" we all say.

I feel so dizzy. The room is a blur. The knife in my hand looks like three.

"Okay, we need to solve this thing quickly," Albie says, blinking quickly, trying to get the disoriented feeling away. "Time is running out!"

We all look at the screen, and it says, *HTE DCEO SI MTHSOEGIN UOY LNOY NDIF NI A IOMRRR!*

"Wh-what is this?" I say. "Some...some kind of language?"

The words then appear to all of a sudden be *ETH ECOD SI MNTIHGSEO OYU YOLN FIDN IN A RRMIRO!*

"I don't know!" Albie exclaims.

As time goes on, we start bending down a little. John, Carlos, Silas, and Kairo are still lying down, afraid that Austin or Albie will kill one of them. The weird letters still show up on the screen. The screen moves down slowly with the wall, and so does the door handle to get out. Albie then yells, "Andrew, type in your first name and last name!"

"What? Why?!" I ask.

"Remember in the journal? The Knife Thrower wants to kill you last! The first part was about his first kill, so the second one might be what or *who* he wants to be his last!"

I then put my name in the lock, and miraculously, it works!

"Get the door open!" Austin shouts.

I push, push, and push at the bottom left until it flies open. "Hurry, get out!" I shout.

We all slide to get out just in time. Once we're all out, I yell, "Let's get out of here!"

We run down from the third level, and once we get to the first floor I see the exit door. We all run into it and crash into a mirror, falling down.

"Ow!" Andrew complains. "Geez! Can we just get out of here?"

I glance behind me and spot the door. We go to the door and finally exit the arena.

"So, why were those words scrambled up? Was it in a different language?" I ask.

"They weren't," Albie says. "It was because of us."

"What do you mean by that?" I ask.

"What I mean is, we hit our heads on the ceiling. *Very* hard. Therefore, it mixed up our brains, and it was as if we all were dyslexic for a moment. I bet we're fine now."

"Ohhh," I say. "That makes lots of sense."

"Do you guys think that John, Carlos, Kairos, or Silas escaped the room?" Austin asks.

"Not a chance," I answer. "We barely made it out."

"There could have been a trapdoor that they escaped out of if one of them is the Knife Thrower," Austin guesses.

"Maybe, but I doubt it," Albie says. "They didn't have enough time. *They did not have enough time. John didn't have enough time.*"

"Albie are you oka-"

She cuts me off and says, "Don't ask me if I'm okay, just-jus-" and she stops talking.

"Well, our only way to know if they died is if we hear news about more murders," I say.

"What if the killer is Ignatius?" Albie asks. "Then, more murders *could* happen."

"He is seriously injured," I point out.

"I guess," Albie says. "Now, let's all go back to our rooms, get some sleep, and meet back at Austin's room at 10:30 a.m."

"Sounds good," Austin says.

"Sounds good," I say.

12

The Wheel of Punishment

I wake up at 10:00 a.m. on Sunday. Nothing happened on Friday or Saturday. Last night, Albie and I had agreed to meet at Austin's room at 10:15. When I get out of bed I look on my desk and there is a letter. Knowing it is most likely from the Knife Thrower, I feel startled for a moment.

The letter says:

I shall see you at the roulette table number 1, which has a special twist on the game at 10:00 p.m. sharp. The actual game doesn't matter. You're not playing to win. You will do three bets. Your bet does not matter. The number it lands on is what matters. I would like to call this "the wheel of punishment." Here's what will happen based on the number the ball lands on…

You getting assassinated – 36

Blackmail you – 27, 12, 8, 4, 21, 15, and 1 (Yes, I know how you followed those two men that day with your stepfather. You almost killed them.)

Someone abducts you for four days on this boat – 26, 34, 2, 13, 5, 6, and 7.

I send out the video I have of you almost killing Ignatius –3, 17, 33, 25, 29, 21, and 9.

I fake my own death and create proof anonymously showing you are the killer – 10, 11, 32, 35, 19, 23, and 18.

Surprise – 14, 16, 22, 24, 28, 30, and 31.

If the ball lands on 36 I will kill you, and the other things that would have happened to you will happen to a loved one. If you happen to land on two or three numbers that are all in the same category, that bad thing will happen only once. Just so you know, I have been in the casino a lot throughout these few days on this cruise when I'm not murdering people. For some reason, 36 is the number that has been landed on most often. Goodbye.

Well, I think, if the cruise didn't have an age-free casino allowing me to gamble, I would have never gotten this letter. I quickly get dressed and run to Austin's room. I barge in without knocking, realizing that his door should have been locked overnight in case the Knife Thrower came in. Albie is already there. Without saying anything, I drop the letter between them.

"Oh, my gosh," Albie says after reading it.

Austin just looks shocked.

"I know," I say.

"I guess we have to go to the casino tonight," Austin says.

"Yep," I say. I then exhale. "What happens if the ball lands on thirty-six?" I say with nervousness.

"You die," Austin says.

"Well, that makes me feel a lot better," I say sarcastically, rolling my eyes.

Austin shrugs while Albie mutters something at him that I don't hear.

"I think you should be fine," she says. Austin and I make eye contact, disagreeing. "What are the odds that the ball will land on thirty-six, huh?"

"Well, actually to save you some math, there is an eight percent chance that the ball will land on thirty-six," I say.

But whatever the ball lands on, three horrible things could happen to me.

"Well...we could maybe live in the casino," Albie suggests.

"What?" I say, completely confused.

"We could live in the casino. It is open twenty-four hours a day and seven days a week. People are always at the casino, so the Knife Thrower wouldn't kill you if you're in an area with lots of people," she says. "It would draw a lot of attention."

"I guess," I say. "I don't want to live in a casino, but I guess it's better than the alternative."

"It would only be for a few days," Austin adds. "It is also, in my opinion, a lot better than dying in some nasty, tortured way."

"You're right," I admit glumly.

"Also, who knows if the ball will even land on thirty-six," he says.

"That is true," I say. "I'm just a little perplexed about the surprise. I wonder what happens if it lands on fourteen, sixteen, twenty-two, twenty-four, twenty-eight, thirty, or thirty-one."

"I think you'll be fine," Albie says, probably just to cheer me up.

"I don't," Austin says.

"Austin!" Albie hisses.

"What? He will most likely not be fine at all, so I'm just being honest to prepare him," he says. "Is that so wrong in a life-or-death situation?"

"Um, yeah, it kind of is," Albie says.

Austin rolls his eyes. "I think that Andrew should take a life-or-death situation seriously and prepare for the worst things that could happen."

Albie scoffs.

"He's right, Albie," I say. "I appreciate what you're saying, but this MMR and everything that's going on is not some game." She looks at me in disdain. "Okay, I said that in the wrong way. What I mean is that honesty is probably the best thing we need right now."

"I guess you're right," she mutters.

"Can you say that louder?" Austin says rudely.

"Austin," I say with annoyance. "We all know that you heard her."

He murmurs something I can't hear.

"Now," Albie says. "What is our plan if the Knife Thrower starts to accuse Andrew of killing Ignatius? He'll send out a video."

"Well, we can probably get a whole video of what happened in the Escape Room. I would think that marshals, detectives, or policemen would believe that a ten-year-old boy tried to kill someone in self-defense," I say. "They went at me first. Also, you guys are witnesses."

"Yeah, but Ignatius has more witnesses. You only have Albie and me. That's two witnesses. Ignatius has Silas, John, Carlos, Kairos, and a video. That's four witnesses and a video of the *crime* scene," Austin says. "You are right, though. I think that the cops would most likely agree with us. We're children."

"Yeah, but that guess is a *little* ageist in a way," I say. "Kairos, Silas, John, Carlos, and Ignatius would call that out."

"What are you guys talking about? They are probably dead," Albie remarks.

"That is true," I admit. "I honestly hope all three numbers that the ball lands on are the abduction numbers."

"W-what? Why?" Albie asks.

"I'll be put in a room for a few days," I say, "then, *boom*, just like that, I'm free."

"Andrew," Albie says in a very serious tone. "You might starve during that time. Maybe even die if you are given no water or food for just a few days. You might get tortured."

"It's better than going to jail for a long time if I somehow get found guilty of murder," I say.

"Better?" Austin says, seeming shocked. "You could die in who knows what room on the ship!"

"To me, the letter didn't sound like I would end up getting killed if I was abducted," I say. "Being killed is what will happen if one of three times the ball lands on thirty-six. Otherwise, what's the point of the numbers for abduction?"

Austin doesn't respond to my question, but says, "Ugh, this dumb wheel. The Knife Thrower is a total imbecile."

"Imbecile?" I say. "Even though I hate the Knife Thrower, I don't think he is an imbecile. He is obviously very smart if we're now stuck in this position!"

Austin sighs.

"Wh-wh-what if we just didn't go?" Albie asks. "Why don't we just never do what the letter says. We might not get killed."

"Yes, we would," I say.

"Okay, but what if we *didn't* end up getting killed?" she argues.

"Let's just meet at Andrew's room at 9:50. Then we'll go to the casino together," Austin suggests. "How about that?"

"That's fine with me," I say.

"Me too," Albie says.

"All right then," I say.

I leave Austin's room. I do think that Albie and Austin are very lucky in this situation. It doesn't matter what number the ball lands on for them, because nothing will happen to them. Only me.

Why me?

As the day goes on, I have a delicious lunch—a burger, fries, and a milkshake.

Then, around 5:00 p.m., I see Kairos and John walking together. How are they alive? I totally thought that they were dead! There must have been some secret door for them to escape! I follow them for a little while, but they don't walk anywhere to kill someone. It's not like one of the two of them are for sure the Knife Thrower, even if it did seem like it in the Escape Room. Kairos, John, Ignatius, Silas, and Carlos all seemed like they wanted to kill me in the Escape Room. That's why I think they could be the Knife Thrower. It's likely they're just killers in general.

* * *

Now it's 9:00 p.m.—only another hour until I go into the casino. I'm in my room, alone, when I realize what happened to Austin's arrows a few days ago. The Administrators stole them! Before we went to Austin's room that day, I saw the Administrators walking down the hall to his room. It was totally them who stole his arrows. Plus, Austin doesn't seem to keep his door locked. That's how the Administrators got in.

Maybe right now wouldn't be a good time to tell him, because all three of us are going to the wheel of punishment soon, but I have to tell him eventually. The arrows were probably stolen for Diana. Austin was right when he said to me a few days ago that the Administrators may have helped us get on the boat, but they still can't be trusted. Now Austin will want to steal all of her arrows.

At 9:50 p.m., I hear a knock on my door. I open the door and there are Austin and Albie.

"You ready?" Albie asks, and I nod. The three of us walk to the elevator and click the button to get to level ten.

As we are in the elevator I say, "Guess who I saw earlier in the casino."

"Who?" Austin asks.

"Kairos and John," I answer.

I hear Albie take a big breath in relief. Even though in the Escape Room she had told John that he meant nothing to her he still must.

When we get to the casino, I see adults drinking wine and beer. People are playing blackjack, poker, and slot machines. The casino is huge. "Well, this place is broad," I say.

Albie and Austin both nod. "Okay, I guess we just go to roulette table number one," Austin says.

"Okay," I say.

"There!" Albie points to a roulette table that has the number 1 engraved on the side.

We walk over, and at the table there are seven chairs. Four of them are already taken by Ignatius, Silas, Kairos, and John. I wonder where Carlos is. Three seats are left for Albie, Austin, and me.

"Oh, hello," Silas says in a creepy voice. "We were just about to start. Would you children like to join us?"

"Yes," I say solidly. "We would."

"Well then. Come play," Kairos says in a persuasive way.

The croupier says, "Are you children sure you want to gamble? Do you have a parent or guardian nearby?"

"Yes," I answer while pointing to some random middle-aged couple at the bar.

"All right then," the croupier says briefly. "Ladies and gentlemen, place your bets."

Everyone puts in their bets. The croupier then spins the wheel. The wheel spins, spins, and spins and the ball goes round and round. The ball lands on a number.

"Oooh," John says triumphantly. "Well, I just won this round. I bet twelve, and that's what the ball landed on."

"Good job, sir," the croupier says happily. "You just won yourself one hundred dollars." The croupier hands John his hundred dollars' worth of chips to cash out. "Now, are y'all gonna play another round?"

Everyone agrees to play another round. Austin then whispers to me, "What happens when the ball lands on twelve?"

I remember from the letter. "I'll get blackmailed," I whisper.

Austin looks nervous.

"Ladies, gentlemen, you may place your bets," the croupier says.

We all put in our bets and the croupier spins the wheel. Everyone gapes as it spins—especially me, because I'm just hoping that it doesn't land on number thirty-six. If the ball lands on thirty-six, I'll get killed, and the other things that would have happened to me happen to a loved one instead. I know I don't like Jonah much, but I worry he might be blackmailed for spying on Chris, John, and Carlos. I haven't seen Chris much on the cruise over the past few days. He seems to be scared of Carlos and John, which I don't blame him for. Jonah and I saw him getting threatened by them.

The wheel is spinning so fast. I can feel my face starting to get red because of how nervous I am.

"Whoa!" the croupier says, laughing. "It isn't the biggest deal if ya don't win."

I ignore him. The ball finally lands on a number. The number is…

"Fourteen!" the croupier shrieks. "Anyone bet on that?"

No response.

Albie then whispers to me, "Do you know what fourteen means?"

"It's the surprise one," I respond. "So, I have no clue what will happen."

Albie nods reluctantly.

"Okay!" the croupier says. "Who wants to play again?" Unsurprisingly, everyone wants to play again. "Ladies, gentlemen, you may place what I hope is a *big* bet."

"So, the house can make more money?" I say.

"Um, that is actually true," the croupier says, embarrassed.

Austin nudges me.

The croupier spins the wheel, and it goes around and around and around, spinning much faster than the other times. I hear John muttering under his breath, "Thirty-six, thirty-six, thirty-six," probably so he can kill me. Or maybe that's what he bet on.

John is staring into the wheel. I can tell he is starting to get a little dizzy when he moves back away from the table and rubs his forehead. It looks as if he has a migraine.

The ball then lands on…"Thirteen!" the croupier says excitingly. "Did anyone bet thirteen?"

"I did," Austin says joyfully.

I didn't even realize that Austin bet thirteen.

"Well, you have won yourself twenty dollars!" the croupier says. He hands Austin twenty dollars' worth of chips. "Remember to cash that out, young fella," the croupier reminds him. "Good job!"

Austin smiles. "Thank you."

"Anyone want to play again?" the croupier asks.

"No," I say.

Everyone else says no, and Kairos, John, Silas, and Ignatius leave the table. Albie, Austin, and I do as well.

"Good job," I say to Austin.

"Thank you," he says victoriously.

"So, what is going to happen based on the numbers that were landed on?" Albie asks.

"I will be blackmailed and abducted for a few days. Then there is the surprise," I say.

"Well, how about we all sleep in the same room tonight and we take turns keeping lookout," Austin suggests.

"Sounds good to me," I say.

Austin cashes out his twenty dollars' worth of chips and seems to be delighted by his winnings.

13

The New Alliance

We walk out of the casino. Albie says, "So, whose room do you want to go to for tonight?"

"We could do mine," I suggest. "How about we all go to our own rooms, do whatever we need to do, and meet back at mine at 10:40?"

"That sounds fine with me," Albie says.

"Me too," Austin says.

"All right then," I say. "And how about when we switch off sleeping, so there's one person sleeping and two guards? I doubt the Knife Thrower can get control of two people at once. Obviously, if he comes in, then the person sleeping will be woken up."

"That is a smart idea," Albie says.

"Yes, that is actually a very clever plan," Austin admits.

We get into the elevator and press the button for thirteen. Nobody is in the elevator besides us, which makes me feel safer for some reason. The elevator doors open, and we start walking to our rooms. I start walking a little faster as I go down the hall, because sometimes it is frightening being by yourself at night on a cruise when a murderer wants you to be blackmailed, abducted, and dead.

When I get into my room, the first thing I do is lock the door. I feel a little relieved. I get in the shower and think. I wonder when I'll get blackmailed. I wonder when I'll get abducted. I wonder what the surprise is. I think there are only about four days of this cruise left, so the abduction attempt will happen tonight or tomorrow. I jump a little thinking that scary thought and slip and fall in the shower. I hit the back of my foot bone badly, which is probably the last part of my body I want to hurt because I'll be running a lot on this cruise. From death. I get up slowly, wobbling. I get out of the shower slowly, dry myself off, and get into my pajamas. I eat an apple because I'm famished.

I look at the clock. Albie and Austin should be here soon. I think I'll ask if I can sleep first.

I hear a knock, and as soon as I open the door, Austin barges his way in and plops himself on the bed.

I say, "Oh, hi—"

"I call sleeping first!" Austin shouts.

"You've told me that about a hundred times on our way here," Albie says. "I know!"

"Andrew doesn't!" he argues.

Albie scoffs and rolls her eyes.

"Well, I guess Austin is sleeping first," I say to Albie. I shrug.

"You can sleep after him," she offers. "I have some energy right now because of my ADHD. I forgot to bring my medicine with me."

"Okay. Thank you," I say.

"No problem," she says.

"So, how is this gonna work? Will we wake up the person who is sleeping every hour?" I ask.

"Sounds fine to me," Austin says.

"Me too," Albie says.

"Put out the lights," Austin demands, even though he says it in a nice voice.

I turn off the lights and the room becomes dark. The only light is the clock next to the bed.

The rotations go on and on and on. It's an annoying process. The two guards usually are in the bathroom whispering or playing games on paper. Even though we are exhausted, we are entertained because we have someone to hang out with. While I am sleeping, I always hold a small ax that Albie gave me just in case. The Knife Thrower had gotten in here somehow before, even though the door was locked. I also hold a weapon when I am hanging out in the bathroom with someone. Albie and Austin do the same.

There are only a few days left on this cruise. The $1 million is coveted. Everyone is determined to find the Knife Thrower and win. I also wonder what Albie thinks about her uncle, John Bryans, possibly being the Knife Thrower. Is she giving him the benefit of the doubt and thinking that he is someone the Knife Thrower forced onto his side? Frankly, I would really like to ask her, but I don't want to put her in an uncomfortable situation. She saw what happened in the Escape Room and how he showed up at roulette. Although the Knife Thrower could have left the Escape Room before the lights came on. Also, the Knife Thrower could have been at another roulette table at the casino watching our table and not even caring one bit about his bet.

As the night went on, I had a moment to tell Austin about how the Administrators stole his arrows. Boy, did he get mad. He was telling me how he wanted to steal all of Diana's arrows soon.

"I just hate those Administrators so much!" he exclaims.

"Shhhh," I whisper, "Albie is trying to sleep!"

"They're just so annoying," Austin says in irascibility.

"Really? You haven't told me that once," I say sarcastically with a chuckle.

"Not funny," he responded firmly. "I'm going to get those arrows back!"

"How?" I ask.

"Steal from them."

"Good luck going up against the four of them to get a few arrows," I say. "What's the big deal? Is it really that terrible that you can't use a bow and arrow? You could use a knife," I suggest.

"Nah, I prefer the bow," Austin says.

"It's not that hard, I could teach you how to use the knife," I offer.

"No thanks," he says, annoyed.

* * *

It is about 6:40 a.m. I am sitting in my room with Albie. We didn't even want to talk or play games, so we didn't go to the bathroom. We just sat in silence, hoping for late morning to arrive. I had a few talks with Albie and Austin over the night, and we all are excited for late morning so we can take a quick rest by the pool where everyone is so the Knife Thrower can't kill us there. The Knife Thrower never kills when others are around. *Never*. Well, he did in the laser tag arena, but it was very dark in there and disorienting with mirrors, so it was easier for him not to get caught.

All of a sudden, I hear a noise coming from my door. The door handle moves! This must be The Knife Thrower.

"Psst!" I whisper to Albie. I point to the door.

The doorknob is being twisted. Suddenly, I hear *clang*—as if the lock on the door was just broken off. The door opens and standing there is a man in a black jacket, wearing navy-blue jeans, black shoes, and a black mask. He is holding one knife in his right hand and one knife in his left hand.

I throw my knife, but he turns out of the way. Then Albie throws one of her axes. It is so close to hitting the Knife Thrower's head, but he swiftly ducks. He then slams the door to my room.

We get up quickly and go out of the room. We run down the hall. The Knife Thrower is waiting for the doors to open at the elevator! They do and he goes inside. I see a glimpse of him pounding the SD button, which stands for sundeck.

I run and take a leap to get into the elevator. I am in the air as if I'm flying. The doors for the elevator are slowly closing. The Knife Thrower is clicking the close button rapidly. The doors are almost closed, but I stick my hand through to trigger the sensor. Then, the Knife Thrower puts his leg through the gap between the doors. He kicks me in the chest, and I fall backward on the floor, knowing there is no chance I can get in the elevator now. It's so close to shutting. At the last minute, though, I throw a knife. It enters the elevator right before the doors close. I know my knife got in there. I just don't know if it hit the Knife Thrower.

Albie, who is a few feet away from me, shouts, "Go get Austin! I'll get the next elevator!"

I don't respond, but she knows I heard her because I sprint back where we came from. I barge into my room, turn on the lights, and shout, "Austin! Get up!"

"Wh-why?" he says wearily, squinting.

"We're going to get the Knife Thrower!" I shout.

That grabs his attention. He quickly gets out of bed, grabs his bow and quiver of arrows, and we run to the elevator where Albie is. Right when the elevator doors open, we get in. I press the SD button. When we get to the sundeck I see the pool, waterslides, mini golf course, and ropes course, but there's no sign of the Knife Thrower.

"Ugh. Didn't we just see him?" Albie asks with annoyance.

"I don't know where he went," I say. "I'm sure I saw him press the sundeck button."

I then eye something not so good. The Administrators are laughing and walking beside the pool. Diana seems to have about thirty arrows. I think now it is very clear that she stole all of Austin's arrows. Austin looks furious once he spots them. "I am going to kill those—"

"Calm down," I say. "Why don't we make a plan on how to steal all the arrows."

"Steal the arrows?" Albie cries. "Shouldn't we be looking for the Knife Thrower at this moment, considering we just saw the guy?"

"He's gone," Austin says. "For now, I want my arrows back. How about we all just sneak behind them and grab a few at a time?"

I personally don't think that's a good plan. "W-wait!" I stammer, but Austin is already running.

He runs past Diana while snatching an arrow, but all the Administrators notice him. Diana grabs an arrow and threads it into her bow. She is posed ready to strike. Is this going to happen? Is Austin going to die? I didn't anticipate any of us getting killed by a fellow Contestant!

I throw a knife. It is not meant to hit Diana, but it does hit where I want it to. It splits the string of her bow in half.

"NO!" she bellows, knowing she can't use her bow anymore.

I run up to her with a knife. I cut the quiver of arrows off her, grab it, and run. Tiberius catches me and pushes me to the ground. I am still holding on to the quiver. Unfortunately, not all the arrows are in it. Most of them spilled out, and only two are left. Tiberius picks up most of them. All of a sudden, I see an ax heading toward Tiberius's head. He ducks right in time, but while it flies over his head, he manages to grab it. I run toward Austin. Tiberius stands in a way that makes him look very tough holding Albie's ax.

Austin has three arrows. He gets one out and is ready to shoot. "A-Austin!" I yell. "Don't shoot him!"

"I'm not going to shoot him. Just give me a second." He seems to be concentrating on aiming at something by Tiberius. Meanwhile, Jack tries to throw a knife at Albie, but she moves to the side just in time. Is this what the Administrators do? Kill kids?

Austin lets go of his arrow. It soars through the air and I'm pretty sure it's going to hit Tiberius right in the arm. But it doesn't—it hits the handle of Albie's ax. Because of the speed of the arrow, the ax flies out of his hand. I see Albie behind Tiberius and she swipes for the ax, kicking

Tiberius right in his mouth. I know Austin and Albie didn't plan that, so it's lucky that Albie just happened to be behind Tiberius right then.

I feel something all of a sudden. In my right arm. A stabbing pain. I pull out a small bayonet from my arm. It didn't dig in that deep, nor was it going that fast. It felt like a shot from the doctor. I see a little blood on my arm. I look behind me and see Jack. For some reason, he is holding Elena's slingshot. I used to think of Jack as just a bully, but he just shot a bayonet at me! He almost killed me! I throw my knife and it spins through the air. The knife carves a long open cut on his arm. "AGH!" he yells, and scurries away with the rest of the Administrators.

Tiberius then hands Elena a spear. She throws it at Austin. He spins his body to the left and shoots an arrow. It is about to hit Tiberius right in the stomach, but Elena pushes him down right before he gets hit.

For a moment nobody does anything. Then out of nowhere, Tiberius and Jack come running up to me and Austin. I can't even see where Albie went. Tiberius pushes me to the ground and puts his hand on my throat. I can't breathe! I put my hands on his wrist, pinching him with my fingers. He has no reaction to that, which is not a surprise. What would a little pinch do to somebody? I then kick up my leg and my kneecap slams Tiberius in the chin.

That gets him off me. I look over and see Jack strangling Austin. I kick him in the head, and he falls over. I help Austin up, and Albie appears next to us. "C'mon!" she shouts.

We dodge bayonets, knives, and spears that whiz past our eyes. Once we get to the elevator, Albie clicks on level thirteen, Austin and I are coughing, and I look over at his neck. It is bright red. I bet mine is the same. We run to my room. Right when we get to my room, I shut the door.

"Oh, my gosh! Did that all just happen?!" Austin roars.

Albie and I look at each other. "They shouldn't have tried to kill us just because we tried to take some arrows. They are literally psychopaths," she says.

"No kidding," I say.

"I…I…I…" Austin stammers. "I am going to go get myself some ice cream for my throat. Do any of you guys want one?"

"No," I say.

"No," Albie says.

"All right then," he says, still gasping for air.

When Austin leaves, Albie says, "Geez, what is their problem? I'll admit that if they stole axes from me, I would run to get them back, but I wouldn't try to brutally murder them. I mean, that's just crazy."

"I know. Well, at least Diana can't use her bow anymore because I broke it," I say victoriously. "*And* Grace and George saw the whole thing with the cameras they put in our eyes."

"Andrew."

"What?" I say, completely perplexed.

"George and Grace saw us start the fight," Albie says in a guilty voice.

"Well, they wouldn't mind if we stole arrows from the people who stole arrows from us. Besides, when we fought against them George and Grace saw how Diana took out her bow first. Our fighting was self-defense," I say.

"I guess you're right," Albie admits.

My Quillix suddenly rings. "That must be Grace or George," I say.

I answer. Before I even say a word, Grace says to me, "We do not think that fight was your guys' fault. We watched through your eyes with the cameras."

"Yes," George says. "They stole from you guys, so you stole back from them. You will also be happy to hear that the Administrators are now disqualified. They don't even know yet, but if one of the Administrators finds out who the Knife Thrower is, they are not winning the one million dollars."

"You guys are very intelligent," Grace says. "Most of the Contestants could never have made it out alive from the laser tag arena or Escape Room. I'm sorry you guys had to go through all that. George and I have never seen a Murder Mystery Race like this one."

"It's okay," I say.

"I wish you the best of luck," Grace says.

"We," George corrects.

Grace chuckles. "I mean, *we* wish you best of luck. The event at the casino with the whole roulette thing seemed so scary. Also, because George and I are responsible for you being in this position, whenever you get blackmailed, you come tell us if you need help getting something to the Knife Thrower.

"Thank you," I say. I smile a little bit.

"And...I have some unfortunate and sad news," Grace says, seeming disappointed.

"What's the sad news?" Albie asks.

"It's about one of the Contestants," Grace says.

"What happened?" I ask.

"One Contestant, Eric, unfortunately passed in the Escape Room," she says.

"Was he crushed to death?" I ask.

"No," Grace says. "I saw a man who seemed about five-foot-ten, with green eyes and brown hair. He killed him."

Albie and I look at each other; we both know that that has to be Ignatius.

"We know who that is," I say.

"Really?" Grace says. Her head pops up so fast that her fancy black hat and veil fall off, but it doesn't look like she even cares.

"Yes," I say. "His name is Ignatius Balquere. He is actually one of the people who we think is the Knife Thrower."

"I hope that barbarous man goes to hell," George says angrily.

"Us too," Albie adds.

"And did you see the other four men with him?" I ask.

"Yes," Grace says slowly. "What about them?"

"Well, we think that all of them could be the Knife Thrower," I tell her. "We don't have one main suspect."

"What are their names?" George questions.

"Kairos Kartyule, Silas Betailu, Carlos Bills, and John Bryans," I say.

"What?" Albie interjects.

"Okay," I say. "N-n-not the John guy."

"All right then," Grace says. "Thank you for your time. Where is Austin?"

"He went to get some ice cream," Albie says.

"Um, isn't it early in the morning for ice cream?" Grace asks, seeming bemused.

"Well, you *know*…because of that incident that happened this morning between Jack and him," Albie explains.

Grace nods and then there is silence.

I nod. "Well, bye for now," I say.

"Bye," George says.

"Bye," Grace says, giving a dismissive wave.

When we hang up, Albie says, "I'm wondering where Austin is. He's been gone for a while…."

"I don't think ice cream stands are open at such an early time," I say, wishing I had thought of that earlier.

Albie nods.

All of a sudden I hear a loud voice speaking. "Attention! Attention! Attention, passengers."

"Who is that?" I ask.

"The captain," Albie responds.

"Attention, passengers!" the captain booms. "It has been rumored that there is a killer on this cruise. We are turning around. Unfortunately, the cruise will be back at Palm Beach at 10:00 p.m. Thursday night. I am sorry for this news. When you get off the vessel your bags will be searched, but while we are still on the cruise look for a man who is about five feet eight inches tall. Do you hear that? *Male*. Five-feet-eight inches tall! Also, a magician was scheduled to give you all a good show at 9:00 p.m. on Thursday night. But that has changed slightly to 8:00 p.m. Goodbye."

"Well, we now have even less time to find the Knife Thrower," I say, with annoyance.

"Yeah, but I guess the cruise was supposed to be back Friday morning. It isn't really a big difference."

I nod. "So, we have four days left, including today, and we have most of Thursday."

"Okay," Albie says. "But again...where is Austin? It's been a while."

"Yeah. It has been a while," I say with worry.

"Do you think something happened to him?" Albie says quickly.

"No..." But the more I think about it, the more I realize that something could have happened to him. "The Administrators could have caught him."

"Don't be ridiculous," she hisses. "If one of the three of us gets kidnapped it would be you."

"What?" I say. "Why?"

"Hello—you're going to get abducted today, according to the wheel of punishment. From last night...at the roulette table. Remember?"

"Ohhhh yeah," I say, feeling like a total moron.

"Mhm...but maybe you're right. The Administrators obviously hate all of us because of what happened recently!" Albie sobs. "Oh, no, no, no, no, no, no! We have to find him!" She gets up and is already walking out of my room, holding three axes in her arms.

"W-w-what are you d-doing!?" I stutter.

"Finding Austin. You coming?"

"I mean y-yeah, of course I want to find him, but don't you think we should plan for what could happen?" I bellow.

"Noooo!" she whines. "We have to search every inch of the ship!" She walks out the door, and I follow her. Oy. This is annoying. I was hoping that maybe we could, I don't know—have a plan or something?

We searched for nearly the whole day! It is about 7:00 p.m. and we still have not found Austin. It is obvious that the Administrators did something to him, or the Knife Thrower killed him. Actually, I think that if the Knife Thrower found Austin he would be keeping him somewhere and planning on giving me a letter saying that he has him.

I am at the sundeck right now and the sun is setting. Nobody is out here. Since the captain's announcement this morning I have only seen about twenty people today. Everyone else is probably in their room dreading the moment they might die. I bet that all the room doors are locked. People are only eating from room service.

I have seen a few Contestants throughout the day. I met this one boy, Everton. He is seventeen and he seemed like a nice person. He doesn't have an ally. I offered him to be with me, Austin, and Albie, but he didn't accept. I even told him how Austin went missing. He wished me best of luck finding him. I saw him holding a few spears. Even though he was nice I felt a little scared during our conversations because of our height difference. He seemed over six feet tall, so I felt like a toddler when he would look down at me. He was like a giant compared to me.

Other than Everton, I have not seen a sign of many other Contestants. I find that very odd. It seems as if the Contestants are staying in their rooms now, but why would they? That would be dumb, because they knew that the Knife Thrower has been on the cruise since everyone got on.

All of a sudden, something swooshes right past my face. It's a spear. I turn left and see Tiberius. "You're next, punk!" he shouts.

I'm next for what? I throw a knife, but Tiberius blocks it with another one of his spears. Adrenaline races through my body. Am I about to die right now? I think about sprinting away, but no. Tiberius has me trapped. If I move one more step, he will throw his spear right at me. I grab another knife and throw it! It is flying right at Tiberius, but all he does is put his foot out and the bottom of the knife hits his shoe and falls down.

Tiberius gets ready to throw a spear, but all of a sudden, he freezes and falls down. Behind him are Elena and Jack. Baffled, I just get up and start running. Did Elena or Jack almost kill Tiberius? I don't know what to think. I run up to the waterslides.

"Andrew, stop!" Elena cries.

I don't listen. I start to go down one slide to get to another side of this ship. I'm getting very wet.

"*No!*" Jack yells. "Get back here!"

Based on their tone, they seem worried for me, but it's obviously a trap. Or maybe not, because it seemed like Elena almost killed Tiberius just now.

There are twists and turns in the slide, until suddenly I am headed straight toward sharp knives stuck into the slide. I hear Elena and Jack yelling, "Get out! Now! Stop it! Stop it! Stop it! Get back here!"

I am about to slide into a bunch of knives. Thinking fast, I grab a knife from one of the pockets in my jacket and stick it to the side! It jams into the side of the slide and I hold on to it tightly. Panting, I shout, "What do you want?"

I hear Elena's voice, "We betrayed Tiberius and Diana! We have been faking our alliance with them!"

"I know this is a trap!" I yell.

"It's not!"

I dive successfully over the knives in the bottom of the slide, but as I'm going down, I see something coming toward my face. An arrow! I quickly turn until I'm going down at a diagonal angle. Arrows keep shooting at me. I turn my head down and take cover. I don't even know how this is happening. This seems like a waterslide of death. I see another arrow going straight to my face. I move my head down just in time, but then something chokes me back. I look up and see the arrow hit the hoodie part of my jacket, pulling me back. While I am still going down, I take the arrow out of my hoodie. When another arrow comes at me, I use the arrow in my hand to deflect it. The arrow I throw hits the other arrow coming at me.

That was a close one.

I'm finally down the slide now, and Elena and Jack are standing at the bottom. "We told you not to go down the slide," Elena says.

"Why were you telling me to stop, though?" I ask.

"Because Elena and I want you, Albie, and Austin as allies," Jack says.

"You're kidding, right?" I say. "You and your murder squad tried to kill me this morning."

"You too," Elena argues.

"You started it," I hissed, so quietly that it was barely audible.

"Well, you guys are kleptomaniacs," Elena says. "I'm not even joking."

"What?!" I yell. "You guys stole from us first!"

"Anyway," Elena says, like I hadn't said anything at all, "Jack and I have been faking our alliance with Tiberius and Diana. We also didn't want you to go on the slide because of what you saw was in there. Tiberius set it up before he just tried to kill you, thinking you would run up there for safety, which you did.

"Really?" I say sarcastically.

Both of them ignore the question. Jack says, "Also, I think that Tiberius and Diana took Austin. Elena and I overheard them saying that they will start to kidnap Contestants so they have a better chance of winning the MMR."

"Do you know where Austin is?" I ask.

"No," Jack says.

"Stop lying," I say. "It's not like Tiberius and Diana knew that you guys were faking your alliance with them."

"We're not lying," Jack says.

"Are so," I say.

"No."

"Yes."

"No."

"Yes."

"Calm down," Jack snarls. He then throws a knife at me. He's not intending to kill me—just to cut a part of my skin thinking that will shut me up.

I catch the knife and throw it back at him, and it slices a little bit of his shoulder. I smirk at him.

"Ow! I don't know where Austin is!" Jack yells.

"Fine, I believe you," I say, annoyed. "And you're lucky I do, because otherwise the next knife would be at your throat."

"I guess we can try to find him," Jack says.

"Do you have any idea where Tiberius might be hiding all the Contestants?" I ask.

"No," Jack answers.

I suddenly hear an angry voice. "What are you doing with *them*?" I turn to where I hear the voice, and see Albie.

"They supposedly have been faking their alliance with Tiberius and Diana," I say. "They now want to have an alliance with us."

"Really?" Albie says, seeming shocked.

"Yes," Elena says.

"Fine," she says cautiously. "But, where's Austin?"

"That's what I asked," I say.

"We don't know," Jack says in a serious tone. "Diana and Tiberius have been kidnapping Contestants, then hiding them somewhere."

"How do you know that?" Albie asks.

"Elena and I overheard them talking about it," Jack answers.

"Where do you think all the Contestants are being hidden?" I ask.

"Unfortunately, that is a statistical question. They have been hidden all over this boat," Jack says. "I can't even think of where one Contestant could be hidden." He seems to be thinking deeply.

"Well, why don't we start looking now?" I suggest.

"That's not the best idea," Elena says.

"Why not?" I ask.

"Yeah," Albie agrees. "How else would we find Austin...and all the other Contestants?"

"Not *all* of the Contestants," Elena corrects. "We need to think of where they might be."

Thinking hard, I come up with an idea. "How about you two," I say, pointing to Elena and Jack, "just go to Diana and Tiberius and ask them about what you overheard about them hiding Contestants. They still think that you guys are all in an alliance together, right? They don't know anything about what is going on right now."

"That is wise, but they might suspect that we know something that was supposed to be *their* secret," Jack says in a guilty voice.

"What do you mean?" Albie asks.

"Well...when I overheard a little bit of their conversation, I opened the door to their room, and they might have seen the slightest bit of my head," Jack says slowly.

"Well...at least confront them," I insist.

"I guess that would still work," Elena says to Jack.

The two have a silent conversation with their faces by moving one eye in a certain direction, rolling and widening their eyes, tilting their heads back and forth, and giving each other ominous and peculiar glances. "Okay, yeah, that'll do," Jack says.

"Great," I say.

"But while you guys are in Tiberius's or Diana's room, Andrew and I will be outside in the hall listening to your conversation," Albie says.

I give Albie a look showing that I am a little baffled. I then say, "What happens if Diana or Tiberius get a glimpse of us? Then they would then hunt us down."

"But it would be four versus two," Elena reminds me. "We would win any fight we get in against them."

I nod. "And we'll need a signal," I say.

"*Why?*" Elena asks obnoxiously.

"Because when the door opens, Tiberius and Diana might see Albie or me, then attack. So, you need to somehow signal us so we know to move out of the way or to go down a different hall," I answer.

"He's right," Albie says, as if she is some leader out of the four of us, probably making Jack and Elena feel like total idiots. "How about you guys fake cough loudly?"

"Okay, we will," Elena says. "Now just follow us."

"Oh, and remember this. If Tiberius and Diana come across us, Elena and I will have to act like we are still in an alliance with them. Okay?" Jack offers. "Even at other points on this cruise, we will not show our alliance with you two if we ever spot Diana and Tiberius nearby."

"Okay," Albie says. She looks at me and shrugs. "I guess that's the best thing to do."

"Okay, thanks," Jack says.

"But if all four of us get in a fight with them tonight, you can no longer act like you're in an alliance with them," Albie points out.

"Well, yeah, of course," Elena says.

As we walk toward the elevator, I think, *Now my alliance with Albie and Austin has grown at least.*

14

The Rooms of Murder

When we get out of the elevator, Elena and Jack just stop walking. They seem a little confused on where Tiberius's or Diana's rooms are. They point in one direction, seeming like they vaguely remember where it is. They seem to be in a state of ambivalence. Jack clicks his tongue and whispers to Elena, "Do you know where to go?"

"This way," she says, then walks down the hall to the right.

I look on the doors to the rooms, and for some reason they aren't in order. There is 612, while next to it is room 633.

"What is all this?" I say, while walking slowly down the hall.

Everyone notices what I'm seeing and how all the numbers on the rooms are not in order. "W-what is this?" Albie says, seeming scared.

"I…I don't know," Elena responds.

"Are we hallucinating?" Albie asks.

We are not. I'm actually seeing things perfectly. I do not feel dizzy at all. I feel completely fine. I don't know why I wouldn't.

We all hear a scream then—a high-pitched scream from a lady. "Please help me!" we hear. We all look to the right, and down the hall we spot the lady screaming. Her door is open, and she seems frightened about what's inside her room.

"Oh God," she keeps screaming. "Please help me! My husband is dead. AH! PLEASE!" she screeches. "PLEASE, SOMEONE!"

The four of us run over to the lady. Elena puts her hand on her shoulder. "Are you okay, ma'am?" she asks.

"No, I'm not okay!" the lady cries. She then hits Elena's hand off her shoulder. "Look!" She points into her room, crying hysterically.

There is a man in there—around the same age as the lady—who seems to have been stabbed. The woman keeps sobbing and yells for a staff member to come.

"It's okay, it's okay," Elena repeats.

Elena gives her a hug, which calms her. "But my husband! My husband—"

The woman nudges Elena away from her and points to me and Jack. She pants, and her panting turns into big gasps. "You!" she cries. "You killed my husband!"

Jack and I look down and see our knives showing through our pockets. We look at each other in shock. Jack says. "Oh, holy—"

"Help me!" the woman yells in terror. She rushes away to the elevator, probably going to the sundeck to find a staff member.

When the elevator doors close Albie yells, "Great! Now, some old lady thinks that you stupid imbeciles stabbed her husband."

Jack and I sigh, feeling embarrassed.

"What were you two thinking?!" Elena exclaims. "Your knives were one hundred percent visible, and you guys didn't even notice!"

"Well, clearly, neither did you!" I argue.

"Well, not till now," she says with annoyance.

"Boys are literally so frustrating. They ruin everything," Albie says.

"Hey!" Jack shouts.

"What do you care about, anyway? You two aren't the ones in trouble," I remark. "Jack and I are."

"Ugh!" Albie scoffs. "Hopefully these two don't screw up anything again," she says to Elena. "Let's just get out of here before someone arrives."

"It seems like people already have," Jack says nervously. He points down the hall, and a bunch of police officers are running toward us.

There are four of them pointing pistols at us. "Put your hands up and don't move!" one shouts.

The four of us do the exact opposite. We run. As we are running, I say, "I never knew police officers can board cruise ships to do their job."

Yep," Albie says. She is about to say something else, but she is panting, running in zigzags like we all are so it is harder for the police to shoot us.

Something makes me shake for a moment. My feet stumble a bit. I look at my pocket and see a knife hanging there. There is a big dent in the blade. An officer must have hit it when he shot. Maybe they weren't aiming for me. Maybe they just wanted to destroy my weapon. Regardless, it is quite concerning that these police officers are shooting at kids, even if we seem like potential criminals.

Albie turns around for a split second. "What are you doing?!" I shout. I grab her wrist to pull her away from where the police are. She then throws an ax at one of them. It doesn't hit the officer, but it knocks the gun out of his hand.

She turns around and continues running. Albie and I start sprinting and pass Elena and Jack, who seem to be way out of breath. We run for our lives, praying that we don't get shot. I run so fast that I'm feeling a little *weird*. It's as if I'm flying, because my feet are hardly on the ground thanks to the big steps I'm taking. I sprint as fast as I ever have before. When I look to my side at all the rooms, they seem blurry because I'm running so quickly. That kind of gets me into a small state of hallucination. I close my eyes and shake my head rapidly, then open my eyes again. Thankfully, everything I see is normal now.

I try to think about how I got into this situation. All that was planned was for Jack and Elena to confront Tiberius and Diana about kidnapping Contestants. Now the four of us are running from police officers who are trying to kill us.

I start squinting. We run to the left, to the right, straight, and down all different hallways.

We've now been running for over five minutes. In that time the police officers have yelled and muttered things into their walkie-talkies like, "*Backup! We need backup*," and "*Code yellow emergency!*" and "*Copy! Do you copy?*" Jack and Elena pant as they run slower and slower. They seem to be crying. They are so tired and scared—or at least it seems like it. All of our breathing becomes louder and louder the faster and longer we run. My throat gets so dry that I start coughing, which makes me stumble for a moment. I am developing cramps in my stomach and thighs. I swallow, clear my throat, and start to pick up the pace.

My cramps get worse. Soon enough, Jack and Elena fall to the ground, completely exhausted. "NO!" Albie cries.

All four police officers are running so fast that they can't help themselves and they trip over Jack and Elena. Jack and Elena get up and sprint in the exact opposite direction from where Albie and I are running. The officers slowly get up and one yells, "You two get the adolescents. Travis and I will get the little ones!"

Albie has a backpack on that rumbles as she runs. While running, she unzips it and pulls out two large bronze knives. She tosses one to me. "Here!" she shouts.

I catch the knife. It is getting hard to breathe so I can't even respond back, but I manage a small nod, which she can understand means *thank you*. I don't even know where Albie got these bronze knives. I thought that Grace and George only gave her axes. Apparently, I was wrong about that, which doesn't even matter right now. We keep on running. The police officers roar at us to come back to them.

All of a sudden, Albie and I come to a dead end. We stand against a wall. Albie points the bronze knife at one of the police officers. I point my bronze knife at the other officer. The officers freeze and aim their guns at us. I whisper to Albie, "I have a plan."

"Well, do your plan now!" she whispers back.

I make myself look nervous. I start shaking and act as if I am flabbergasted. The two officers look at each other, seeming baffled. "The Knife Thrower!" I cry. I point to the left and the officers' eyes look to the left. "Run!" I shout.

We charge the police officers. They are so distracted that they don't seem to know what's going on. Albie and I push the officers down and we dash away.

We keep running to get as far away from the police as fast we can. As we run, Albie and I call out to each other things like "*Left*," "*Right*," "*That way*," and "*This way*." Sometimes even, "*Catch up! You're so slow!*"

Running at what feels like a gazillion miles per hour, Albie and I knock heads into two other people. "OW!" I shout.

I see who we knocked into. It's Jack and Elena. "Man!" Jack shouts. "Watch where you're going!"

"Sorry!" I say, in pain.

Everyone whines for a few minutes about how they are hurt so badly. "Well, at least we're all safe now," Elena says in relief.

We all nod. It takes me a couple of seconds just to get a little bit of my voice out because I need to get some air. Finally, when I feel fine talking, I say, "How long did it take you two to escape from the police?"

"Not long," Jack says. "What about you two?"

"Just a few minutes ago," I answer.

He nods. We all sit down in the middle of the hallway. "Don't worry, we'll find Austin soon," Elena promises.

I forge a smile to thank her, even though she didn't really do anything besides make me feel better. I then ask, "So, what do you guys think about the mixed-up room numbers?"

"I'm not sure," Albie says with bemusement.

After colliding heads, we're not even sure if our befuddled minds saw the numbers right. My head rocks back and forth, disoriented. When my eyes catch the bright light of a light bulb, I shut my eyes and shake my head.

"Are you okay?" Jack asks.

"Yes," I say. "Now, why don't we look around and see what's going on with the rooms."

We walk down different halls, and the numbers are still mixed up. As we walk past one room, something drips at the bottom of the door. A red liquid. "What is that?" Elena asks.

"I'm not sure," I say.

"Let's find out," Jack says gruffly.

"Are you suggesting we go in?" Albie asks.

"Yes, I am," Jack says resolutely.

"I'm not opening the door," I say, creeped out.

"Neither am I," Albie says, while backing away.

"I'm not," Elena says. She sounds surly.

"Fine," Jack says with annoyance. "I will."

He slowly starts opening the door. The door screeches. I can feel my heart pounding, and I wonder what lies in Room 49.

When Jack opens the door, he backs up. Elena looks at the room in shock, while neither Albie nor I can see what is in the room because of our short heights compared to Elena and Jack.

Albie and I nudge our way into the room. "What is it?" I ask curiously.

"Oh my gosh," we say at the same time.

One person is dead. There is a small amount of blood. Bleach covers the room. The bleach has a nasty smell; it makes me grimace in disgust. Not only because of the bleach, but because the room looks grotesque. I notice a piece of parchment taped to the wall. It says:

Killed room by room by room and Prosecutor by Lawyer by Judge by Guilty.
K. T.

"What's that?" I ask.

"I don't know," Albie says. "Some kind of hint about why the Knife Thrower killed this man and why the room numbers are scrambled up?"

"What could 'prosecutor by lawyer by judge by guilty' mean?" Jack asks.

"I'm not sure," Albie says with worry.

I think really hard about what this means and if it even hints at who the Knife Thrower is. My feet move carefully around in the pool of bleach in the room. I concentrate very hard. *Silas*. He's been in court many times. Not only because he sold drugs, but also for "accidentally" killing people while performing surgery on them. Or he could have also been trialed for the other murders he is suspected of. The people who died during his surgeries included his alcoholic father and ex-girlfriend. He probably hated most people in court, such as the prosecutor, judge, the jury, or even his lawyer, who may not have defended him well. He obviously hated the prosecutor who went after him in court. The judge, though. What did the judge do to hurt Silas? Silas served time in jail for selling drugs. The jury in that trial made the decision about whether Silas was guilty or not. If he wasn't guilty, he would for sure hate the jury. And his lawyer too, who didn't protect him enough so he would be found innocent.

Maybe Silas was innocent. In his case there could have been other people who were suspected of selling drugs. Silas could have been somewhere with those people. Therefore, he was a suspect in the trial, and he was found guilty of selling drugs, too. What if he got so angry that he became a murderer? Now, Silas wants to kill all lawyers, prosecutors, judges, or anyone who has been in a jury before. Is Silas the Knife Thrower? The mastermind killer?

I know how Silas could even find out who on this cruise is a lawyer, judge, or prosecutor (though not anyone who has ever been on a jury). This is because now, before a person gets on an airplane or a cruise, one piece of identification isn't enough. If you're employed, you have to have another piece of ID from where you work saying what you do. This is just so the people who work at airports and for cruise companies are certain about who you are. That change in the United States was made in 2039. It is just so weird how, back in the day, only one piece of identification was needed.

Back in the crazy room we all just found, Albie sighs. "I don't even understand this."

"Me either," I say, even though it's not totally true. The reason why I am not sharing my theory is because it could easily be wrong, and if everyone were to agree with my idea and it turns out Silas is not the Knife Thrower in the end, I will seem like a total idiot.

"Wait a minute," Jack says. "I have an idea. What if the Knife Thrower was falsely accused of something in a trial? Is that maybe why he might hate judges, prosecutors, lawyers, and jurors? Then, maybe he got so mad that he decided to start killing people."

And Jack just said everything in my head.

"Oooo," Elena says with excitement. "That might be true."

"That does make a lot of sense," Albie admits. "What if we narrow down people in Wayverlyn who have had a part in a trial? Maybe they know some things? Even if they were falsely accused of something. Even a lawyer, judge, or prosecutor."

Now, everyone is complimenting Jack for an idea I was supposed to say. Unfortunately, though, I had my chance.

"What do you think?" Jack asks me.

I shrug. "Yeah, I think it sounds good," I say with a little bit of annoyance.

"Why aren't you more excited about this?" Albie squeals.

"I am," I lie.

"Also, we still need to find Austin," Albie reminds us.

"Oh, yeah," Elena says. "I forgot."

"Now, does anyone know who in Wayverlyn has been falsely accused of something?" Jack asks.

I take a deep breath and calm myself down so I can resume my motivation for finding the Knife Thrower. I am going to tell them about Silas.

I tell everyone about him and mention how Austin told me about him.

"Also, any suspect for the Knife Thrower may not just be upset for being accused of a crime. They could have also been neglected by a loved one or have had a rough childhood," Albie adds.

"Silas was for sure neglected when he was growing up, because his father was an alcoholic," I add.

"That does make a lot of sense," Jack approves.

"I wish Austin was here," I say, the stress in my voice clear. "He probably has the most information about Silas. So, does anyone have any ideas on how to find Austin?"

"Not a clue," Albie says gloomily.

"Wait," I say. "I have an idea about what is going on with these rooms."

"What?" Elena asks.

"It says in the letter on the wall 'prosecutor by lawyer by judge by guilty,'" I say, while pointing to the letter. "What if the room's numbers were changed by the Knife Thrower and he is now after all prosecutors, lawyers, judges, and people who work in the court system? Why don't we try to find this guy's identification for where he works?" I ask.

"Okay, let's start looking around," Albie says.

We all snoop through drawers and under furniture. I find lots of clothes but nothing else. I'm starting to get a little annoyed. This guy must be protective of his identification, as if suspecting someone were trying to steal it...which now that I think about it, the four of us are kind of doing.

As I throw clothes on the floor from drawers, I see something a little thick in the side pocket of a backpack lying on the floor. I open the pocket and find the man's passport. His name is Jim Margelt. His identification for where he works must be in his backpack too, I figure. I find an iPad, an iPhone, and a lot of other expensive items. As I look through everything, I find a wallet. It must be where the guy's work identification is. I look through his wallet and find only a few ten- and twenty-dollar bills in it. No work ID. Not even a driver's license.

I then have an idea. I say, "I know where the work identification might be."

"Where?" Albie says, while bursting out of a pile of clothes.

"In the safe."

"In the safe?" Jack says, seeming confused. "That will take forever to unlock."

"Not unless we use Elena's slingshot," I say in a scheme-ish voice.

"Huh?" Elena says.

"I mean you shoot a bayonet at the safe, then boom, it opens," I say, feeling like a genius.

"All right. I'll try," she says hopefully.

She gets her bayonet ready to launch at the safe. As the seconds go by, her face gets a little red. Elena gets perfect aim, then boom! She lets the bayonet go from the slingshot.

Bang!

It bounces off. The safe doesn't open.

Elena scoffs. The bayonet only made a small dent in the safe.

"W-well, what do we do instead?" Albie says.

"Oh, I've got an idea," I say.

I go up to the safe. I pull out a small knife. I don't have many left. I shove it through the tiny seam of the small door. I give the knife a good jab. The door flings open and there is the safe. Open.

"Good job," Jack says, obviously impressed.

"Thanks," I chuckle. "Now, let's see what is in here." I take everything out of the safe and drag it onto the floor. I look at the stuff. There is a stack of money. We count it quickly. It equals $10,000.

"Whoa," Albie says, seeming shocked. "The guy must've got some big winnings at the casino."

"No kidding," I say, feeling a little jealous.

"Should we take it?" Albie asks.

"Take it?" Elena shrieks.

"Yeah," Albie says.

"Why?" Elena argues.

"The man's dead!" Albie exclaims.

"Fine," Elena says.

We all split the $10,000. We each get $2,500. Well, when I get my share of money, I feel very guilty, so I just put it back in the safe.

"So, what else is in there?" Albie asks.

"Let's see," I say. I move my hand around in the safe and I feel a card. "This must be it," I say. I pull out the card. It is black and it displays a picture of Mr. Margelt. We all read what it says. LAWYER AT KOPP & COHEN LAW FIRM. SINCE: 2039.

"He's a lawyer," I say, I stare at the card for a moment, familiar with the firm. I'm pretty sure that it is an extremely successful law firm that started in Pittsburgh by a man named Mike Kopp. I have relatives in Pittsburgh and my aunt works at that firm. I think my aunt mentioned that Mike retired and went to Naples, Florida to be a tennis instructor at a local tennis club.

"So, the Knife Thrower's goal is to kill all prosecutors, lawyers, and judges," Albie says.

"Yup," I say lightly.

"I still don't understand the mixed-up rooms," Jack says.

"Let's go to the other rooms and see if people are dead and find out whether they are a lawyer, prosecutor, or judge," I suggest.

"That sounds like a good idea," Albie says.

As we walk out of the room, I look to the right and see the four police officers who we recently just escaped from! I jump back into the room and we fall down like dominos. I shut the door quickly.

"Ow," Albie hisses. "Watch where you're going!"

"I just saw the cops that we escaped from a little while ago," I whisper seriously.

"Oh, shoot," Elena says.

"Don't worry," I say. "I don't think they saw me."

I hear voices outside. "Ay. You just see that kid who we chased?"

"Um, no, sir. What are you talking about?"

"Yeah, I didn't see no kid," another says roughly.

"I don't know, Martin. I thought I saw the young boy."

"Mmm, I don't think so. I would have seen him."

"I'm just gonna take a look in the room where I thought I saw the youngster."

"All right, but don't be annoyed when you don't find him."

"They're coming!" Albie whispers with worry.

"They'll see the dead body and messed-up room!" I whisper.

The officers come in. They see nothing except for a guy sleeping in his bed with a nice thick comforter on him. Some clothes are around the room, and bottles of wine are next to the pool of bleach. Lots of wine bottles.

"Huh?" one says, seeming baffled.

"Told ya," another says.

"Shut up!" the other one demands. "The guy must've gotten drunk with all this spilled wine."

"Let's get outta here."

"All right."

Once we hear the door slam, we get out of our hiding spots. I get out from under the dead man's body feeling like I was just suffocating. Jack burst out of a pile of clothes. Elena gets out of the cabinet under the sink. I hear an, "Ow!" She must've bumped her head on a pipe.

Albie then gets out of the closet. She had quickly put on an extra-large suit with a hat that covered most of her face and stood with the man's hanging clothes.

"Are they gone?" Jack asks.

"Yep," I say, relieved.

"Ugh, this suit made me feel like I was a million degrees warm," Albie says. She takes off the suit and is now in her normal clothes. She's sweating after being in an extra-large suit for less than a minute. I look at her in confusion for a moment wondering how she got so sweaty.

Elena comes out of the bathroom. "Ow, I hit my head on that pipe hard," she complains.

"I was under a pile of clothes," Jack adds.

"I was under a dead man's *body*," I add.

We debate for a while on who went through more pain in their tiny, narrow, uncomfortable hiding spot.

"Well, at least we found spots to hide quickly," Albie says thankfully. "Those cops are dumb. I would've looked around the room a little more considering the lights were on."

"Yeah," I agree. "Although the cops thought that the guy was intoxicated so they just left the room thinking that he will just be hungover tomorrow morning."

"Why don't we wait a few minutes so the cops can get away?" Jack insists.

"Good idea," I say, while rubbing my back because it hit part of the ground hard.

I know that Jack and Elena seem like nice people now, but because of all the things the Administrators had done to us before those two joined our alliance, I still don't like them that much. Although, I guess that Jack and Elena produced cogent reasons why they wanted to be in an alliance with us and ditch the other two Administrators. Shockingly, the alliance is going well, considering our circumstances. I bet that when I was going down the waterslide just a little while ago, Diana was shooting arrows at me. That doesn't seem quite possible because I did break the string in her bow. Unless she reattached it somehow. It would have to be a super tight string.

I feel something in my pocket and pull it out. Ah, it's the Satan Svare. I remember using that a lot in the laser tag arena. I should be using it more.

"How about we leave now," I suggest.

"Yeah, sure. I bet the cops are away by now," Elena says.

I slowly open the screechy door and look left and right just to double-check that no cops are nearby. I pull out a knife from my pocket and place it out in front of me, as if I am ready to fight someone. "Okay," I say, relieved. "No one is here."

We slowly wander down the hallway to room 273. We look in the room and see a dead woman. As we explore, we find out that she is from Carson, Nevada. She works at Trial & Mystery Law Firm. She has been working since 2042.

As we go on, we look through many rooms. There are dead bodies in most of them, with the same sign about killing room by room and those other words. In rooms 98, 553, 777, 63, 434, 364, 588, 203, 637, 616, 742, 302, and 252, the dead people inside were either a judge, prosecutor, or lawyer. I don't know, but something about the numbers triggers me for a moment.

Albie, for some reason, breathes heavily. She is grumbling, muttering, murmuring things very quickly. She seems very worried, as if she is having a feeling of anxiety. "Are you okay?" I ask.

"Yeah, yes, I am, totally. Why don't you think I would be? Of course I am. Why shouldn't I be?" she says quickly.

We stop walking and she starts panting. "Albie," Jack says in a serious tone. "What is wrong?"

"N-nothing."

"Yes, something is," Jack corrects.

"Okay, fine," she says. "Seeing all those dead bodies creeped me out so much," she says, while rapidly itching her arm for some odd reason.

"What have you been muttering the past twenty minutes when we've been searching for the rooms and walking down halls?" Elena asks.

"I was counting by sevens," she says nervously.

"Huh?" Elena asks, completely confused like Jack and me.

"I was counting by sevens," Albie repeats.

"Why?" I say slowly.

"I don't know, it just calms me down," she says awkwardly.

"Okay," I say. Something seems wrong, though.

Albie keeps counting by sevens. Minutes go on with her counting, while Elena, Jack, and I stare at her, or exchange looks of confusion.

All of a sudden, I feel like Albie's counting is related to the numbers. She has so far said 63, 98, 203, 252, 273, and 302. I realize that those numbers are rooms that dead bodies have been in and the dead people are either a prosecutor, lawyer, or judge! How does Albie know this? What is going on? What are the odds of this happening? Has the Knife Thrower somehow forced Albie to do this?

I signal Elena and Jack to get away so I can tell them my crazy thought. I do, and they gasp. I can tell they're both thinking for a second.

"Eh," Elena says. "I think that is just a coincidence."

"I don't know," I say with worry. "It seems a little..." I pause. "Suspicious."

Elena and Jack exchange doubtful looks.

I then remember something that might have to do with what's going on now. The afternoon before we went to the Escape Room, Albie said that she felt a pinch on her back. We ended up finding a letter that someone stuck on her that was probably the Knife Thrower. Of course, I thought it was weird that Albie felt a pinch when someone just put a piece of paper on her.

But what if the Knife Thrower put a quick shot in her or something like that that is making her like this? For giving us a clue meant for this time. To hint that all prosecutors, lawyers, and judges on this boat are being killed, but only in rooms that can be divided by seven. I have heard about studies that show seeing the color red makes you see the number seven. Could the Knife Thrower have put a quick shot into Albie making her see red in her brain at certain times? Then, maybe it would make her do something that had to do with sevens to give us a hint that murders of prosecutors, lawyers, and judges are only in room numbers that can be divided by seven. Albie even could've kept on saying seven, seven,

seven…numerous times. Then, when the needle went through her shirt into her back to hide what would have been a trickle of blood, the Knife Thrower stuck the letter on her back not just to give us a hint about the Escape Room but also to press on her back so the blood would be wiped away right on the back of her shirt! Oh my gosh. Could this be true? It makes a whole lot of sense.

I tell Jack and Elena about that, which takes a long time.

They both are very shocked after hearing my theory. "That does make a lot of sense," Jack says. "I just don't understand why the room numbers are mixed up!"

I look behind me, and twenty feet away Albie's back is to me, and I can hear very little of her muttering, murmuring, and grumbling of numbers that can be divided by seven.

"I'll tell you why the rooms are mixed up," I say confidently. "The Knife Thrower did it to make his killing easier!"

"What do you mean by that?" Elena asks.

"I mean, let's say all the rooms are in order. Number after number after number. The Knife Thrower is killing prosecutors, lawyers, and judges seven rooms apart, right? So, not that far away. But now that the room numbers are mixed up, the Knife Thrower has organized his killing. I guess the plaque for the rooms number is removable. Two room numbers that can be divided by seven would be about twenty rooms away from each other! Very far," I exclaim.

"I just don't understand why the rooms need to be far away from each other," Elena says.

"The purpose is so no one would catch him!" I say reluctantly, because Elena wasn't following what I was saying so well. "If the Knife Thrower sorted out room numbers that can be divided by seven and are far away from each other, he won't get caught. One kill there, one kill all the way over there. Okay, I think you guys get the idea what I am saying. Point is, if he just killed someone in every seventh room, then he would get caught because he would spend a lot of time in such a small area of space!"

"Ahh, that makes sense," Elena says. "Now, why again does he want to kill prosecutors, lawyers, and judges? He clearly has a grudge against them all, but why?"

"We went over that," I say, annoyed. "It's because we are assuming that the Knife Thrower was once falsely accused of a horrible crime. He may have gone to jail, or was probably very close to. We also assumed that he had a complex childhood and was neglected by a loved one. That is how you solve a mystery!"

"I guess that helps," Jack says, "but we need to narrow down a list of suspects."

"Okay, we'll talk more about that later, but first let's notify Albie about this," I suggest, and then we tell her everything.

"Oh my God," she says, as if she is about to burst out in tears, which seems like she might. "I was b-basically drugged!"

I was about to say, *Well, at least it gave us a hint about the Knife Thrower*, but considering Albie is just finding this out, I decide to just cheer her up. Plus, the more I think about it, the more I realize I should never say that. It would sound like I told her she was used or something, or she was acting weird, and unexpectedly getting a shot was useful. I would never say that.

"Well, we know now and you're okay, right?" Elena says hopefully.

"Yeah," she sniffles.

"Now, why don't we all get some sleep," I insist. "We've had a long day."

"What about your friend Austin?" Jack asks.

"Yeah!" Albie exclaims. "What about Austin?"

"We'll find him tomorrow," I promise. "Let's sleep in pairs in each room."

"I'll go with Albie," Elena says, probably because she wants to make Albie feel better.

"I guess Jack and I can go to my room," I say.

15

Room 800

Jack and I are in my room. Jack got his pajamas from his room. We both showered and brushed our teeth and are now in our pajamas. "So," I say, "what do you want to talk about?"

"I think your theory about the Knife Thrower's door system strategy was quite clever."

"Thank you," I say. "Now, I am starting to think that if the Knife Thrower did not go to jail or prison because he wasn't found guilty, why would he hate lawyers?"

"Well, when people are being accused of a crime and are on trial, they live in jail temporarily while the trial goes on. If they are found not guilty, then they are released," Jack answers.

"So, what's your overall point about that?" I ask.

"My point is they still could have hated that they were a suspect of a crime they didn't commit and that they had to stay in jail for however long the trial went on," he says. "And some trials can go on for months."

"So, how do you think we're going to find Austin?" I ask.

"I don't know," he says in a dejected voice. "But we will. Don't worry."

I smile.

We then hear a thundering voice from the overhead speaker. The captain. He says, "Attention, passengers! Attention! A woman on this boat reported the death of her husband just an hour ago. Not all evidence has been found for this mystery, but she said she saw two young children who look about ten to twelve years old and two adolescents. Two had knives sticking from their pockets. Also, the woman said that she saw a glimpse of an ax. Look for a girl who is about ten to twelve years old. Long brown hair and blue eyes who looks about four-foot-ten. Look for a ten- to twelve-year-old boy. Brown hair and brown eyes. About four ten, just like the girl. Then look for a girl, about fifteen to eighteen years old who has *dark* brown hair and green eyes. She is about five-foot-five. Also, look for a boy who looks about sixteen to eighteen years old. Black hair and blue eyes. He is about six-one. Report if you see *anyone* who looks like that. They are assumed to be working with the Knife Thrower.

"Murders have also been occurring left and right. Law-enforcement officials used to think that the Knife Thrower has been behind these kills, but maybe not anymore after learning that four kids could have murdered a poor, innocent woman's husband. It is assumed that these kids are not the Knife Thrower because photographs of him have shown he is taller than these kids, but they could possibly be working with him or just causing confusion. We have no video, fingerprints, or other evidence of their crimes, only witnesses, which is not good enough. Have a good night everyone. Stay safe."

"Well, we are now fugitives!" I exclaim.

"Ugh, we have to disguise our looks," Jack complains.

"What do you mean by that?"

"Like, wear big shoes to make us look taller...or we could share the truth."

"What do you mean by 'share the truth'?" I ask.

"I mean, we could go around telling everyone on this cruise when they're at the pool, mini golf course, ropes course, or casino that the four kids who the captain claims murdered some man are innocent. We need to convince people!"

"We can't start doing that quite yet," I say. "We have to find Austin."

"Okay, first we'll find him. *Then* we'll spread the truth and hopefully find out who the Knife Thrower is. We only have tomorrow, Wednesday, and most of Thursday to find the killer. We must find the Knife Thrower."

"All right," I say.

"Now, let's get some rest. I'll take the first watch," he offers.

"Okay," I say.

We turn out the lights and I plop down on the bed. I shut my eyes. Everything goes pitch-black.

The jury has found Andrew Mikaelson guilty of the murder of Owen Robbins, the judge says. I stand up. *He will be taken into custody*. The judge then bangs her gavel.

I wake up and realize that was a nightmare. Before I had that dream, there had been many rotations with the whole sleeping-and-guarding situation. Jack and I had switched off every hour and a half.

It is currently 8:00 a.m. Jack is sitting in the chair at the desk. "How'd you sleep?" he asks.

"Fine," I say.

"Elena told me that she thinks it's a good idea if we split up."

"What do you mean?"

"Well, we need to find Austin and the Knife Thrower. We were thinking that Elena and I look for the Knife Thrower and you and Albie find Austin."

I think about that for a moment. I really want to be the one to find the Knife Thrower, of course. Elena and Jack have already found a killer prior to the Murder Mystery Race. In fact, they have had several chances to participate in the MMR. I know Austin is more important, though. Even so, why can't Elena and Jack just be the ones to find him? Why does it have to be me and Albie? That is unfair.

I'm about to point that out, but I realize that if Elena and Jack find Austin, that could be a fatal decision. Austin has no clue about this whole new alliance. He would be confused and scared about why Jack and Elena ditched Diana and Tiberius. He might think it's a trap if Elena and Jack said they would help him escape the room.

"All right. Fine," I say, guessing this is for the best.

"Okay, great. Now, we're all going to meet at the sundeck in one hour. In that time, we need to go get some breakfast."

"Okay."

After breakfast, which was honestly boring with Jack, we go to the sundeck feeling tired. I bet Elena and Albie are really tired too. It's what happens when you switch off sleeping. I then see Albie and Elena. "Over here!" I shout. Jack and I wave and shout their names.

Finally, we get their attention. They jog over to us. "So, does everyone know the plan about the whole splitting up situation?" Elena asks.

"Yeah," I say.

"Okay, great. Where do you guys want to meet back at and at what time?" she asks.

"How about at 9:00 p.m. at the mini golf course?" Albie suggests.

"Sounds fine to me," I say.

"All right. See you guys at the golf course," Jack says, then gives a dismissive wave.

We all say bye, then split up. "So, where do you think we'll find hints on where Austin is?" Albie asks.

"Diana and Tiberius will probably give us some, but probably not right now during the day when people can see us have a big fight with them or something like that," I answer.

"Well, we need to look for the Knife Thrower now because we already have so many hints about him and who it could be. On the other hand, searching for Austin might not be successful until we get any hints."

"Okay, then let's start looking for the Knife Thrower," I say.

As we walk around the cruise looking for anything suspicious, I have a knife in my hands ready to throw when I catch sight of the Knife Thrower.

As we approach the golf course, all of a sudden Albie starts tapping my shoulder. "Hey! Hey! There!" She points near the booth where they hand out clubs, balls, and score cards. There I see Diana and Tiberius purchasing a golf club. I can see something engraved on it that I cannot make out.

"This is perfect," I hear Diana say excitedly.

"Yeah," Tiberius agrees.

Albie and I look at each other in confusion. "What are they talking about?" Albie asks.

I shrug.

"Okay," Diana says. "Let's bring it to the room."

"Let's follow them," Albie suggests.

"Okay," I say. "I think they might be going to one of our rooms. It might be something that has to do with Austin."

"Yeah, I bet so," Albie says.

We follow Diana and Tiberius to the stairs. They go down a few levels, and we see them walking to my room.

Albie and I look at each other in shock and nervousness. As I walk closer to them, Albie says, "Stay back! You don't want to get in their sight."

"Okay."

We crouch down about ten yards away from my room and watch them go inside. After a few minutes, Albie whispers to me, "What do you think they could be doing that's taking so long?"

"I don't know," I say.

"We'll find out."

Diana and Tiberius eventually leave my room giggling. "This is probably some stupid prank," I say, with annoyance.

"Eh, I think otherwise. Whatever is in your room is something important," Albie says.

We slowly walk to my room. So slow that I can feel my legs shake. Like an earthquake ready to explode through my body. Albie notices my shaking. "Calm down. I'm sure we'll be fine," she says.

Truthfully, I don't think we'll be fine at all. When we get into my room, we see something on my bed. "What is this for?" Albie says in disgust.

"I don't know," I say, gaping at what's on my bed. It's a golf club—the one Diana and Tiberius bought at the mini golf area. There's a bright red ribbon tied around the long, expensive-looking club. Something is engraved on the club. I can see it clearer now.

It's the number 800.

"What could this mean?" Albie asks.

"We might need to go somewhere that has to do with…I guess the number 800?" I guess.

"Okay…I'm trying to think of why eight hundred is significant," Albie says deeply.

"I know!" I say. "The room eight hundred. That's where Austin must be."

"Are you sure?" Albie says, looking at me as if I am the most stupid person in the world.

"We might as well go check," I say.

"I don't see why not," she responds.

I slowly peek out of my room, scrutinizing every angle around me to make sure Diana and Tiberius aren't there.

"Is anyone out there?" Albie asks.

"No," I say. "I don't think so."

We slowly creep upstairs and go down halls to find our way to room 800.

Once we get to room 800, I slowly open the door. I see Austin. He's strapped to a chair with thick rope and has duct tape covering his mouth. Obviously because of the tape I can't make out what he is saying, because all I hear is "MMMMM! M-M-M-M-M-M-M!!!! MMMMMMMMMM-MMMM!" He twitches his head around and shakes it many times.

"I'm gonna get you out, don't worry," I say. "Don't worry!"

I pull out the bronze knife Albie gave me last night and cut the ropes. Finally, Austin is out of the chair. He rips the piece of thick tape off his mouth. He gasps for some fresh air. He coughs. He has a big red rectangular-shaped mark above his chin, under his nose, and over his mouth.

"Come on," Albie says. "We need to get out of here."

When we turn around to the door to get out, I see Diana and Tiberius. "Going somewhere?" Tiberius asks.

After a few seconds, I run and slide under Tiberius's legs. Albie and Austin run and slide under his legs too. Diana and Tiberius attempt to chase us, but I slam the door. It seems to collide with both of their heads. We run as far as we can, but Austin is way ahead of us. He seems to be running faster than a cheetah. Albie says to me, "Um, how is he so fast?"

"I don't know," I say. "It's kind of weird."

"I have never seen a human run so fast in my entire life," she says, seeming astonished.

Albie and I try to run faster so we can catch up to Austin. Finally, after many turns, going down flights of stairs, and sprinting through hallways, we stop. "Are you okay?" I ask Austin.

He nods. "Yeah, I'm fine."

"Did they do anything to you?" Albie asks.

"No," he says. "Nothing, but just kept me strapped in a chair with duct tape covering my mouth."

"At least you're safe now," I say, relieved.

"Yeah," Albie agrees.

"Anything happen while I was gone?" Austin asks.

Albie and I make eye contact, then exchange looks of tiredness.

We explain the whole situation to Austin. Everything about Jack and Elena. The woman whose husband was killed. How Albie, Jack, Elena, and I are prime suspects of a murder and the captain's announcement about searching for us. How we think that the Knife Thrower had a hard childhood, was neglected by a loved one, and was once accused of a crime he didn't commit. We went on about the mixed room numbers. We talked about why the Knife Thrower hates all prosecutors, lawyers, and judges. It gets a little tiring speaking so much. We mainly focus on being chased by the police officers. We said that it was so psychotic, brutal, and terrifying. We said how Diana and Tiberius hinted to us that he was in room 800 and how it was a trap.

"So. That's it," I say proudly.

"Wow," Austin says, seeming flabbergasted. "I never knew that so much could happen in such little time."

"You never know what can happen. But we're not done with the mission of finding the Knife Thrower," I say firmly. "We still have the magician Thursday night."

"Now, let's try to find Jack and Elena," Albie says. "They will be happy we found you."

Austin backs up, still a little scared of the other half of the Administrators, which I don't blame him for. He didn't leave off on a good note with them before he got abducted.

"Come on. They're fine," I say, talking about Elena and Jack.

"Okay," Austin says bravely.

We wander around the gigantic cruise ship. We're on the sundeck and I see Elena and Jack about sixty feet away. "Hey!" I shout. "OVER HERE!" I put my hands up as high as I can and jump as high as I can to get their attention.

"Andrew?!" Jack shouts.

I wave them to come over.

"You found Austin!" Elena says happily. "Are you okay?"

"What do you think?" he hisses.

"What's wrong with him?" she asks.

"Well, as you know, he didn't really leave off on a good note with you guys before his abduction. So, you can't blame him for disliking you," I say while shrugging, because if I were Austin, I would have done the same exact thing.

"Are you okay?" Jack asks.

"Yesterday you strangled me. Why do you think I would want to even talk to you?" Austin snarls.

Jack puts his hands back as if Austin is going to harm him, which unfortunately he might. Austin seems to be flushing with anger and building up fury in his head, planning on how he wants to attack Jack. Austin's face turns bright red. Crimson. He then punches Jack in the face.

"Hey! What's wrong with you?" Jack says.

"Okay, okay, okay, okay, let's not fight right now," Elena says.

Jack and Austin give each other nasty looks that seem to mean *I will kill you later. I am not even kidding.*

I whisper to Austin, "I don't blame you for throwing that punch, but maybe when we're in public and need to find a murderer, it isn't the best time."

"Okay," Austin says, annoyed. "Fine."

"Okay, now, try to relax a little bit," I say. "That should be good for you."

"Good for me?"

"Whatever."

"So, what should we do now?" Elena asks.

"Start looking for the Knife Thrower," Albie says in an obvious tone. "How about we all split up?"

"Okay, let's plan to meet at the ropes course this evening?" I suggest.

Everyone agrees to do that. I start my way to the casino. I remember the Knife Thrower said in his letter that he likes to be at the casino when he isn't killing people. I'm not exactly sure if he is killing someone now, but I might as well check the casino. I start to feel butterflies fluttering in my stomach. I don't even know why. I don't feel nervous, shocked, or terrified at the moment. I just feel like I have a stomachache.

When I arrive at the casino, I wander around for a little bit trying to find anything suspicious. I look over at the blackjack table and I see Silas, John, Kairos, Ignatius, and Carlos. I walk over there. There is one seat left. I try to look confident when I approach the table of what could be crazy murderers. "Hello," I say as I hop in the seat.

No one responds except for the dealer, who says, "Hello, young man."

The five murder suspects just look at me.

I notice a big bandage wrapped around Ignatius's leg. I decide to leave after I spot that, because for some reason it creeps me out. I look around the casino. Some adults are drinking alcohol while I bet other people haven't even had breakfast. Craps is a very popular game. Many people are playing it. There seems to be hundreds of slot machines, and at least two people are at every machine. I don't get why people blow their money on slot machines. They are rigged. When playing poker or blackjack, you use your mind, and you actually have a better chance of winning. I bet no one so far on this cruise has won twenty bucks or more from a slot machine. But that isn't really important to me. I guess I am not the one wasting money in a dumb machine. Not many people win big from slot machines.

I don't find any suspicious things about anything really. I just hope to find the Knife Thrower. Time is running out. Maybe George and Grace were wrong. Nobody might capture the Knife Thrower. Nobody! Saying that to myself gets me thinking that I unfortunately might not win the Murder Mystery Race. But so far, I have made friendships that will last forever. Some are really close to my age and some aren't. I know this whole Murder Mystery Race thing has been a scary journey, but also one that makes me proud for surviving it so far.

If I win, I can only pick three people to participate in next year's Murder Mystery Race. I wonder who I would choose. They all have been great friends. Actually, I don't want to get ahead of myself, because who knows if I will find the Knife Thrower, but I sure hope so.

16

The Knife Thrower

I am supposed to meet Elena, Jack, Albie, and Austin at 9:00 a.m. at the Pancake Hub diner. Yesterday, on Wednesday, nothing much happened. There were no corpses found and nothing sketchy. I brush my teeth and change my clothes. I look at the big bronze knife I have. Something tells me that I will be using it tonight...something in my brain, heart, and soul.

After spending a lot of time worrying about what awaits me today, I leave to go to the Pancake Hub. I don't need a sweet and fluffy pancake in my body. Or greasy, oily bacon. That would make me nauseous, and I would probably end up hurling all over the diner. I honestly don't feel very hungry. My stomach is still tied in knots that feel unknottable.

The Pancake Hub is on the tenth floor, where mostly everything is. Well, except for the mini golf course, ropes course, pool, and waterslides that are on the sundeck.

I walk down a flight of stairs to get to the tenth floor, and for a moment I stop. I stand there scrutinizing every single person. I don't know why. Maybe because I think someone in my sight could be the Knife Thrower.

I walk into the Pancake Hub and see the image of a pancake on a big menu at the front of the restaurant. It makes my stomach queasier than it was. I see a few people waving to me at a table. They're all smiling: Austin, Albie, Jack, and Elena. I walk over to them and take a seat.

"How did you guys sleep?" Albie asks.

"I slept okay," I say.

"Me too," Austin says wearily.

"Me too," Jack says tiredly.

"All right, so what are you guys ordering?" Albie asks.

"I'm going to look at the menu for a little longer," Elena says.

"Me too," Austin says.

"Me too," Jack says.

As the meal goes on, I stay quiet. I wonder how Uncle P's CIA trip is going. I think he is flying home tomorrow. As for me, I don't know what my plan will be for going home.

As I walk out of the restaurant, I see a familiar face. Ms. Rolenstein. My teacher. I start to walk in a different direction so she doesn't catch sight of me, because who knows if she saw my mother before she left town to go on this cruise.

"Andrew?" I hear.

Uh-oh. That's Ms. Rolenstein. I start speed-walking away, but I can hear the clicking of footsteps jogging behind me.

She gets ahead of me and turns around. I look down. "Hi, Andrew," she says happily. "What are you doing here?"

I ignore the question and keep staring down.

"Right before I left for my flight to Palm Beach I went to a diner for an early breakfast, and I saw your mother there and she said that you were at a lake house. What are you doing here?"

I need to come up with an idea for how to get away. I do. I say, "Excuse me?"

"What?" Ms. Rolenstein asks.

"My name is not Andrew," I say. "It is Josh, and I don't know who you are."

"Oh, okay," she says, embarrassed.

"I'm sorry," I say.

"Okay, then," she says, a little mystified. "Bye. Sorry for the mix-up."

"Bye," I say.

As I walk away, all of a sudden I hear Ms. Rolenstein's voice again, which makes me stop. "Yes, this is," responds a familiar voice from the phone. After a moment I realize it is my mother!

I am just a few steps from Ms. Rolenstein so I stop and I take out my Quillix to make it seem like I stopped to focus on something, when really I am trying to listen in on this phone conversation. I hear a voice on the phone that I recognize is my mother. "Hello, how are you?"

"Good," Ms. Rolenstein answers. "I just saw a young boy on the cruise I am on, and it looked exactly like your son, Andrew."

"It can't be him," my mother says. "He is at that lake house right now with his step-uncle."

"He might be lying to you, Jamie," Ms. Rolenstein says with worry. "I'm sure it was him."

"All right then," my mother says. "I'll call his step-uncle and find out what is going on."

They hang up and I feel so nervous.

A moment later I hear Ms. Rolenstein's voice again. "Hello, Jamie."

"Hello, Karry," my mother answers. "He is okay. Andrew is tubing right now."

"Oh, okay," Ms. Rolenstein says.

"Thank you for checking, though," my mother says kindly.

"No problem."

They hang up, and I get away from my teacher as quickly as I can.

The day goes on, and we are all very excited to see the magician. Well, actually, not exactly excited, but we know that the Knife Thrower will be there. After breakfast, everyone goes on about their delicious food, except for me, who got nothing.

"So, what is the plan for today?" Elena asks.

"I think we should look around for anything that might have to do with the Knife Thrower. We could also meet at my room at 7:50 p.m. and get ready to see the magician," I say.

"Magician?" Elena says, confused.

I realize I forgot to tell Jack and Elena about the magician. Or maybe I did, and they just forgot. "Oh, before we became an alliance, we found out that tonight we're seeing a magician," I say.

"Oh, interesting," Elena says. "But why?" she says, seeming bemused.

"We think that the Knife Thrower will be there," I say. "Most likely."

"Well, then we'll all be another step closer to finding him," Jack says.

The day goes on. Lunch was okay. I had a hot dog—which was very greasy—and a lot of water. Then, I looked around for Carlos, John, Kairos, Silas, and Ignatius. I am prepared to reveal tonight that one of them is the killer. I will catch him. I *know* I will.

* * *

It is now about 7:30 p.m. Elena, Jack, Austin, and Albie should be here soon. I throw everything back in my backpack carelessly. Underwear touches quarters, and many other odd things are touching each other. I just showered, which was nice, except for the bit of shampoo that got in my eyes. I start to get very hyper for some reason. My heart beats quickly. I'm getting a little nervous for tonight. Well, not a little. Very. I'm very nervous about what might happen tonight.

I hear a knock on my door. I open it. It's Austin. "Oh, hi. Come in. Nobody else has arrived. You came here pretty early."

"Yeah, well, I had nothing else to do. Are you scared?" he asks.

"For what?"

"The magician thing. Tonight, I feel like a big event will happen," Austin says confidently.

I have been thinking the same thing throughout the day. It is the last night on the cruise, and the Knife Thrower knows about the Murder

Mystery Race. Something crazy will strike. I just feel it. "Yeah," I agree. "I have actually been thinking the same thing throughout the day."

"Really?"

"Yeah. I think it's because tonight is the last night of the Murder Mystery Race." I notice a backpack on Austin. "Oh, did you pack already?"

"Yup."

"Me too."

Once the clock turns to 7:50 I hear a knock on my door. I open it. Albie, Elena, and Jack are standing there with backpacks on. They must've packed up too. "Are you guys ready to go?" Albie asks.

"Yep," I say. "Come on, Austin."

The five of us walk down the stairs to get to the tenth floor. We walk in silence. The only noise is our footsteps, heavy breathing, and hearts racing. "So, where is the magician performing?" Jack asks.

"I didn't think of that," I say. I then spot a staff member. "Um, excuse me," I say to the woman.

"Yes, dear?" she responds cordially.

"Would you happen to know where the magician is performing?"

"Yes. It is where bingo is." She points to a big door where I see the illuminated word Magician.

"Thank you," I say.

"No problem at all," she says happily. "Enjoy the show."

"We will!"

The five of us head to the big doors, and when we open them we see a big room. There seems to be about 150 seats and a big stage with a man off to the side of the stage. He is wearing a black hat and has a table in front of him with many supplies on it. He also has a curtain. A few feet next to him is a square that seems a little cracked with duct tape around it.

We see a woman who is telling everyone where to sit. "Hello," Albie says to the woman. "May we get five seats, please?"

"Yes, of course. A-and what are your names?" the woman asks.

"Albie, Andrew, Austin, Jack, and Elena," Albie answers while pointing to who is who.

"I will put you five in the farthest row back," the woman says. For some reason she leads us in a way that makes sure I get a seat right in the middle of everyone, which makes me feel safer. "Have a fun time," she says in delight.

After a few minutes of my heart racing, the lights turn off. I hear a voice thundering from a microphone. "Ladies and gentlemen, get ready to see the one and only Fred Gotherson!"

Spotlights hit the stage and there is the magician bowing. "Ah, thank you, thank you, thank you, everyone," Fred says.

There are many claps throughout the audience.

Fred begins his act with some adult jokes. He then starts his first trick. He makes roses come out of his mouth, which was fascinating. He makes cards disappear, then reappear in what everyone thought was his empty pocket. He laughs at his own tricks. He makes a fancy black scarf float in the air. He asks someone in the audience to name a card, only to find it in his shoe. He makes half a dozen birds fly out of his hat, then go back in a cage.

Fred is a pretty good magician. His tricks are very impressive and he's very humorous. It is very entertaining. I don't think I've seen a better magician than him in my life.

I look over to my right and glance at Jack's watch. It is 8:50. With all the tricks Fred has done I can't believe it's only been fifty minutes! That's how many tricks he's done.

"Now," Fred says in a way to get the audience excited, "I am about to present the final trick. I will make one of you in the crowd disappear."

There are many "oooohs" throughout the crowd.

"Oh, calm down," Fred says in a teasing way. "Now, one of you guys. One! One! One of you guys has a red envelope under your seat. Check under your seats."

Everyone bends over. I look under my seat, and there I find the red envelope. Albie, Austin, Jack, and Elena look so shocked, just as I am. I remember last week when Grace told me not to ever volunteer for a trick, but I can't help myself. I shout, "I HAVE THE RED ENVELOPE!"

Some people look at me with excitement, while others envy me. "Come up here to the stage!" Fred shouts. "Come on! Don't be shy!"

I walk to the stage with the red envelope. I can feel myself shaking, but I need to take a deep breath and just calm down. I forge a smile as I walk onto the stage with lots of people in the crowd cheering. Fred moves the microphone to my mouth. "What is your name?" he asks.

"Andrew Mikaelson," I answer.

"And how old are you, Andrew?" Fred asks.

"Ten," I say shyly. I can feel the big bronze knife in my jacket pocket, and for some reason I think about it for a moment.

"Well, would you do me a favor and stand right here?" Fred asks. He moves my body to an area lined out with duct tape lines. Fred moves ruby-red curtains in front of me and no one can see me.

"Well, folks, watch this! I am about to make young Andrew here *disappear*." He then leans over to me and whispers, "Relax. Stay where you are the whole time and don't move." He then turns to the audience and says, "3-2-1!"

What I am standing on moves down. Like an elevator. It goes left and right. What is going on? I am standing on a floor that is moving around, and it is pitch-black. It feels like part of an elevator going to the sundeck. I don't even know how.

I then see the Knife Thrower with his black mask on, one knife in each of his hands. I take out my bronze knife from my jacket pocket. Slowly. The Knife Thrower then throws a knife at me! What is going on? I should be in the bingo room reappearing in Fred's trick. I duck so the knife doesn't hit me. I roll under the Knife Thrower, and in that time, I go for a slash with my knife. It cuts right through his pants, leaving blood trickling. The Knife Thrower growls like an angry bulldog. I have my bronze knife pointed at him. He then pulls out a bronze knife from his pocket and we start slashing at each other.

I whack my knife around trying to cut his face, but he ducks every time. I then slice a cut on his wrist as he sends a screech out of his lungs. The Knife Thrower then throws a knife. I duck, but because my back is at a diagonal angle it cuts a bit of my shoulder. I fall back, and when the Knife Thrower runs to tackle me, I kick him right in the chest! As he falls back, he seems so startled, as if he skipped a heartbeat, which I think he might have.

I draw a hunting knife from my pocket and throw it! I aim for the Knife Thrower's shoe so it will hit his foot to prevent him from walking, but he avoids the throw and the knife sticks in the ground. He quickly picks it up. We pace around, hissing at each other, ready to attack at any moment. He throws a knife straight at me, but I lean to the right just in time. He laughs at me, probably thinking I am weak. We hold our bronze knives and try to slice each other with them but dodge it every time. I then roll under his legs and lean up and get a good kick in his back. He quickly gets up and throws a knife that is going straight to my forehead. I lean back and the heavy knife zooms over my head.

He throws another knife that spins in the air, ready to slice the skin of my left arm. Right before it is about to hit me, I catch it on the blade with my left hand. Miraculously there is no blood from my hand—just a sting. I throw the knife back at him, but he easily dodges it.

We stare at each other. We're seven feet apart and ready to attack one another. I pretend to throw a knife. The Knife Thrower moves and right then I throw the knife and it zooms over his shoulder. I may have just lost another knife in this fight, but I have to keep fighting. Adrenaline is living in me right now. The Knife Thrower throws another knife at me, and I jump to the left to avoid the fast-coming blade. We stare at each other, planning on when to attempt a kill to end this crazy fight. He throws another knife at me. I catch it on the handle. *Ha-ha*, I think. I smirk at the Knife Thrower, which fills him with anger. He comes charging at me. I move just before he runs into me and I kick out my foot, tripping him.

Here is my moment not to kill him, but to injure him and find out the truth of everything. In seconds I have so many thoughts before I throw a knife. I aim. I put my hand out and throw the knife! It glides through the air, then stabs in the Knife Thrower's left arm. Sharp red blood pours out of his wound.

I dash over to him and pin him down on the ground. I look through his black leather jacket for any knives. Any knife I find I throw over into the Atlantic Ocean. We're near Palm Beach. I see land! But that is not my main focus right now. "You're coming with me!" I snarl.

I can barely see his face, but I can tell worry lives in his eyes. I sit him down on a chair at the pool. I stand in front of him, pointing a bronze knife at him, implying that if he moves, I will throw it at him. The Knife Thrower breathes rapidly.

"Take off the mask!" I demand.

The Knife Thrower takes off his mask, and there I see Jonah.

How could this be true? There is no way! How? What?!

"You were meant to die on this cruise," Jonah says.

"There is no way this can be true," I say while trying to hold back my tears, which is a tough challenge.

I then realize how it all made sense. Jonah was good at knife throwing because he always did ax throwing, which wasn't much of a difference. He never practiced throwing knives because he knew it would be suspicious. And growing up with a bad childhood—when Jonah was a kid his parents got divorced, and I remember him telling me that he had a cruel stepfather, which is what he has now become. Also, he had been falsely accused of something. Jonah was almost put in jail for murder. This is why he hates prosecutors, lawyers, and judges. Then, he had been neglected by a loved one. I neglect Jonah. I never cared for him, I have a rude attitude toward him, and I talk back to him.

I take a deep breath and say, "Fifteen years ago when you were accused of murder, did you murder the person?"

"No," he says. "The prosecutor did, yet he was the person accusing me in court. Only I knew, but no one believed me. That is why I killed Mr. Smith. He was the prosecutor. I murdered the rest out of anger."

"Okay, now, I'm sure you know who Grace and George are. Would you like to share how they know you are the Knife Thrower?" I ask, still holding back my tears.

"They once saw me murder someone. I tackled them and put the cameras in their eyes they put in you so I could see what they were doing. I told them that if they dare to ever tell the police I would kill them. It was the only thing I could do so my secret of who I really am wouldn't get revealed," Jonah says. "But congrats—you found me."

I don't respond.

I think for a moment. "Wait…what about John, Carlos, Kairos, Silas, and Ignatius? With the whole Escape Room thing? What's that about?"

"I drugged them," Jonah says, in an obvious tone.

"What?" I say, shocked and confused.

"I drugged them," he repeats.

"W-what do you mean you *drugged* them?" I ask, completely confused.

"I abducted all five of them. I forced them to do things. I forced them to take medicine."

"What medicine?"

"Two types. One that makes the human body hyperactive and one that makes people hallucinate. They thought in the Escape Room that knives were dodgeballs and you guys were playing a friendly game of dodgeball. I know you're shocked, but it's true."

"What about that day when we spied on Carlos and John?" I ask. "Does anything have to do with that?"

"Yes. Before I had rounded up all the guys and forced them to take the medicine, John and Carlos hated you and me for spying on them. If you got in their sight, they would go crazy."

"And what about you mainly murdering judges, prosecutors, and lawyers on this cruise," I say. "I know you hated them for their jobs, but they all couldn't have been involved in your trial. So, what was the need to even kill them? They're innocent. They have done nothing to you."

"Those kinds of people have accused innocent people in trials or didn't defend them well in trials. They're all like that. All of them!" Jonah snarls.

"Well, when you're a suspect of a murder, I hate to tell you this, but you go to court and are either found innocent or guilty. That is a part in lots of people's lives unfortunately, and you handled it very poorly," I say with a surly tone.

"What'd you expect? Me not to be angry for being accused of a crime I did not commit?" Jonah asks, while giving me a questioning look.

I don't answer him. "I could just kill you now. If you didn't know, you have no knives on you, and you are sitting in a chair while I have a big bronze knife pointing at you. And I will not get in trouble with the police. If I do, I still will never regret killing you."

"Okay, then," Jonah says. "Kill me!" I just stand there perplexed. "Go on. Kill me." I do nothing. "Yes, that is what I thought," he sneers.

"Tell me this too," I say. "Why was the red envelope under my seat at the magician show?"

"I told the lady who seated you that I was a part of Fred's show. I put the envelope in a certain spot and told her to seat you there. I told her that you are my son and that you'd love being involved with a trick."

"I'm your stepson," I correct. I'll never let him say we are part family unless he uses the word "step," but now that I know his true identity, I don't want him to be a part of our family at all. "Also, Grace and George said that you told someone that you were going on a cruise to start murders and you made it sound like you're working with him. Who is this person?"

"A police officer. We worked together for a little while. Then I killed him. We fought over who would get to do most of the killing."

I realize that I forgot to ask about the abduction from the wheel of punishment. I also realize Tiberius and Diana could have been working with Jonah. They abducted kids on this cruise. "And what about the abduction that was supposed to happen? Were you working with Tiberius and Diana?"

"Yes. On the first night, only those two were together at one point and they found me. I begged for mercy, and they showed mercy. But then they wanted to commit murders with me and do kidnapping."

Oh my God. Is that true? Contestants from the Murder Mystery Race working with the Knife Thrower? I am speechless.

We sit there in silence while I point my bronze knife at him. I think about how crazy this is. What will my mom think? What will Uncle P think? I feel like this is a dream, but unfortunately it is not. Jonah is the Knife Thrower. Out of all people, who would even suspect him? I hope he gets the death sentence for his crimes and burns in hell. Jonah, who I remember as the too kind, outgoing, friendly, mature person, has all this time really been a crazy killer. A psychopath whose soul does not deserve mercy from God.

I hold back my tears. Jonah can see in my eyes that I am in pain and that I am hysterically crying in my head. I am dreading this abhorrent, scary, and worst moment I have ever felt in my entire life. Who knew this is what was going to happen? Who knew that I would be screaming in my head after finding out who the Knife Thrower is? The plain answer is, no one.

I am waiting for Albie, Austin, Elena, or Jack to come and see this. They might not know who Jonah is, but I need someone to comfort me right now, which no one can…no matter who. Not even my mother or real father can make me feel better in this horrifying moment. I don't regret any of those times of correcting "father" to "stepfather" when I was around Jonah. He is a horrible person who I wish was never born in this big universe. Sadly, though, things happen in life. Terrifying, scary, abhorrent things.

I don't want to kill Jonah. I'll let the police take care of what happens next.

Finally, the boat docks and I can get off the cruise of horror. I hold Jonah by the back of his neck and slowly walk off the boat. His body will be scarred forever because of me. My body will be scarred forever because of him. The Knife Thrower.

As we walk off the boat, I see two familiar faces—Grace and George—with many police officers. "You found the Knife Thrower," George says.

"I did," I say firmly.

Red, blue, and white lights flash in the dark night through Palm Beach because of the police cars. Police officers come over. They handcuff Jonah and walk away. I run up to Grace and George and give them a big hug. Now I feel slightly better.

"Congratulations," Grace says gloomily. She pauses for a moment. "I'm sorry that this is who the Knife Thrower turned out to be. You deserve way better."

"Thank you," I say. "And you guys did not deserve getting those cameras in your eyes from Jonah. I'm sorry you were threatened."

"Don't say sorry," George says kindly. "It is not your fault one bit. Okay? If you need some space right now, we understand that."

"Thank you," I say, while giving a smile. A very real smile.

I walk about fifteen feet down the beach and that's it. I grab some sand and it slips through my hands. I look at the waves in the distance. I play with the seashells. They make a nice clicking sound. There are so many beautiful colors of the seashells—white, black, sea blue, violet, crimson, red, silver, bronze, and gold.

Grace and George walk over to me. "Oh, and I am sorry that you are about to hear this, but you will not get the million-dollar reward for finding the Knife Thrower," Grace says.

"Why?!" I exclaim.

"Well, you did not call me or George when you found him," she says, with sorrow.

"Then, for next year's Murder Mystery Race I get to pick four people to participate. Not three," I negotiate. I was completely scammed. Had they done this before? Austin hadn't told me if they had, but this is completely unfair.

George and Grace have a quick conversation with their eyes. "All right," George says, "you may choose four people to participate in next year's Murder Mystery Race."

"Thank you," I say with a smile, when, really, I am irritated.

"You're welcome," Grace says happily. Then we all say our goodbyes.

I sit around waiting for someone to come. I don't know who, though. I see big crowds around the beach.

Everyone wants to find out who the Knife Thrower is. A police officer runs over to me asking a bunch of questions. I don't respond with words. I just shake my head or nod lightly, not even paying attention most of the time.

I haven't even bothered to go find Albie, Austin, Elena, and Jack. They obviously assume something happened to me, which something did. Uncle P will have to admit now that he is in the CIA because my mom doesn't have a job, and my mom also thinks that I still see Uncle P as some guy who is my lazy, unemployed uncle who likes to sleep in very late. My mother will be worried that I am nervous about money problems because Jonah won't be around anymore. I hope that the police have called my mom and Uncle P. Although my mom still won't arrive for a couple of hours. And, Uncle P? He is still in Saudi Arabia, so he is very far away.

My hypothesis is that the Murder Mystery Race will not be discussed with my mother. Unless I am telling her about next year's Murder Mystery Race.

After about twenty-five minutes I lie down in the comfortable sand.

I stare up at the dark sky and glistening stars. I feel exhausted. Those nine days on the cruise felt like nine years of fighting and mystery.

The only noise I focus on is the calming waves that go swoosh-shhh-swoosh-shhhh-swoosh-sh-sh sh-sh-sh wwwuuu-*shwoo-shwoosh-shhhh.*

Someone then taps me on my shoulder. I turn around. It is Uncle P!

"H-how'd you get here? How'd you find out about this? I, uh, thought you were in Saudi Arabia?"

"Well, the trip ended four days earlier and last night I got a call from these people named Grace and George. They told me about the whole Murder Mystery Race. Don't feel mad about lying. You told a pretty good one, all right." He gives me a fist bump. "Anyway, they told me that they thought you'd be the one to find the Knife Thrower, so they asked me to be here Thursday night at this time."

"Wow. That's a story. But what happened on this cruise could fill a book," I say sadly.

"Also, I gave your mother a call and she is taking a flight here right now. She got the last seat left on the plane. I haven't heard from Jonah, though, but I bet he is coming with your mother."

"That's false," I say.

"W-what do you mean 'false'?"

"Because Jonah is the Knife Thrower."

"Wait, what?" Uncle P responds. "How can that be possible when—"

"Don't ask," I say miserably. "Someone will tell you the story. I just won't be the person to tell you."

Uncle P spends a while trying to cheer me up, but he fails. There is pandemonium on the beach. No one from Florida knew about the Knife Thrower. It was mainly the passengers who were on the cruise going crazy. Everyone else was just very confused on who the Knife Thrower is.

Who knew that the Knife Thrower had always been right under me and I never bothered to look down?

What will my mom think about Jonah being the Knife Thrower? If I had to guess, I would say she will be horrified.

I still can't believe who the Knife Thrower turned out to be. It is too shocking. Why did it have to be Jonah? Out of everyone in my town, why him? Why did Jonah have to torture John Bryans, Carlos Bills, Ignatius Balquere, Kairos Kartyule, and Silas Betailu? I know that they were bad people, but Jonah just made them get into more trouble.

All of a sudden, I feel a light tap on my right shoulder. I turn around to find Albie and Austin. "Oh," I say gloomily. "Hey, guys."

"We're sorry about who the Knife Thrower turned out to be," Albie says lightly. "I was also very shocked to find out that Diana and Tiberius had been working with your stepfather."

"Yeah," Austin agrees.

"It's okay," I say. "It's not either one of your faults."

We sit on the beach in dark silence in the dead of the night. "Here," Austin says. He hands me a gold bow, along with a quiver of eighteen arrows.

"Wow," I say, astonished. "But no. This bow belongs to you." I put the bow back in his hands.

"I brought two on this cruise. And two quivers of arrows. Of course, I forgot about it when I was complaining about the low number of arrows I had. Remember when the Administrators stole arrows from me?"

"I remember," I say.

I take the gold bow back and strap the quiver on my back. "Why don't we all go for a little walk on the beach?" Austin suggests.

Albie and I both nod.

The three of us walk down the beach, staring down at the sand.

All of a sudden, I can sense danger coming toward me, when I look straight ahead to see something soaring at me. Something shaped like a skinny cylinder with a point at the tip. It looks a lot like a sharp pencil. That is when I really see it. A sharp, metallic, shiny silver arrow. The arrow slides past my cheek, opening a long, stinging cut. Due to all the pressure from the arrow, I fall back on the soft sand, now looking up at the dark sky, feeling disoriented. I sit up and catch sight of two peculiar figures in the distance. It's a little hard to see, as if the figures are coming out of fog. Once they get a little closer, now about twenty-five yards away, I can see them much better. Two people. Two very tall people. They both let smirks curve across their faces.

I get up, drawing back the bowstring and sending an arrow straight toward Diana's throat. She moves aside as the arrow cuts through her left arm sleeve, and I see a long cut that stretches up to her shoulder.

An ax comes hissing from my right side toward Tiberius's heart. He turns and releases a spear toward Austin's neck that Austin averts with his bow while ducking for extra protection from the harrowing spear.

I draw a knife from my pocket and throw it at Diana's chest. She reflexively moves her quiver of arrows in front of her and the knife darts in the quiver. Diana pulls the knife off her quiver and lets it fall to the sand.

I'm busy delivering an arrow to Tiberius's thigh. I succeed, seeing him collapse to the ground and hearing a big screech from him. He pulls out the metal arrow and snaps it in half as he starts to flush with anger. He chucks a spear at my rib cage that I halt by throwing a knife at it. The spear sits on the ground with the glistening light from a star on the dent that was created by my knife.

An arrow is zooming to Albie's chest. She ducks as she draws a dagger with a wavy blade, making it look like a slithering snake. She guards herself with it anytime a spear or arrow comes toward her.

I throw a knife toward Diana and it spins through the air. She swerves around it, but not quite. Diana's braid of hair flies through the air and my knife cuts about six inches off and her hair falls down, blending in with the sand. I'm stunned at the moment. Since when have I ever thrown a knife, cutting off some hair? She sneers while pulling the knife out from the sand, and she chucks it into the ocean with all her rage.

All of a sudden, Diana and Tiberius charge straight toward us, planning in seconds on how to give us sadistic deaths. As they sprint toward us, Tiberius draws a long knife from a pocket and points it at us.

I throw a knife at Tiberius that is guaranteed to plunge into his chest, but he ducks down as the knife whistles over his head. His eyes narrow toward me and we make eye contact.

Finally, Tiberius and Diana get to us. Tiberius punches Austin in the face, which leaves Austin sitting on the ground in pain. Diana trips over a rock, making her fall to the ground. It looks like she sprained her ankle, and she wails in pain.

Tiberius grabs me by the neck and picks me up like I'm some little toy. I kick around and try to squeeze his wrist. I am completely helpless. He then throws me into the Atlantic Ocean. The water is quite warm, and now I'm completely soaked. I still have cuts all over my body, and that cut on my cheek from the arrow is the worst. Salt enters the wounds and stings. The sharp stinging feeling rushes through my body, but I get up and I see Albie give Tiberius a nasty look. She draws a long bronze knife and constantly whacks it at Tiberius's face. She opens a cut on his temple and goes for another swing at his arm. Albie carves a red scratch through his sleeve that displays an X. She then slices Tiberius's palm with her knife. Tiberius grunts.

I haul myself out of the water, and I feel the pressure of a small wave push the back of my legs, which leans me forward a little. My feet make footprints on the heavy sand. I finally reach where Albie and Tiberius are. I pull out a small knife from my jacket pocket and throw it down at Tiberius's foot. The knife buries in the middle of his foot. I know it got deep into his foot when he groans loudly. Tiberius limps away, helping Diana off the ground.

I load an arrow in my bow and attempt to shoot at Tiberius, but I don't have such a good aim, so I miss. They scurry away to something that is shaped like a sphere. It is still kind of hard to see because it is very dark. Our only lights are from the cars all the way down the beach by the cruise ship and the shiny stars that gleam on our silver weapons.

The sphere-looking thing I see is really a black helicopter. Diana and Tiberius jump in and rapidly start the engine. The helicopter floats up into the air. Austin slowly gets up and shoots an arrow that bursts through the helicopter window. Glass shatters around the beach.

The helicopter soars away high in the sky going west.

West.

I have to remember that the helicopter is going west.

Only one thought sits in my brain....

Diana and Tiberius have escaped.

Acknowledgments

Thank you to Jon Ford who edited my manuscript. Jon helped me to become a better writer.

About the Author

Andrew Cohen was born in 2010 and resides in a suburb of Chicago, Illinois. Andrew is an avid tennis and ping pong player and enjoys cooking extravagant meals for his family. Andrew loves archery and is the recipient of six awards from the Camp Archery Association of the United States. A thrill seeker who enjoys skiing black diamonds and riding rollercoasters, Andrew's bucket list includes riding the top five tallest coasters in the world.

Andrew loves mystery, action, and suspense novels and movies. His writing journey began in second grade when he started writing comics and short stories. When Andrew was in fourth grade, he began writing chapter books. In sixth grade, Andrew chose to submit his latest manuscript to publishers for their review. His journey from writer to published author has officially begun.